THE MANIFESTATION OF CALEB LEWIS

TIMOTHY D. TIMS

THIS BOOK IS DEDICATED TO THE LOVES
OF MY LIFE

AMBER, TYLER, KARA, RYKER & BECKETT
TIMS

ACKNOWLEDGMENTS

MY WIFE AMBER, WHO HAS PUT UP WITH ME MOST OF MY LIFE AND NEVER KNOWS WHAT I'LL DO NEXT. SHE IS NEVER A DISCOURAGER, BUT ALWAYS AN ENCOURAGER.

A BIG THANK YOU TO CARRIE OTT, MY EDITOR SUPREME.

OTHER OPINIONS AND OR CONTRIBUTORS OF THOUGHTS OR WORDS INCLUDE: MERRELL KNIGHTEN, AIMEE WILEY, AND STEVE WAGNER.

I WOULD LIKE TO HEAR FROM YOU.

BOOKOFCALEB@GMAIL.COM

Table of Contents

CHAPTER 1

"MOM, WHO IS THAT MAN?"

Caleb heard the bedroom door open. His heart skipped a beat, and he quickly dodged into his mother's closet. He pulled the door closed. *Mom will be mad at me for forgetting my present to Willie's birthday party.*

He heard a strange man's voice and sounds he wasn't familiar with. Squinting his eyes, he looked through the slats in the closet door and saw his mother naked and in the arms of the stranger. Caleb stood deathly silent in the dark closet. The bedroom was illuminated only by the sunlight filtering through the window shades. He stood there trembling, beads of sweat dripping from his forehead, taking shallow breaths, trying to be as quiet as possible. He kept squinting through the slats and quickly turning away. Deep inside he knew he was watching something that he shouldn't see, but he wasn't sure why. He kept trying to look away, covering his eyes with his hands, but he was too curious not to look and at the same time, too repulsed to look.

As he stood there in that hot closet, his heart pounded so hard he could feel it in his throat. He kept watching his mother in all kinds of odd positions; Caleb struggled to discern what was happening. The sounds of passion puzzled Caleb; the groaning and moaning of Lillie, and the grunts and quick breathing of the man—that man was hurting her. But why didn't she scream? Cry for help? His eight-year-old instincts told him to burst out of that closet and help his mother. But she didn't seem like she wanted help.

He watched them have sex for over an hour. When they were finished and left the house, Caleb slowly swung open the closet door, took a deep breath, and just stared at the bed. He was trying to figure out what had just happened. After a few minutes he quietly left the room, perplexed and crying. The present he'd come home for lay forgotten in the dark closet.

* * *

"Caleb, my mom said your mom likes to kiss all the boys!" shouted Tobert Johnson in the park. "I want to kiss her too! Will you please ask your mom if I can kiss her?"

Lillie's affair had become news around town a few months earlier when some women saw her and the man kissing in her car. In a small town, your sins will always find you out.

The other boys at the park overheard Tobert teasing. They'd heard similar comments about Lillie from their parents. All the children swarmed together, held hands, and started dancing in a circle around Caleb, chanting, "Who wants to kiss Lillie? I do, I do! Who wants to kiss Lillie? I do, I do!"

Caleb felt crushed. He just bowed his head and broke out of the circle, stomping away. The children's chant followed him out of the park. Kicking a rusty can down the street as he headed home, he was embarrassed and mad at his mother and wished he had different one.

A couple weeks later, Caleb was at the baseball park waiting to play a little league game. He lay on the soft grass, tossing a ball up and catching it with his mitt. Ronald Obete, Waylon Forsight, and Bobby Fastner, all sixth graders, found their way over, but Caleb ignored them.

"Hey Caleb," Ronald said, breaking Caleb's concentration. He dropped his ball. "Everyone says your mom is easy. She'll have sex with anyone, right?"

"Shut up!" Caleb snarled, bolting to his feet. "That's a lie!"

"Yeah," Waylon interjected, "my big brother told me she's a whore, and for $10 she'll have sex with anyone. I have 10 bucks saved up; ask her if she'll have sex with me, would ya?"

 Bobby giggled, smacking Caleb on the arm. "I heard everyone in town's having sex with her."

Caleb grabbed his ball out of his mitt and threw it as hard as he could, beaming Bobby right between the eyes. Bobby fell to the ground and started crying. Then Caleb charged Ronald and tackled him. "You talk about my mother again and *I will kill you*. I will kill all of you!"

CHAPTER 2

LIFE IS A STRUGGLE

Life continued to wear Lillie down. The same routines day after day as one year rolled into another. Of course, Lillie loved her family very much, but deep down inside she had never wanted one. As a little girl she had always imagined getting out of Enapay and starting a new life for herself. Oh how she daydreamed about going to New York and being a model, being on magazine covers and modeling clothes—it just sounded so glamorous to her! Then the pregnancy came, and so she ended up the same as many small-town girls—planning a very quick wedding whose joy was quickly subsumed under years of working, homemaking, and taking care of children.

Lillie had become indifferent, everything and everyone nothing more than lackluster. And of course Lillie, gorgeous as ever, had no shortage of men eager to go to bed with her. The man she got involved with at work wasn't anything special; it was just something different, something to add some excitement to the drudgery of her life. She didn't love him—he was a diversion. With him, she could pretend to be something special, completely detached from herself and her normal, mundane routines. No, it wasn't a model's life, but it was a temporary escape from the grind.

Sitting on the edge of her bed, Lillie started her routine for the day. She slipped on her well-worn clothes, looked in the mirror, and sighed at the wrinkles that were forming on her face—*so much for all those childhood dreams*. She trudged out of the room and down the steps to prepare breakfast for her family. After she'd finished her plate and tucked it away, Jack gave her a hug and she left for work. He held her just a second longer than usual—he felt uneasy, as if he wasn't the only one putting his arms around her. But if that were true, how could he prove it? And more importantly, did he even want to?

***

Jack Lewis had grown up in a typical American family, whatever that is. He'd always been a good athlete—all-state in football and recruited by a few colleges—but he wasn't interested in going to school anymore. Not to mention his girlfriend Lillie was pregnant, and he needed to go to work to support his new family. Jack was a good father, and though not rich by any means, he took care of his growing family by working long hours. He was absolutely in love with Lillie; he felt lucky to have such a beautiful woman.

Jack normally got home around seven every evening. He made sure that the first thing he did was kiss his wife and hug his three children. They would eat supper as a family, then Jack would take the boys out back to play. Not surprisingly, his children had the same sort of skill for athletics that he did; he took every chance he had to coach them and share his experience in basketball, baseball, and football. His little Amanda was never too interested in such rough play, so she took to helping Lillie around the house. Lillie loved to play dolls with Amanda and taught her how to cook and clean. Despite her general dislike of rough sports, Amanda did have a bit of a weakness for basketball; she played throughout her elementary, junior high, and high school years. It was the perfect family, or so it seemed.

***

 The year was 1971, Nixon was president of a country embroiled in fighting in Vietnam, and John would soon be off to join the conflict. John was the perfect son, he never drank, smoked, or did drugs, his faith in Christ was strong, and he definitely showed it in his life. Like his father Jack, John was tall and had been raised with the motto "God, family, country." Despite his smarts, John may have been a bit naïve—he believed every word that Nixon and the politicians said about the Vietnam conflict. He had a true sense of duty, and when he was drafted he considered it an honor to serve his country. He always tried to act brave and "be a man" around Jack. The truth was, though, that John was petrified of going to Vietnam; there wasn't a hateful bone in his body, and the thought of killing a man was something he could not stomach.

Amanda, on the other hand, had just turned 15 years old and was all about peace and love. She'd gotten caught up in the war protests that were exploding around the country, mostly because one of her friend's brothers had been killed in Vietnam a couple of years ago and she'd seen the terrible pain and heartache it caused their family. She didn't understand—why were we sending our young American men to a foreign country to die, and more importantly, die for what? She thought about these sorts of things perhaps a little too often, and so it goes without saying that she was absolutely livid with her brother John. She pleaded, cried, and threatened him if he didn't burn his draft card and move to Canada. She begged and begged John not to go, but Jack and John thought that was nonsense and most un-American. You get drafted, you go fight for your country—that's what young American men do. Jack would have no draft-dodger as a son.

Lillie seemed apathetic about John going to Vietnam; really, she seemed indifferent about everything these days. Something wasn't normal with Lillie, and Jack was trying desperately to figure out what the problem was. Lillie was downing valiums like candy, but he figured if the doctor said she needed them, she needed them. What did he know about it? One thing he did know, though, was that the pills or something else were changing her personality. Little by little things would pop out now and then; Jack could almost feel the signs of discontent emanating from her. She seemed to be depressed a lot, and even mere mentions of lovemaking had pretty much vanished; she did it more out of marital duty than love. He'd tried to talk with her about her recent lack of interest in him, but she'd acted like nothing was wrong. He knew for sure something was off when she quit getting the kids up on Sunday to go to church; Lillie had always been a very spiritual person, and the sudden cutoff was too strange. He didn't bring it up much, though, and so Jack still got up every Sunday, got the kids ready for church, and off they went to worship—without Lillie.

***

Then, that one summer day a few weeks after Caleb had seen Lillie with that man, it all just came out. Caleb, still confused by what he saw, went to talk to his dad about it.

"Dad, do you and Mom like to wrestle?"

Jack looked down at Caleb. *Well that's an odd question.* Leaning down, Jack smiled and said, "Caleb, what makes you ask that?"

Caleb looked up at his dad, shuffling his feet back and forth, still not sure if he should say anything. Finally he managed, eyes diverted, "Well, I was in your room, and I saw Mom and a man wrestling." Jack's heart sank as he looked down at Caleb, this innocent little boy who didn't even have the words to say what had happened. After a few seconds, Jack sat down on the floor so he could be eye to eye with Caleb. He put his hands on his son's shoulders.

"Caleb, can you tell Daddy everything you saw? Don't be afraid, I won't be mad at you."

"Well, I forgot my present to Willie's birthday party, and…and I came back home to get it. I went in your room to get it out of the closet. I heard Mom open the door, so I hid."

Jack's heart was beating fast, even though he really already knew the answer to all the questions buzzing around in his head. Caleb must have been able to sense a piece of his father's fear, because tears were welling up in Caleb's eyes and he suddenly lunged forward, burying his face in Jack's neck and bawling.

"Mommy didn't have any clothes on, and I hid for a long long time 'cause they wouldn't stop wrestling." Caleb sniffled. "Daddy, I thought maybe the man was hurting Mommy! I didn't know what to do…I'm sorry Daddy. I'm sorry!" Caleb completely broke down sobbing, his little fingers constricting the fabric of Jack's shirt into wrinkled balls. He'd never seen Caleb this scared—*the poor kid must have had this building up in him for weeks*. Jack closed his eyes tightly, his teeth clenched, though he didn't make a sound for fear of scaring Caleb more. Teardrops were spilling down both of their cheeks, and he held onto Caleb like it was the last time he would ever be with him.

"Caleb, they were just having fun. It's nothing to be worried about." Jack pushed Caleb back a little so that he could muster a smile, however fake, for his son. When Caleb gently buried his face into Jack's neck again, Jack bowed his head and silently pleaded to God for guidance and for peace of mind for Caleb. Jack already knew how this story was going to end, and he didn't want Caleb to talk about it anymore; it was too much for him to understand.

That day when Caleb told Jack the story of his mother with another man, it changed everything. That's usually how it goes, after all—the spouse is the first to suspect it and the last one to know.

***

Jack went upstairs and packed his bags slowly. Each piece of clothing, each stupid little thing he owned, seemed duller, more frustrating. *Why do I have all this stuff?* After a few deep breaths, he walked into the kitchen to see Lillie.

"Caleb saw you and your boyfriend in our bedroom on Saturday." Lillie said nothing. When she didn't respond, Jack frowned. "He watched you have sex until you left." His eyes betrayed the sense of failure he was trying to hide from his face. "The divorce papers will be here soon. Goodbye."

Caleb stood in horror on the front porch, watching his dad walk down the steps. He frantically ran to him, screaming for him to stay. "I'm sorry, Daddy! I didn't mean to tell you! I'm sorry! Please don't go, Daddy, I'm sorry! I'm sorry!" Caleb grabbed onto Jack's leg, trying to pull him back to the house. Jack stopped, bent over, and looked at his son.

"Caleb," he said in a soft voice, "you didn't do anything wrong. None of this is your fault—your mother brought this all on herself. I'm not leaving you; I will never leave you. I'm just moving to another house, and you are always welcome to come over whenever you want. You are my son, and I love you more than you know." Jack wrapped his big arms around Caleb and gave him a hug, then he stood up, turned away, and left. Caleb cried to himself, a low, droning whine as he let his head fall down. It seemed like he would never run out of tears, but finally he was just too tired to cry any more. He trudged back to the house, casting a eerie glance at Lillie. Daddy said this is all my mom's fault. I don't like her any more.

The tears that Caleb cried that day were far from over. The next five years of his life went by with one tragedy after another. His older brother John—the brother he adored more than anyone else—got killed in Vietnam. His sister Amanda overdosed on drugs (supposedly LSD—jumped off a balcony thinking she could fly), and his mom and dad were divorced. Life changed dramatically for him between eight years and thirteen years, and Caleb had become a bitter child.

CHAPTER 3

LIFE PAINFULLY MOVES ON

During the years following Lillie's affair, Caleb withdrew from everyone. The only time anyone saw him was when he was playing sports, in school, or going to a sibling's funeral. His time was spent mostly with reading, reading, and more reading; he read like someone was going to destroy all the books and he had to read them all. He was at the library every day checking out new titles, especially if he could find things on psychology or true crime. Naturally, he shot way ahead of his class (which was so incredibly boring, he thought) and was reading at college level by fifth grade.

Caleb was a remarkable young man with a truly photographic memory. He could recall every line of every book he had ever laid eyes on. To him, his reality had become the books he read and the sports he played—his only escape from the demons inside him. He didn't have or want any friends; most kids were scared of him anyway and thought he was weird. Even in sports, which he excelled in, he didn't hang out with his teammates. When they were all huddled up before the game started, Caleb would stand far away by himself, waiting for the game to start. He didn't talk much and his social skills were lacking, but if you wanted to discuss psychology, science, math, or crime with him, you had better be on your A game. By the time he was thirteen, his knowledge of these subjects had blossomed into something a PhD might have.

Why had this even happened to Caleb? Maybe it could be blamed on Lillie or maybe it was just the way he was, but Caleb had become a loner. Loners aren't just less outgoing than most; they view the world in a completely different way. Whereas most people enjoy friends, social events and group communication, loners focus more on their own mindsets and don't distinguish between what is generally right or wrong. Above all else they generally lack a conscience; they are limited to what existence they have shaped for themselves. And so Caleb sat at the corner table and opened a new book.

***

At home, Lillie had a garage apartment in the back yard separate from the main house, and as she promised, she let Caleb move in when he was thirteen. He'd decorated it with black light posters everywhere—it looked like a hippie den. He could come and go as he pleased, because Caleb devolved into a furious ball of rage if she tried to confront him about his comings and goings, so she just left him alone. She never really knew where he was, but what could she do?

Jack was still living in Enapay and still working at the hardware store. He'd become the manager and had remarried to a wonderful, loving woman named Mary, fathering a child with her named Billy. Caleb regularly went to see his dad and always did his best to act like an all-American boy; more than anything, he wanted his dad to be proud of him—yes-sir, no ma'am, and thank you. He really had two personalities—one was perfect around Jack, but away from Jack, the other was mean, spiteful, and angry.

As had happened so often in the past, Lillie felt another wave of helplessness come over her following another one of Caleb's rages. For the hundredth time, she went to talk to Jack about him.

"He's out of control, Jack. I'm finding alcohol, marijuana…the other day I found two pairs of girl's panties out back in his room, and they were different sizes; for goodness sakes Jack, he's only thirteen years old! I get calls from the teachers, well, it seems like every day saying Caleb is a bully picking on the other kids!"

Jack scoffed. "I wonder why he's like this, *Lillie*? Surely it couldn't be because he saw his mother having sex with some random man."

Lillie felt a pang in her chest, a little adrenaline rush of anger. Oh how she wished Jack would stop throwing that in her face! As if she didn't how much she'd hurt Jack, or that her affair had destroyed the family.

She sighed. "Jack, I made a terrible mistake. I know that, all right? But I've changed. I've apologized to you a thousand times, Jack. What else I can do Jack? What do you want from me? What can I say to help you understand that there is something terribly *wrong* with the *only* child we have left?" A stream of tears slid out of the corners of her eyes, and she had to hold back the quick flashes of

Amanda and John's beautiful faces in her mind. She stepped into Jack and put her hands around him, laid her head on his chest trying to find comfort; she needed to be protected and loved by someone. Her arms were shaking, and her voice was breaking up.

"I can't lose Caleb, Jack. I just can't. What do I have to do to help you understand?" She sniffled and grabbed the edge of her skirt, lifting it ever so slightly. "I have calluses on my knees from praying for Caleb so much. He hates me, Jack, and he scares me. He looks at me with such contempt in his eyes." She clenched her teeth to try to stifle the tears. "His beautiful blue eyes are full of hate, Jack."

Jack took a deep breath and held Lillie close. His mind meandered back to a time when they were so in love and life was perfect. He stayed that way for a while, letting Lillie cry out all of her tears.

"I think you're overblowing the situation," Jack said at last. "He's always the perfect kid around my family. He makes good grades in school and he's a great athlete. I just can't see the side of Caleb that you're talking about." Lillie held Jack tightly, as if trying to make up for the years apart that her one mistake had brought, but after a few minutes Jack let go of her and nudged her away. As she watched him step back, Lillie gave one final sigh and then brushed herself off. She wiped away the tears and stood up straight again.

She is not going to lose Caleb.

CHAPTER 4

GETTING HIS DUCKS IN A ROW

Caleb began experimenting with alcohol and drugs when he was thirteen. He found it gave him some relief from his anger. His thoughts and actions had become dangerous, not only to himself but to the people around him. Caleb was mad at the world, mad at everything and anything and somebody was going to pay. He needed money for the alcohol and drugs, and he'd learned that taking lunch money from kids wasn't enough to feed his cravings. He tried to work and earn money the old-fashioned way, but it just wasn't enough. He had read a bunch of crime books about blackmail and extortion, and it was time to put his knowledge to work.

If he had learned one thing from his reading and being a bully, it was that, *fear is the great equalizer*. He shut the book he was reading with a thud.

Emerging with a vengeance from his five years of isolation, Caleb is on the hunt.

***

Caleb mowed Mrs. Daisy Belview's lawn to earn extra money. She lived in the wealthy part of Enapay and had a spacious, well-kept home. Mrs. Belview was a petite woman, maybe 4'8 or 4'9, and couldn't have weighed much more than 90 pounds or so. She grew up in Birmingham, Alabama and was a proper southern woman. Her husband passed away about two years ago, but he'd been sick for quite a while before that (in contrast to Mrs. Belview herself, who was 65 years old and still a very beautiful, healthy woman). Her perfectly-styled hair, impeccable makeup, and pressed clothes just screamed "southern."

One day Caleb was mowing her lawn and had stopped to put gas in the mower. Mrs. Belview sat busily chattering away on the porch with a man on the phone. Caleb slowly, quietly unscrewed the gas cap and set it in front of a mower wheel. Crouching down and making himself seem busy, he listened. The huge number that sprang out of Mrs. Belview's mouth when she talked about her bank account didn't go unnoticed.

 Caleb finished mowing and went to the library. Maybe it was the years of suffering and isolation he'd been through, but he had a man's mind in a child's body. Too cunning for his own good. He found his way to the little-used part of the library and grabbed every book he could find that covered Oklahoma law on rape, statutory rape, and child molestation. Caleb had, after all, noticed that Mrs. Belview was always watching him. At first he didn't think anything about it but, after two years of her attention, he was pretty sure she had a thing for him. But making it work in his favor was easier said than done.

The next week, when it was time to mow again, Caleb brought along the miniature tape recorder he got for Christmas. After mowing a while, Caleb let go of the mower, stuffed his tape recorder in his pants, shuffled over to the door and knocked. Mrs. Belview opened it eagerly.

"Come in, Caleb!" she said with a smile. "May I offer you a glass of cold lemonade?"

"Thanks, it's hot outside," Caleb said, walking in and shutting the door behind him. His gaze darted around the house while Mrs. Belview was fixing his drink. *Man, what a house!* he thought. *This place is something else.* He finally set his eyes on a doily underneath a lamp, so he quickly scurried over, put down the recorder, and hit the record button. He wasn't sure if anything would happen today—he intended to only plant a seed in her mind—but he thought he would tape it just in case.

Mrs. Belview walked back into the living room with the lemonade (on a sterling silver tray, he noticed).

"Caleb, you are just a *wonderful* worker. I bet your mother and father are very proud of you."

Caleb proffered a smile and said, "Yes-ma'am!"

She quickly set the tray down, eyes fixed (as always) on Caleb. He smiled at her as she grinned turning to look out the window. Mrs. Belview had been observing him through those windows, watching Caleb mow that lawn now for almost two years. He never wore a shirt and had the most beautiful bronze skin, and long silky black hair, and all those muscles. Sweat just dripped down every inch of his body as he pushed that mower, and…well, it was just more than she could take sometimes. Mrs. Belview would perhaps hesitantly admit that Caleb had crossed her mind more than a few times when she was alone and in bed at night, but afterwards, she was always ashamed of herself for thinking such thoughts about a child. But still, she looked forward all week to watching him mow that yard. Blushing a bit, she sat down next to Caleb on the couch.

"Do forgive me for speaking so boldly, Caleb, but you are just the most handsome 14-year-old boy I think I've ever seen. You have the most engaging blue eyes and you are so tall, and those muscles! I just bet all the teenage girls are falling all over themselves to date you." She then reached over and brazenly placed her hand on his thigh.

"I don't know about that, Mrs. Belview," Caleb said.

"Please, call me Daisy," she said. "That's my first name." She was slowly rubbing her fingers up and down his inner thigh. Now, Daisy hadn't had relations with a man in ten years, and she knew that having relations with a 14-year-old was certainly against the law—and more importantly to her, it would be morally reprehensible, perverted, and a horrendous crime against a child.

Caleb looked at her and then down at her hand. *She's older than my grandmother, but then again my grandmother doesn't have 180k in the bank.*

Caleb reached over and grabbed Daisy's hand and placed it on his abdomen. Daisy heaved a sigh and rubbed around for a few seconds, then abruptly pulled her hand away.

"Oh my, Caleb! I just can't. You're just a baby!" Caleb took a deep breath. *Here goes nothing.* He rolled her over and started kissing her neck. "Oh Caleb…it's been so long for me, but I do feel this is so wrong." Caleb let nature take its course, though, and Daisy was so aroused she didn't complain.

When they were finished, Caleb stood up and ran his eyes over a very satisfied Daisy basking on the couch, walked a few feet to his tape recorder, and turned it off. Daisy was watching and said, "What in the world is that contraption, Caleb?"

His gaze penetrated deeply into her eyes. "This is a tape recorder, Daisy." Her eyebrows peaked. "I need some real money, Daisy," he said. "In fact, I need about $1,000 a week. I bet you can give me that much money, can't you?"

Daisy's mouth fell open a little. "Why Caleb Lewis, do you believe I'm so desperate for intimacy that I have to hire a gigolo? I assure you I'm not, and I don't think I have *ever* been so insulted!"

Caleb sat back down on the couch and put his arm around her. "I wonder what my parents would think about a woman your age having sex with their baby boy? You know what the law calls what you just did? Statutory rape. Let me just define that for you real quick. *Statutory rape is sex between an adult and a sexually mature minor past the age of puberty.* Daisy, guess what, you qualify! You just knowingly raped a 14 year-old-boy! Now, you don't want everyone in Enapay to know about this, do you? How about your family, friends, and oh, the church! How would you feel if everyone in town knew you're a child molester? I have it all right here on tape, would you like to hear it?"

Caleb had her, and he knew there was nothing she could do about it. Daisy quickly started adjusting her dress and brassiere and violently shoved Caleb's arm off of her. She angrily stared at him for a minute, and let out a long sigh. She leaned back on the couch, looking at the ceiling, and started shaking her head back and forth. Tears started rolling down her cheeks as her mind wandered back to a time long ago. She remembers being a little girl in Alabama sitting with her father on their front porch, and she could hear his voice saying, *"Daisy, it takes a lifetime to build an honorable character, but just one second to destroy it. When it's all said and done, your honor and character is all you will have left in this world, so protect it at all costs."* It didn't matter that Caleb had planned it all—she, the adult, had still given in. She had no choice but to give Caleb what he wanted.

She found him on her porch at least once, sometimes twice a week. When Daisy passed away a few years later, she was broke and couldn't even afford a decent funeral. She was buried next to her husband in a plain pine box. Caleb didn't show up at her graveside service.

***

Now that Caleb finally had all the money he needed, he wanted to get a few things straight with the liquor store. Buying drugs was easy, but buying liquor was always a hassle and he was tired of it. He grabbed his baseball bat and headed out.

John and Amy Wills owned the Drop and Shop Liquor store on the south side of town. He could see them chatting behind the counter as he approached the little shop. A bell jingled as he walked through the door.

"Caleb!" John sighed. "How many times do I have to tell you, you can't come in this store! You're too young to buy liquor." Caleb didn't say a word; he swung the bat and hit John in the arm. John stumbled back, bent over in pain, clutching his arm.

"WAIT A MINUTE!" he shouted. "Have you lost your mind?" Caleb swung the bat again, sending a whole shelf of liquor crashing to the floor. Amy lunged for Caleb, but he pushed her back and reached across the counter, grabbing John by the hair. Caleb slammed John's head down next to the register and put the bat to his face.

"Your head is next if you ever deny me liquor again."

"Caleb LET HIM GO!" Amy screamed as she dove to grab the bat. Caleb slapped Amy and knocked her to the floor; she landed with a splash and a yelp in the puddle of broken glass and booze. Caleb reached down and dragged her by her hair across the room, picked her up, and smashed her against the wall. He pressed his weight against her, his mouth next to her ear.

"This is real simple, woman—I will buy what I want when I want it. If you give me any trouble or even *think* about calling the cops, I will make sure you, your husband, and your kids live *just* long enough to regret it. Do we understand each other?"

"We got it," John and Amy said in unison, both clutching their bruised bodies. With an entirely fake, frightened smile, John said, "Would you like anything today"?

Caleb stepped back and huffed. "Are you stupid? I can't be seen buying liquor in your store or you'll get closed down, moron. I'll call you with what I want, and one of you will deliver it to my room in the back yard of my mom's house. I'll pay for what I buy. It's that simple." With a final scowl, Caleb turned around and left.

Amy and John just stood there a minute looking at each other, then finally John started sloshing through all the broken glass and liquor on the floor.

"What the heck was *that*?" Amy said.

John reached for the phone. "I'm calling the police."

He didn't even have time to reach for it before Amy slapped his hand away. "YOU TOUCH THAT PHONE AND YOU WILL LIVE TO REGRET IT, MISTER! I WILL GO BUY A BAT AND HIT YOU MYSELF!" Amy took a few deep breaths. "That kid is dangerous; let's just give him what he wants. What difference does it make, anyway?"

CHAPTER 5

THIS IS JUST TOO EASY

For many young men, sex is something you're always on the lookout for. For most teenage boys, any sex with any woman is good sex, but not so much for Caleb. The incident with Lillie when he was eight had twisted his view on sex and women, so he hated the idea of sex, but his natural instincts were always at odds with his brain. Caleb was an exceptionally good looking young man, and girls were asking him outright for sex, falling all over themselves trying to get to him. But Caleb was still socially challenged, and the thought of being with a girl by himself could be disturbing to him. Sometimes if Caleb was just *with* a girl, his mind flashed back to traumatic memories of Lillie and her lover and he could become violent. Generally speaking, if Caleb was alone with a girl and having sex, he was after something else.

The odd thing, though, was that if the girls were bisexual, that worked much better. Not in a freaky kind of way, but in a way that Caleb could cope with sex. He had learned that with two girls they would do all the talking without expecting him to say much—just lie there and look pretty and that was fine with him.

 One night his sophomore year after a football game, Caleb was reluctantly talking to a reporter about some of the more impressive plays of the night. Two of the cheerleaders, Nia and Jamie, started walking towards him as the reporter left.

"Hey Caleb," Nia said, "what are you doing tonight?" She leaned in with a pleasant, and obviously nervous, smile.

Jamie elbowed her way past her friend and chimed in, "So, do you have any beer? Nia and I are looking to party a bit, and we thought you could maybe help us out."

"Sure, I've got beer and stuff," Caleb said. "Why don't you girls come over to my room in about thirty minutes? We'll party till morning," he said with a wink.

"Great!" Nia said. "We'll see you then."

At about 10:30, he heard the girls pull up outside the garage. He made his way to the door, a couple of beers in hand, and ushered them in. Jamie wasted no time in snagging the beer from Caleb and chugged it down in seconds; Nia wasn't far behind.

Caleb was wearing a tank top and hip-hugger jeans with a thin roped headband on. "*Whew, this is one hot man*, Nia thought to herself.

"What else do you have around here?" Jamie said, waggling her empty beer bottle.

"What else do you want?" Caleb said. "I have it all."

Jamie giggled. "Got any weed? We've never tried it, but I'm dying to!"

Caleb laughed out loud at that. "Please. I have weed, LSD, PCP, heroin, cocaine, uppers, downers, and all the alcohol you can possibly drink. It's a den of iniquity in here!" He flopped down on the couch and put his arms on the back, nodding them over. "So, girls, what kind of music do you like? I have a great stereo system."

"Oh!" Nia shouted, "I *love* Cheap Trick, The Knack, and Bad Company! Do you have any of that?"

"I have all of it!" he laughed. "Let's turn it up!" He gave each of them a joint and a few paper tabs of LSD, turned on the black lights, and let the music blare.

"What's this, Caleb?" Nia flipped the paper tabs over in her hand.

"Don't worry about it let's just have fun," Caleb said with a smile. They both slid the paper under their tongues and lit up their joints. Nia coughed for a minute when Caleb lit hers, but soon enough they were all kicked back in bean bags chilling out to the music. After about thirty minutes, both girls were as high as a kite and hallucinating.

Caleb didn't take any pills, just smoked a joint. Someone needed to watch out for them, after all—this was their first time. Caleb leaned back and watched the chaos unfold with a slight grin on his face. Nia stood up, put her hands out to her sides, and started twirling in a circle, giggling, "Look at all the beautiful colors! *I* am a beautiful color."

Jamie started dancing and taking off her clothes. She walked over to the bed, laid down, and looked at the posters above her. "Whoa! Freaky, dude! I've never…never felt like this before. It's so pretty." Soon after that, Nia had her clothes off and was lying on the bed with Jamie.

Caleb could feel his skin start to tingle, and his face flushed as his heart started beating faster. He smothered what was left of his joint and climbed into bed with them. Soon, everyone was having sex with everyone. Whenever the high started to subside, Caleb would go off and fix a shot of heroin, another joint, whatever he felt like giving them.

They went on and on the entire weekend. None of them got dressed; they just laid there and drank, took drugs, and had sex. Early Monday morning, Jamie shook Nia out of a stoned sleep.

"Wake up. We have to go home. We have school in a few hours."

Nia opened one eye and said, "I'm playing hooky today. You go ahead." As Jamie started to leave, Caleb ran over to her and set her up with one more fix of heroin before sending her on her way.

From then on, Caleb would call the girls every day to come over and party. An addiction to drugs is elusive—the girls weren't mature enough yet to know what they were getting into. They thought they were just having fun. Soon enough, those two girls wound up wholly dependent on Caleb to give them their fix, and he used them to live out his sexual fantasies. Nia and Jamie were always with him, asking, begging for another shot. Once he had them hooked, they had no choice but to do whatever Caleb wanted whenever he wanted it. They were kicked off the cheerleading squad—you have to practice to cheer, and they didn't have time for that anymore.

CHAPTER 6

SUPERSTAR

Like most kids in small towns, Caleb played sports growing up. Unlike most kids, he was something really special from the moment he started. All the way up through little league, coaches were tripping over each other to get Caleb on their teams. It made no difference to them that he was a bit different—this boy could flat out *play*. In football, basketball, and baseball, he was so dominating that it was discouraging for the other kids that had to play with him. If Caleb was on your team, the other one usually just gave up. Might as well hand him the championship and skip all that exercise.

For some, God reaches down when you're born and touches you with a special gift that is unexplainable—a gift that goes above and beyond human understanding. It's a gift that is so frustrating to those who even hope to match it, and at the same time, it's so magical to all who witness it. Such was Caleb Lewis.

As a senior in high school, Caleb was a menacing 6'5," 235-pound beast with a rocket for an arm. He could run a 4.4 40-yard dash and had moves that could make NFL running backs jealous. Caleb never lost a football game— not one. In baseball, pro scouts were scouting him because of his 34 home runs in 26 games in his senior year. He was a projected first round draft pick in Major League baseball. The awards were pouring in for Caleb; a three sport All-American, Oklahoma High School's "Athlete of the Year" and the National High School "Athlete of the year." He could pick the college and the sport he decided to play and he'd get in, no questions asked.

***

The regional television station sent a reporter named Rhonda Boaz out to talk to Caleb about winning the National High School Athlete of the Year. This was a big deal, of course—only one person in the US gets the award every year, but Caleb was still a little uneasy about the interview. He was just such a private person, and he loathed the thought of talking about himself, but he understood that the award was a big deal to folks in town and so he reluctantly agreed.

Rhonda shook his hand as she sat down, her big, toothy grin spreading from ear to ear. The two passed a few minutes in (mostly one-sided) chit-chat before moving on to the real topic.

"So when did you first find out about winning the National Award?"

"I didn't even know I was nominated for it, and I still don't know how I got it." He kept his hands on his lap and his face bland.

Rhonda opened her mouth to start her next question, then decided against it. She'd have to loosen up his standoffish demeanor first. "Let's have some fun, okay?" Caleb didn't seem enthused. "Just tell me the first thing that pops into your mind when I say something. Hmm…favorite color?"

"Black."

"Short or tall?"

"Short."

"Favorite artist?"

"Peter Max."

"Favorite band?"

"Pink Floyd." Caleb leaned forward.

"I never get tired of?"

"Reading." A shadow of a smile crossed his face.

"What does every child deserve?"

"Love."

"Do you believe in God?"

"No."

"Every person needs?"

"A place to get away by themselves."

"Something you know you need to stop doing?"

Caleb glared at her, "no comment."

"So, what's your dream job?"

"NFL quarterback."

"Are you going to the prom?"

"No."

"What are you afraid of?"

Finally, Caleb smiled. "Nothing."

"Well then, it sounds like you're a brave man," Rhonda said. "Have you always been so dominating in sports, or was it something you really had to work on?"

Caleb scratched the back of his neck, nervous. "I don't really like talking about myself, but I don't know, sports have always come easily for me. I mean, I worked on weights and stuff, but it just came easy. I like playing and all, but I would be just as happy sitting and reading a book, I think."

"We all know about your gifts as an athlete, but who are *you*? What is the essence of *Caleb Lewis*," Rhonda said with an emphatic jab of her pen.

Caleb cocked an eyebrow. "Who am I?" he said, rolling his eyes. "I have no essence, I smell a little I guess, maybe I need a bath." he said laughing. I'm a guy who can throw a football and hit a baseball. In the grand scheme of things, that seems pretty trivial to me."

"I know you had some tough times growing up," Rhonda said. "Can you tell us about your brother?"

Caleb's face immediately darkened again. "Hmm. My private life is really my own business"

"The nation is clamoring to know who you are, Caleb! Isn't your family important to you?"

Caleb grumbled, his glare deepening. But finally, he said, "John…he was killed in Vietnam when I was 10 years old." Rhonda leaned back, perhaps regretting she'd asked. "It was hard—I loved my brother so much, and I still get angry about it. Man, we used to play basketball out in the backyard; we nailed an old hoop to the garage, and I learned a lot playing one-on-one with him. We would play until the sun went down, and then," Caleb chuckled, "Dad would come out and turn on the headlamps on the car and we'd all play till we were plum wore out or until the battery in the car went dead, whichever happened first…Dad and John and Amanda and me. Man that was fun. He taught me how to play chess, too. I got pretty good at it, so we'd play for hours and hours until Dad made me go to sleep." Caleb ran a hand through his long hair, his smile fading. "It all seems like such a waste. What the heck did he die for, anyway?" Rhonda leaned in and reached a hand toward him, but he shot her a threatening look. "Can YOU answer that question, Rhonda? Because nobody else seems to be able to. Tell me, Rhonda. You're a reporter. Why did my brother die in Vietnam?" The tension in the air was palpable. Suddenly, Caleb took a deep breath, leaned back, and with a wave of his hand said, "Next question."

Rhonda hesitated. "I know this is another sensitive question," she said, casting a quick glance over to one of the producers, "but people in Enapay have heard the stories and are curious about you, Caleb. If it's not too much trouble, could you tell us about your sister?"

 "I loved my sister," Caleb said, never breaking eye contact. "Amanda was 6 years older than me, and she was so passionate about the things she believed in that I always wished I was more like her. She had a sense of right and wrong and would fight for it—believe me, she would fight for it. I can remember boys always calling and coming over and Dad was just livid about it. He protected her, probably a little too much, and ran off all those boys, he said laughing. She could sing, too…boy she had a beautiful voice. She got to sing solos in the youth choir at church. That's really why she went out to Los Angeles, to be a singer. I don't know all the details about what happened to her because I was eleven when she died. I only know what my dad has told me. But one thing I know for sure is that she didn't deserve it. No one with a soul so full of life should die so young. I know it crushed my father—two kids dead in two years, it was just too much, too- too much." Caleb paused. "Everyone I love dies. Maybe I'm the grim reaper and that's not meant as a joke." Rhonda smiled slightly, but Caleb's simmering look shut her right up.

Rhonda folded her hands on her lap gently. "You said it crushed your Dad; what about your mother?"

Rhonda's gaze connected with Caleb's in that moment and the shine of those icy blue eyes chilled her so much that she sucked in a breath. You could hear a mouse pee on a piece of cotton. The whirling of the cameras was the only sound in the room——Caleb sat in silence. When Rhonda opened her mouth to ask the question again, Caleb interrupted, "If you want to talk to me about sports, that is fine, but I won't talk about my family anymore, it is just painful." He looked at Rhonda with a very chilling, trance like stare.

"Caleb," Rhonda said, "I know you've had a hard life, which makes your story even more extraordinary. Being able to overcome and conquer all that to become the National High School Athlete of the year is truly something special." Caleb shrugged, so Rhonda continued, "Have you decided which college and what sport you're going to play?"

Caleb sighed, relieved. "I'm not sure about the college yet, but I know I am going to play football, and baseball too, if they let me."

"Is there anything else you would like to say?" Rhonda asked.

"Are we done now?" he responded.

Rhonda nodded, feeling the tension in her shoulders melt away as he left. She had heard the rumors about him, but as she packed up her materials, she thought to herself, "That boy needs help."

***

Yes, Caleb Lewis had a bunch going for him. But that didn't mean he was the all-around popular sort of guy. In school, his teachers were so terrified of him and what might happen if they scolded him that they just left him alone. People in authority walked on eggshells around Caleb; they just wanted him out of school and out of Enapay. His junior year in high school, he supposedly raped a seventeen-year-old girl. She was so frightened of him that she wouldn't talk about it to her parents, friends, or counsellors. The girl committed suicide that same year.

The closest Caleb ever came to being arrested was the day he got into a confrontation with his science teacher, Mr. Swoho. The principal called the police, and Caleb was escorted off the campus and sent home, where he was to stay for the rest of the semester on suspension. Caleb could have cared less about being suspended but there was one downside—he couldn't be in sports. That was the only thing that kept Caleb somewhat sane.

***

Caleb stood outside the principal's front door, clenching and unclenching his fingers. Whether it was from a little twinge of nerves or because of the chilly evening air, he didn't know. Finally, he pushed the doorbell.

A rather rotund man in an ugly green shirt opened the door.

"Mr. Johnson," Caleb said before the principal had time to speak, "I just want you to know that I apologize for hitting Mr. Swoho. I shouldn't have done that."

Mr. Johnson just stared at him, not entirely sure if Caleb was going to attack him. "Caleb, you can't just intimidate people and hurt them. That's not how civilized people act. I hope you take time while you're off this semester and search your soul and come back next semester a better man and a better student."

A dark shadow flickered across Caleb's face, but he just stood staring into Mr. Johnson's eyes. "You know what else I've been thinking, Mr. Johnson?"

"What's that?" the round man said.

"Your daughter sure is beautiful—what is she, a sophomore?" Mr. Johnson's lazy expression grew a little more intense, but Caleb only smiled pleasantly. "Since I'll have so much free time this semester, I think I'm going to date your daughter. How does that sound to you? I mean, if you're absolutely positive there isn't a way I can get back into school, I think I'd like to date her. She's pretty sexy."

The frown on Mr. Johnson's face was so deep it looked like he had weights strapped to his lips. He'd heard the stories about Caleb and women and there was no suspension in the world worth putting his daughter in danger for.

After a long pause, Mr. Johnson replied, "Caleb, what you did was wrong, and you are *very* lucky that Mr. Swoho didn't file assault charges on you." The principal took a deep breath. "But that being said, I accept your apology, and I will see you in school tomorrow." Caleb smiled.

"I thought you might."

Mr. Johnson was fired the next day and Mr. Swoho quit, sued the school, and retired in the Bahamas.

Chapter 7

POOR LILLIE

Lillie tried the best she could with Caleb, but to say he was totally out of control was an understatement. She would threaten, yell, try to take away privileges—pretty much anything that she could think of to "pull in the reins" on him. But nothing worked; Caleb had no respect for Lillie whatsoever.

Then another event happened that forever changed Caleb.

It was a beautiful Sunday morning in spring. Lillie was bustling about getting ready for church, and the only thing she had left to do was try again to wake Caleb for church. She'd left this for last intentionally—it was always quite unpleasant, and he never went to church, but she asked him every week if he would go. She reached for the doorknob, then paused.

Caleb had long forgotten his church. He no longer believed in God. If there was a God, why would he pick on a child and cause all of the heartbreak, confusion, and utter devastation that had happened to his family? His brother and sister dead, his mother an adulteress, and his parents divorced—not really a "blessed" life. Of course, Caleb himself also felt responsible for the breakup of the family; if he just hadn't told his dad about what he saw, they might still be together. Caleb believed if all this is God's plan, he didn't want anything to do with him. He is sure if there is a God, he is worse than him.

Lillie stood frozen, hand halfway to the doorknob, lost in thought. Even though Caleb was a bad kid, a mother's love always holds out for hope. Lillie's life had gone so badly since the affair—the deaths of two children are enough to destroy most, but then watching the only child she had left making nothing but bad decisions and then feeling so helpless to do anything…she had repented to God and all the people in the church. She prayed for Caleb unceasingly; after all, people turn to God in their darkest, most desperate hours. Lillie is heartbroken and so tired of all the grief and suffering she has endured the last few years. But she has trust that God can fix him and restore his faith. She just needed to get him in that church house. She has to help him turn his life around, and she has to do it *now*.

Lillie finally seized the handle to the door and pushed it open quickly. She sees all the beer bottles and smells the weed that has now permeated itself in all the drapes and carpet. She walked over, quietly weaving through the maze of trash to sit on the edge of Caleb's bed. She stared at her baby boy, asleep, and reached over to run her fingers through his hair.

Caleb always told her he loved her, back when he was that innocent little boy who ran and played without a care in the world. *I love you*. It had been such a long time since she'd heard those words, from him or from anyone else. Lillie softly lay down next to Caleb. She sighed deeply, catching a hint of his smell mixed with the stench of pot and booze. She wrapped her long arms around him, she can't remember the last time she held him like this and is savoring this moment. She squeezed him tightly and tears started dripping from her eyes. Holding him felt so right to her and it had been so long since she even touched him. After a few minutes, she leaned in to whisper in his ear.

"Caleb. Caleb, it's time to get up and go to church." Caleb lazily opened one eye, turned his head and looked at Lillie, turned back, and went to sleep. Shaking his shoulder she repeated "Caleb, Caleb it's time to go to church." Caleb huffed and shrugged her off, shoving her out of bed as he rolled to stand up. He was hung-over, tired and angry. He slowly got up from his bed and looked at his mother. Suddenly, all the heartache, contempt, and disgust for his mother came pouring into him at once; his veins were throbbing in his forehead. Caleb was a strapping man now, not a child anymore.

Lillie looked at him and immediately knew she was in danger. She tried to run—a bad idea. Maybe it was instinct, maybe it was rage, but the sight of her as she turned made him snap. Caleb lunged, grabbing her by the hair and threw her against the wall, "Whore!" he screamed at the top of his lungs. "Whore! Whore! Leave me alone, you cheating whore!" He threw her down on the floor; clawing at his face, she tried to fight back, but he was too strong. She moaned as his fist connected with her jaw, then her eye, her nose—Caleb raged totally out of control. All the resentment, anger, and vengeance that had built up in him over the last ten years came pouring out with a fury of punches. Blood peppered the wall as he drew his fists back again and again. Lillie looked at him one last time and gasped her final breath.

Caleb had killed his mother.

CHAPTER 8

THE COVER-UP

While Caleb may have been crazy, he wasn't stupid. Oddly, he felt no immediate remorse for killing his mother—just a focus on the task at hand, which was to figure out how to cover it all up. He knew that he couldn't intimidate the Oklahoma State Bureau of Investigation.

Should I make it look like an accident? Should I just get rid of the body and tell the police I don't know where she is? How do I cover up all the blood in my bedroom?

He sat on the edge of his bed looking into the motionless eyes of his blood-covered mother, deep in thought. He had read so many true crime stories in his life that it didn't take him too long to come up with a plan.

"Well, with Mom dead," he said aloud to himself, "I would get the house to live in and I wouldn't need this apartment anymore." He always had some candles burning in his place, and Lillie would always come and clean his apartment when he wasn't home. *I'll burn it down with her in there*, he thought.

It wasn't an easy fix. The fire needed to be intense enough to destroy his bedroom where the murder took place and cover up any signs of abuse on his mother. It had to look like it burned naturally, though, and the use of any accelerants like gasoline was risky. He had an official visit for football scheduled in Stillwater, Oklahoma the following day, so he had to make up his mind quickly. *Wait,* he thought, eyebrows peaking. *If I can start a fire while I'm out of town....*

He grabbed the phone and called Nia, telling her that he "had something to show her." When Nia showed up, he took her in to where Lillie was lying. Nia gagged when she laid eyes on the body.

"If you don't want to wind up looking like this," Caleb said, "then this is what I want you to do tomorrow." She stood trembling, looking first at Lillie, then at Caleb, then back at Lillie, terrified. She thought of running, but where could she go? Plus, Caleb supplied all her drugs. Caleb wrapped an arm around her shoulder—she tensed—and explained all the details, exactly how and where to start the fire. Then he handed her the only thing she'd ever really wanted from him—drugs.

Nia took them then wiped her forehead, breathing quickly and afraid. *This is going to send me to hell for sure.* But she was already in so deep with Caleb, what difference did it make now? *Here or there, my life is already hell.*

***

Once he had the plan in place and all the details under control, Caleb's mind snapped back to what he'd just done. His legs felt weak, and he fell to his knees with a dull thud. Tears were tickling the corners of his eyes as he stared at Lillie. Blood was seeping into the carpet and walls, and his fists had disfigured her skull. The realization of what he had just done hit him, like a ton of bricks, and he could no longer control himself. Tears rolled down his face and off his chin. He lifted Lillie up in his arms, scrubbing desperately at her face as his sobs intensified. He cried, "Momma, I'm sorry." His fingers kept getting caught in her blood-soaked hair as he frantically tried to straighten it. He just kept saying, "I'm sorry, Momma. I'm so sorry…" over and over again. Caleb was the most unemotional guy Nia had ever known, and she'd often found herself wondering if he actually had feelings. Seeing him like this—it was just incomprehensible. She couldn't stand it. She stood up quickly.

"I know the plan, and I'll do it exactly like you said," as she turned and left. The house was silent but for Caleb, sitting there for an hour sobbing, grief-stricken, rocking back and forth, holding the mother he once loved so much in his arms. How had things come to this? For the first time in a long time, Caleb felt remorse.

Caleb wanted a fresh start and was so tired of what he'd become. It was just a destructive, painful way to live.

Caleb bent over, kissed his mom on the forehead, and whispered a real, honest apology in her ear. He finally said the words she longed to hear—"I love you"—for the last time and left

***

While Caleb was in Stillwater, the apartment went up in a spectacular, fiery explosion. The fire marshal ruled it a gas leak ignited by a candle burning near the wall-mounted room heater in the bedroom. It took the fire department a few minutes to get there, and by then, all they could do was watch the fire and keep it from spreading. Included in the report was mention of one body in the room, a Lillie Lewis. She was incinerated completely by the intense heat.

Nia was found dead three days later of an apparent drug overdose. Jamie supposedly left town and was never heard from again. Caleb was sure of one thing—dead bodies don't talk, and who can trust heroin addicts anyway?

CHAPTER 9

COLLEGE IS GOOD!

Caleb had decisions to make about his future. He was touted as a first-round draft pick in the Major League baseball draft, or he could go to the college of his choice in football. Pro scouts were calling him the next Mickey Mantle, and college coaches were telling him he would be the greatest college football quarterback in history.

The only way to make it to the NFL in 1981 was to go through college first, so that's where he wanted to be. Caleb's house is a beehive of activity that spring. Between MLB scouts and NCAA coaches, it is a bit overwhelming. Caleb was the #1 High School QB pick in the United States in every scouting report and magazine. Jack, unceasingly proud of his son, was helping him with the decision. American Legion baseball was just getting underway, and that kept Caleb busy, so Jack footed a lot of the work and the talking. Caleb didn't seem all that interested anyway and could probably care less where he went—he just wanted away from Enapay.

Caleb had visited the University of Oklahoma, Oklahoma State University, and Missouri. He wanted to play in the Big Eight Football Conference because he was familiar with it. The City of Angels University in Los Angeles or the CAU Panthers was hot on his list, and after he returned from a visit there one week, he told his dad that he was going to CAU. Caleb had loved the QB coach, Bob Axom, and the head coach, Joe Richert.

Jack, of course, thought that all of this was just great. CAU had a great tradition of football, one of the powerhouses of the nation, not to mention they had high academics and were a well-respected university. CAU is right behind Notre Dame, Oklahoma and Alabama in National Football Championships won.

Caleb had been the perfect gentleman throughout all of the recruiting. The coaches thought they had an all-American young man that any university would be proud to have, an excellent example for young people and the university. A few weeks later, Caleb and Jack made the announcement in town to great fanfare from everyone. Everyone in Enapay was thrilled with the idea because Satan would be thousands of miles away and they could let their girls out of the house again. There was only a few days left of high school, and the university wanted him to move out there as soon as he graduated so he could begin work on getting their system down.

In June of 1981, Caleb was 18 years old and heading out to new adventures in a new town. He had a brand new 1981 model red Corvette. Everyone assumed CAU bought him the Vette, but he never said one way or the other. He was ready to get out of Enapay and all the destruction, abuse, and sorrow it had caused him. He still had over $30,000 left from his extortion of Daisy's money, and Jack had agreed to sell Lillie's property for him and file the life insurance that she had from her federal job. He would put all the proceeds in a bank account so Caleb would have money while he was in college.

Caleb was ready to turn over a new leaf—for once, he felt like he knew right from wrong and was just sure he had a conscience…it just didn't always work right. A new life in front of him, that's just what he needed. He packed a couple of bags full of clothes, drugs, and money and headed west to start his new life.

CHAPTER 10

HEADING WEST

Just about the only places Caleb had ever traveled to were
his sporting events, so he was a bit nervous about the trip to
Los Angeles. He packed his new Vette with a couple of
suitcases, got out his road map, and headed to Interstate 40.
Jack had told him not to drive past Albuquerque, which
was about 490 miles away from Enapay.

Caleb was itching to press down the pedal on this Vette. In
1981, the speedometer in all cars read to a maximum 85
mph, mandated by a new (and controversial) federal law.
He wanted more of a muscle car, but this was what was
available for the time being, and he looked good in it.
Caleb kept on driving west through the boring stretch of
nowhere between Enapay and the Texas border, always
bumping up against the speed limit. After an hour or so, he
turned onto the quiet Highway 256 heading to Memphis
Texas, grinned a devious smirk, and put the pedal down to
the floorboards and shredded past that 85 mph on his dash.
He laughed out loud, a big smile stretching from ear to ear.

A couple of lights spinning in the reflection of his rear-
view mirror wiped that smirk right off his face. A deputy
sheriff on his bumper—this was bad. He had over $30,000
in Daisy's cash and a pound of heroin, weed, and cocaine
in his luggage. No more than an hour away from home, and
trouble had already found him. He pulled over to the side of

the road, running a hand through his hair and taking a deep breath so as not to let his emotions get the best of him. Just play it cool. Be nice and see where it goes.

Deep in his mind Caleb is prepared to kill this deputy if he asked to search his luggage, but he didn't want to resort to that. Killing a law enforcement officer in the first hour he'd been gone was not exactly what he had in mind when he thought about a fresh start.

"Sir, would you step out of the car?" the deputy said as he approached. He looked to be around 5'10, 60-ish, fat and out-of-shape. Caleb knew he'd have no problem killing this man if he had to.

"Yes, sir," Caleb said, staring closely at the deputy.

"Do you have any idea how fast you were going, young man?"

"No, sir. I just got this car, and I was seeing what it would do. I'm on my way to play football at CAU, so I guess I was just a little excited." Caleb sighed. "I'm sorry, sir, it was a dumb thing to do. I promise I'll be careful the rest of the trip."

The deputy paused. "Are you by any chance Caleb Lewis?"

"Yes sir, I am."

The deputy's face broke into a grin. "Ah! I've watched you play football a couple of times! You're quite the athlete, young man. But I sure am disappointed you didn't go to the

University of Texas to play ball," he said with a serious look.

Caleb leaned back onto the Corvette and smiled. "That's where I wanted to go, but my dad would have nothing to do with it!" (This was a lie—it would be a hot day at the North Pole before Caleb would consider going to UT).

The deputy took a quick glance inside the car and saw the two suitcases. "That all you're taking with you?"

"Well," Caleb said, "you can't get much luggage in these, so I just put some clothes in and took off."

The deputy looked at him, eyebrows furrowing together. "Did them boys in California buy you this car?"

"Sir, no disrespect to you, but I promised I wouldn't comment on that," he replied, wiping off a bug on the Vette.

The deputy rolled his eyes but still smiled. "Shoot, son, UT would have bought you a garage full of these cars if you'd gone there!"

"Well, I did what my dad thought was best for me. I try to respect my parents as best I can," Caleb replied.

"Well at least you didn't go to Oklahoma University! I can't stand that Barry Switzer, so I'm thankful for that." The cop gave Caleb a friendly nudge on the shoulder. "Now you slow down that car and put on your seatbelt before you get yourself killed." Caleb nodded. "Oh, and one more thing, though, before I let you leave. Could I ask you for an autograph?" Caleb smiled and signed away. The deputy wished him the best of luck at CAU and off he went.

As he started to get back to speed on the road, Caleb leaned back in his seat and thought, *maybe my luck is changing.*

***

Caleb pulled into Albuquerque a few hours later, a bit tired and ready to relax. He pulled into a hotel, got a room, took his bags up, and hopped on the bed. The cool sheets were a welcome change from the hot air. He called the front desk and asked for a 7 A.M. wake up call, then hung up the phone and locked the door.

Grabbing his drug kit out of his luggage, Caleb shook a pack of heroin into the spoon, heated it up, and pushed the needle into his vein. He'd shot in just about every place you can get a needle: arms, hands, front of fingers, back of fingers, palm, chest, abdomen, legs—wherever there's a vein, there's a shot. Caleb had always been fascinated with human anatomy and had studied it quite a bit, so he knew where to find veins to shoot up. One of the great myths of injecting is that it marks the body. Yes, it will if you continuously shoot in the same places, but with new, fresh veins there are no marks left. If you inspected his body, you wouldn't notice any obvious marks on him; once again, Caleb did his homework.

Caleb just did heroin occasionally before bedtime, but he was in no way addicted to it. He could go weeks without giving it a thought. In reality, he'd only purchased the heroin for Nia and Jamie's habit—he truly thought about throwing it away before he left. But, you never know what the future might hold, right? When he got up every morning, he took a shower, dressed, and snorted coke to wake up and get going. He would usually have few beers during the day and some more coke. Caleb called Jack to let him know he got there safely, and his plans were to drive to Flagstaff in the morning and then on to L.A. the following day.

CHAPTER 11

FLAGSTAFF

Caleb jolted awake the next morning, startled, sweat pouring down his face, screaming his mother's name over the ring of the 7am wake-up call. It had been the same recurring nightmare since he murdered Lillie. He sat on the edge of the bed for a moment trying to catch his breath. After his nerves had calmed down a little, he got up and went through his normal routine—showered, dressed, and snorted some coke. He loaded up his car and drove to a local mom & pop café to get some breakfast.

As he was sitting alone at the counter, two local men swaggered up to him.

"How'd you get that nice car there, boy?"

"My dad bought it for me for college," Caleb replied, not really looking at them.

"Mind if we take a look?" the two asked.

"Sure," Caleb said with a shrug. "Let me finish my breakfast and I'll show it to you." The waitress, who'd been listening nonchalantly, brought Caleb's food. She knew these two guys were bullies and could make trouble for this young man. Little did they know they were about to pick on the biggest, baddest bully of them all.

The two men sat down on either side of Caleb, nudging in close.

"You a spoiled rich boy, kid?" Caleb didn't reply, just sat there eating his breakfast. One man snorted. "Hey boy, you deaf?"

Caleb looked at him with those piercing blue eyes and said, "No, I ain't deaf. I just don't like talking to two uneducated rednecks this early in the morning." His blood pressure was starting to rise, adrenaline kicking in.

The waitress, losing her patience, said, "Why don't you two leave this poor boy alone and let him eat his breakfast in peace? Why do you always have to be making trouble for people?"

Caleb looked at the waitress and with a relaxed smile said, "Don't worry about it, ma'am. I can kick both their asses, and I will as soon as I finish my breakfast."

The two men sat there flabbergasted, and one of them picked up a glass of water and poured it over his head. "Well boy," he said, "you've done the easy part, talking about it."

He no sooner got the word "it" out of his mouth before Caleb's fist hit him square in the nose and knocked him across the floor. Caleb heard his nose snap. The other guy grabbed him from behind and Caleb elbowed him in the jaw with such force that he thought he might have broken it. One man was crawling on the ground with blood gushing out of his nose, and the other was screaming that he broke his jaw.

"I don't think I've ever whooped two guys in less than a minute!" Caleb said with a laugh. "Can I give you boys some words of wisdom? Ya ought not to be picking on people if you can't fight any better than that."

Caleb asked the waitress if he owed her anything for the broken glass, but she just giggled at the two men on the floor. "No sir, you don't owe us anything and your breakfast is free."

He looked down at the guys, making sure one foot came precariously close to their faces as he passed. "You men still want to look at my car?" he said and walked away chuckling. The smile stayed on his face for most of the way down I-40 toward Flagstaff.

***

When Caleb pulled into Flagstaff, he couldn't help but pause to look around at the beauty of it. Situated in a dramatic location beneath the San Francisco Peaks halfway between New Mexico and California, Flagstaff was more than he'd imagined. He saw a Holiday Inn just off the interstate and pulled in to get a room.

Caleb laid down for a bit after he smoked a joint that afternoon. When he awoke, it was around 6pm, and he was starving. He'd noticed a place that looked cool when he first arrived, so he bustled over there to grab some food.

Caleb had grown into an outrageously handsome man—very tall and masculine, with that same beautiful bronze skin as Lillie. He had transparent blue eyes, big dimples, and jet-black hair down to his shoulders. He was the "bad boy" that women seem attracted to. It was no surprise, then, that as he scanned over the menu, a girl in a light, airy skirt floated over.

"Mind if I sit here?" she asked, putting a hand on the chair next to him.

"Whatever you want to do," he said indifferently.

She slid into the chair and spun toward him. "So what's your name?"

"Why do you want to know?" Caleb mumbled. Women were constantly hitting on him, and it was tiresome. She just sat there twirling her hair and smiling.

"My name's Carmen, and me and a friend are on our way to San Francisco for the summer. We're just looking to party a bit on the way there, you know?" Caleb said nothing. "What about you? You like parties?" His eyes stopped scanning the menu for a moment.

"Sure. What did you have in mind?" He followed her gaze to what must have been her friend—a total knockout, and Carmen wasn't too bad either. Both girls had long hair, stood about 5'3" or so, and had nice, curvy bodies. Around 20 or so, probably.

Carmen lightly put a hand on his shoulder. "Wanna hop on over to our table?" Caleb slid out of his chair and followed her. Thank goodness there were two of them—he knew he wouldn't have to talk much. The other girl (whom he discovered was named Robin) seemed very shy and uncomfortable with Carmen's boldness.

"You know, you never answered my question about your name."

"It's Caleb."

"Well, Caleb," Carmen drawled, "wanna smoke some weed?"

Caleb's eyebrows peaked, and he smiled knowingly. "Sure, but I don't have any." (He had a pound back at his hotel, but why waste it? They wouldn't have asked if they didn't have some themselves.)

"Don't worry," Carmen said, "we do. Let's eat a bit, then we'll go back and have some fun." After eating their fill and drinking too much they hopped in Carmen's car and headed off to their hotel.

***

When they were done and he'd had everything he wanted from them, Caleb told the girls he had to leave and got up, walked out of the hotel, and wandered a few blocks back to his Vette.

Once Caleb left the room, Carmen leaned over to check on Robin. She was lying on the bed just staring up at the ceiling, her eyebrows contracted —confused, high, something. Carmen snuggled up to her, laying her head softly on her shoulders.

"You do know that regardless of what just happened, I'm not a lesbian, right?"

Robin bewildered by what just occurred said "I didn't think I was either, but now I'm not so sure."

Carmen wrapped her arms around Robin. "Was it just me, or did you get the feeling that something bad was going to happen to us if we didn't do what he wanted?"

"There was something very disturbing about that guy," Robin slurred, still a little high and drunk. "It felt like he was on the edge and about to go mental at any second."

They lay there in silence for a few minutes, and Robin quietly dozed off. When Carmen shifted and yawned, she woke again.

"Hey Robin?"

"Yeah?"

"Have you ever been with a guy that big?"

Robin grumbled "Nope. And I hope I never am again."

They both just shook their heads and laid there in each other's arms, feeling like they just danced with the devil and somehow escaped.

"Oh, and Carmen? Never tell anyone about this. EVER." That night with Caleb forever changed how they regarded men. They wound up getting married to each other a few years later, but secretly, they always said, "If it wasn't for that freak forcing us to make love, we wouldn't have known we were soul mates." Caleb didn't get an invitation to the wedding.

Chapter 12

CAU HERE I COME

Caleb pulled into Los Angeles, ready to tear his map in half trying to figure out how to get to CAU. He had never seen such a mess of roads before. There were roads in every direction going up and down and all over the place. He got on Highway 60—somehow it led him to the CAU campus. He kept his eyes peeled for the CAU stadium—that's where he thought the coaches were. As he made the final turn down Highway 60, he caught a glimpse of the City of Angels Stadium. He smiled; he was a country boy in a big place, but he felt like he belonged here.

Pulling into the CAU stadium, he opened the door and walked in. There were signs on the wall, and one said Football Offices. He followed the directions to a receptionist sitting at the front desk. Her shiny nameplate said "Susan Smith."

"Hi," Caleb said as he approached her, "my name is Caleb Lewis, and I'm going to be playing football here this fall. What am I supposed to do now?"

Susan looked up, a little shot of electricity jolting over her as she caught an eyeful of his good looks. She giggled. "My name is Susan; nice to meet you. You need to see Anni Vohem. Her office is the first office on the right."

Caleb walked into Anni's office, surprised to see another secretary named Beth Owens (as per the name tag). Caleb cleared his throat. "I'm here to see Anni Vohem, please."

"Take a seat," Beth said without looking up. "Mrs. Vohem will be with you in just a bit." Caleb slunk into a chair, looking around the office. He noticed a brochure—"CAU Football: The Making of a Champion." *What a cheesy title,* he thought.

Inside were numerous bios, but the one that caught his eye was the one on Mrs. Anni Vohem herself. It said that she was 38 years old, had her MBA, and was Vice President of Football Operations. She was married to a Dr. Rod Vohem and her picture was good-looking—Rod was a lucky man.

After about 10 minutes, Beth's phone buzzed. As she answered, she actually took the time to look up at Caleb. For once, her face changed expressions.

"My goodness!" Caleb heard her say under her breath. Whispering into the phone she said, "A Caleb Lewis is here to see you, and boy have you got to come out here!" A few moments later, Anni swung open the door of her office and looked at Caleb.

What an astonishingly good-looking young man. Anni couldn't take her eyes off of Caleb; she was like a teenage girl. This is the exact man that was with her as a teenager when she was in bed late at night learning about her body. And now he was in front of her.

"What, uh, p—" she stammered, then cleared her throat and mentally smacked herself for her giddiness. "Yes, what position were you recruited for, Mr. Lewis?" She could feel beads of sweat pearling on her forehead, and she wanted so badly to fan her face, but she thought that would look awkward. She leaned to the side and whispered, "Is the air conditioner working, Beth?"

Beth giggled and said "I'm freezing."

"Quarterback, ma'am," Caleb replied proudly, forcing her to focus.

She nodded and, pointing a finger in the air, told Caleb to wait for a minute. She picked up the phone and rang for Coach Axom. "Coach, you have a young man waiting here with me. Could you come down and help him?"

A few minutes later, the door flew open as Coach Axom happily blasted into Anni's office. "Welcome to CAU, Caleb!" Coach said, grabbing Caleb's hand for a firm shake. "Are you ready to be a champion?"

"Thanks, coach," Caleb said with a smile. "I'm excited about being here, but I'm not sure what I'm supposed to do now."

Anni stood off to one side, just staring at Caleb, spellbound. Maybe she had other work to do. She didn't really know or care.

"I have everything prepared for you, so you don't have to worry about it," Coach Axom said. "Just do what Anni tells you. Beth will get you into your apartment and show you around campus. Just listen to what she says. And stay out of trouble," he added, the smile on his face fading into a more serious look. "It's a big place with lots of temptations, and you are a target of the press because you play for CAU. Be very careful with your statements and your actions. Don't do anything that will embarrass CAU or yourself and you'll be fine. It's time to grow up now and take on a new level of maturity. We have all the confidence in the world in you or we wouldn't have recruited you."

Caleb nodded, so coach gave him a thumbs up and then walked around to Beth behind her desk. She was getting her things together to show Caleb around, but he put a hand on her arm and drew her a few steps to the side.

"Be careful how you speak to Caleb," he said quietly. "He can get irritated easily, I hear." Beth paused and looked up at him. She'd shown football players around their dorms many times, but she'd never gotten a warning like that.

Caleb didn't feel the greatest about being shown around the dorms and the football program by a woman, but he just sighed and kept on. *Be nice. Be a gentleman. She's just going to help me.*

Caleb and Beth headed about, but no sooner were they on their way to the parking lot than Anni ran out of her office and grabbed Beth.

"You know, Beth, I was just thinking. I know you're busy, so I don't mind getting Caleb settled in." Beth rolled her eyes and giggled. Anni NEVER took ball players to their dorms.

Anni, prancing clumsily with her high heels, caught up with Caleb, who was still kind of floating along taking a slow look at the big campus. Finally, Anni scurried to his side and waved goodbye to Beth. "You have a new car, don't you?" she said, breaking the silence.

"Yes ma'am," Caleb said, beaming. "A brand new Corvette!"

"I know," she said with a laugh, "I paid for it! And you must be quite the ball player. That's only the third Corvette I've bought in 14 years."

As they walked to the car, Anni made a special effort to swing her hips and walk as sexily as she could remember— it had been a while. Anni patted the car. "Do you mind if I drive?"

"Heck no!" Caleb said. "You bought it, and I have no idea where I'm going anyhow." She smiled and slid into the driver's seat; her short mini-skirt barely covered her butt to begin with, and as she drove, it kept riding up higher and higher until she was basically sitting there in her pink panties. She knew it, and more importantly, she knew Caleb knew it.

She drove him to the football athletic dorms, took him up to the second floor, and said, "You're staying in #232 with another QB we recruited by the name of Billy Thompson from San Diego." As they opened the door, Caleb was both surprised and relieved; it was much bigger than his apartment at home. Each person had their own bedroom and study desk, a nice T.V., a common living area with a couple of couches and a small refrigerator, and they shared a large bathroom with two sinks and a big shower.

"Billy isn't to arrive for another few weeks or so," Anni said, snapping him out of his daze, "so you'll have the place to yourself." Her eyebrows may or may not have perked at that—he wasn't sure. "Downstairs there are pool tables and foosball tables along with some pinball machines. There's also a study hall with tutors available to help you with your classes. We've got a cafeteria where you can eat three meals a day, and of course, everything is free."

Caleb sat down on the edge of the bed as she continued talking. In between sentences, she reached into her handbag and pulled out the Athletes Code of Conduct book. Her face became serious quickly.

"Read it until you know every word in it. You and only you are responsible for your actions at CAU, and the excuse 'I didn't know' is unacceptable. Everything you need to know is in that book." Before he could skim through it, she reached back into her bag and pulled out another very thick book. "Here is your bible—this is the CAU playbook for 1981. You must study, study, study, and then study some more until you know every play. You must know what every player does on every play, not just what you do. You will spend hundreds of hours on this book with Coach Axom; you must know it by instinct. You will guard that book with your life—it is yours and only yours. You will be expected to turn it back in at the end of the season. You can take until Monday to get acclimated to your surroundings, but on Monday you are to meet with Coach Axom at 9 A.M. in his office…and I wouldn't be late if I were you.

Oh, and there's one more program you need to be aware of. Every game each player receives four tickets to the game. You can give them away to family or friends, but you can also sell them back to my office for face value. I need you to understand that if you are caught selling the tickets to anyone else but my office, you will be dismissed from the football team and of course lose your scholarship. This is private information and the tickets aren't to be discussed with anyone. The NCAA, let's just say, frowns on this. Now, do you have any questions?"

"No, ma'am," he said.

"Good," she said, bringing a warm smile back to her face. She took a few steps toward him. "Now, do you need any money?" she asked with a purr.

"Uhhh…not yet," Caleb said, slightly confused by that.

She waltzed up to him, leaned in close, ran her fingers through his hair. "You might want to get that hair cut," she whispered in his ear. Her lips were just inches away from his, her breathing heavy.

Caleb leaned back from her, surprised by her boldness, and said, "Well, thanks for your help. You folks sure are friendly around here."

She just giggled and said, "Bye, and I'll see you on Monday."

"Hey, you need a ride back, don't you?" he said.

"Don't worry about it," she said confidently. "I don't have a problem getting rides around the athletic dorm." Then she left.

***

Caleb started unpacking his bags around 3 that afternoon, but what he really wanted was to talk to some other athletes to get a feel of what these dorms were all about. But before he ventured out to find some others living nearby, he reached in his bag, got his small spoon out, and snorted some coke. While he was still riding the drug, he reached for the phone and called Jack, swapping pleasantries about how he's safe and settled in and promising to keep in touch often. Caleb told Jack he loved him and hung up.

He hung all of his clothes in the closet and put his other stuff in the drawers, but he was especially meticulous with his drugs—he was worried about someone finding them, so he looked thoroughly for a good place. He spotted a hole underneath his desk where the paneling had come loose from the wall a bit. He tugged on it a bit more, and after it came loose with a little puff of dust, he hid his drugs and money in between the studs.

A little relieved that he'd found a good place for his stash, he wandered through the halls and ended up down in the cafeteria. It was pretty empty, save for a big fellow playing pool. This guy was HUGE—about 6'7" and he must have weighed over 300 pounds.

73

"Hi," Caleb said, coming up behind the giant. "My name's Caleb Lewis and I just got here from Oklahoma about an hour ago. I'm wondering…when do we eat?"

The big guy took a shot, scratching the cue ball into the corner pocket. He huffed in fake frustration, and then turned to Caleb. "I'm Lavon Jackson from Bossier City, Louisiana," the guy said with a smile. "I just got here a couple of days ago myself. The best I can figure, they open around 4:30 till around 7:30, but man, I'm always hungry!" Both boys chuckled. "I tell ya one thing; you ain't ever gonna eat as well as these folks feed you. Just tell them what you want, and they cook it up and it don't cost nuttin'. Last night I asked Miss Pecking if I could have a steak, and all she said was, 'How big a steak you want, Lavon?' I said, 'How big a steak you got?' Then she looked at me and said, 'I got a whole side of beef, you just tell me what you want and I'll cut it for you.' So I said, 'How about a T-bone steak?' and I put my hands up and said, 'this big.' After she cooked it, she said it's a 36-ounce T-bone, and it didn't cost me nuttin'! They gonna fatten us up like cows going to slaughter around here. I promise ya that!"

Caleb laughed. "So we have about an hour before we eat, then. Mind if I join you in a game of pool?"

"Sure!" Lavon said. "But I'm terrible at it, and I don't really know how to play, but that's okay." Caleb smiled and nodded—he wasn't sure how bright Lavon was and figured he hadn't read any of the procedure books yet, so he would just wait until some sophomores or juniors showed up and ask them some questions about living here.

As Lavon randomly racked the balls, Caleb said, "So what position do you play?"

Lavon, thinking hard, said, "Well, if they determine I'm fast enough they say they're putting me at defensive tackle; if I'm not fast enough, they'll put me at offensive tackle. I played both those spots in high school, but here you only play one or the other. It don't really matter to me, though; I feel like I'm living in a mansion, eating all the food I want, TV in my room. Man, who would have thought playing high school ball for fun would turn out like this! I feel luckier than a man with two peckers."

Caleb laughed loudly, leaned in, and placed the cue ball. "Let's play some pool."

CHAPTER 13

SUMMER WORK

There were about 20 or so guys staying in the dorms that summer, all of them incoming freshmen. There were a couple of dorm supervisors living there, and their job was to keep these kids in line. That's tougher than it might seem—most of these young men had never been away from home and were out to sow their wild oats. Dorm rules stated NO WOMEN allowed inside; CAU learned long ago that women in the dorms were just trouble. If you wanted to see a girl, you had to go to their apartment. One supervisor stayed downstairs while the other guarded the stairwells, so it wasn't easy to sneak a lady up there. And if you actually got caught with a girl in your room, the punishment was pretty harsh.

To his own bemusement, Caleb wasn't even trying to mess with any girls; he didn't trust himself with women, and he wasn't familiar enough with the dorm layout and rules. That and he truly wanted to turn over a new leaf and try to live like an average 18-year-old. He just wanted to play football.

On Monday morning, he arrived at the stadium at 8:30 to be greeted by the receptionist, Susan, who motioned him to wait in the coach's office. He had studied both books that Anni gave him and was already pretty familiar with both.

When Coach Axom walked in, he greeted Caleb with another massive hand shake.

"Getting settled in all right, kid?" Axom asked.

"Yes, sir!" Caleb said. "Everything is great."

"Well, let me show you around," Coach Axom said, walking off quickly. Caleb followed. "You're going to be spending most of your time in the athletic facilities, and CAU has the best in the nation." Caleb had seen some of this before, but it truly was immensely impressive. The CAU stadium was only five years old but was the most modern stadium in the country. It held around 90,000 fans, and the entire upper east side of the stadium was filled with everything from the football offices, training rooms, weight rooms, film rooms, and even medical facilities.

They passed by the weight training facility, and Caleb sneaked a peek through the side window. There must have been a hundred different machines, free weights, and other gadgets. Coach paused, waiting for his enamored freshman to get a grip.

"You'll be in this room every day for the next four years. Weight training coaches will tailor a workout for you that you must do religiously, so be prepared to step up your game." Caleb nodded and skipped after Axom, who had already begun to leave. He caught up to him in front of the locker room.

"Okay coach, where's *my* locker?" Caleb said, but he didn't need to hear the answer—his gaze fell upon a shiny silver engraved name plate: "Caleb Lewis #11." He flung open the locker door, and inside he already had shoulder pads, a helmet, and a practice jersey. Caleb picked up the practice jersey and looked it over; on the back, it said Lewis 11. He'd never had a jersey with his name on it! He was tempted to put it on and just wear it for the rest of the day, but he decided against it.

They left the confines of the inner stadium and ventured back out to the open air. There were two full-size fields, one with Astroturf and the other with natural grass. A couple of freshman receivers were practicing out on the field.

"Want to toss a few?" Axom asked.

"Sure," Caleb said with a grin. "That's what you pay me for."

Coach Axom's pleasant face suddenly fell into a glare. "Don't *ever* say those words again, please. We don't pay you anything, and if the press heard you say that, all kinds of questions would break loose." Axom sighed and put a hand on Caleb's shoulder. "Caleb, you have to pick your words very carefully around here."

"Sorry, coach," Caleb said, a little surprised at the outburst. "I'll be more careful."

"Good." Axom's smile slowly returned. "Now, why don't you go throw some 10-yard, then 20-yard passes until your arm warms up?" Caleb started to jog away, but Axom quickly called out to him. "And don't just go out there throwing 50-yard passes with a cold arm!" Caleb stopped and grabbed a ball. "We're all about working smart and not getting hurt. A hurt football player does us no good. We always warm up before we go full blast."

Caleb looked at Coach, grinned, and said, "See that little guy at the other end of the field?" Axom looked, and while he was turned away, Caleb picked up a football and flung it about 70 yards downfield and hit the receiver in the back of the head. The poor receiver didn't even know there was someone throwing, much less 70 yards away. He knocked him to the ground.

Coach Axom stood stunned for a moment, but that didn't last long. "Exactly what part of the warming up speech did you not understand?" Maybe there was a little smile hidden underneath that frown.

"Sorry coach, I haven't thrown a football since November, and I just had to sling it."

Coach just shook his head. *This kid is going to be the greatest QB in history.*

Caleb and the coach headed back to the office and spent a few hours on the playbook and looking at some film of last year's CAU team. The starting QB, Jason Allgood, was going to be a senior this year, so he had lots of experience. CAU was primarily a power running team. They've had two Heisman Trophy winners, both running backs. The place had even taken the unofficial name "Halfback University" in the last decade or so. Caleb hoped he could turn CAU into a passing team over the next four years, but if given a chance, he could run and scramble with the best of them. It would be almost impossible to break into the starting lineup as a freshman, but he planned on doing everything he could to convince the coaches that that would be the best move.

On the way out of the practice facilities, Caleb said goodbye to Axom and stopped in to Anni's office for a visit. She showed him around a bit, and he wondered what she did to deserve an office like this. It had a private bathroom, a small bedroom, and it even overlooked the game field.

As Caleb wandered through her place (rather intrusively, actually, but she didn't particularly care), she leaned back and tried to take an objective look at herself and where she was. Anni grew up in Los Angeles and went to school at CAU, so she got to know some important people that hooked her up to this job as Vice President of Football Operations. But she wouldn't let them take all the credit. She was a disciplined, focused professional executive who worked hard to get where she is. Anni is the first female in the country to rise to a job like this and that's just the beginning—she was on track to become the first woman athletic director of a major university. She pretty much ran everything anyway, and all the coaches went to her for questions about policy or procedures. She could pull just about any strings she wanted for coaches or ball players without explanation. It was power.

The coaches didn't want to know what she did because of the NCAA, and her only bosses were the head football coach and the athletic director (who just left her alone, usually, because they were always trying to put out their own fires). Still, despite all her power—or maybe because of it—if anyone got into trouble with NCAA, it was going to be Anni. Players' grades, homesickness, law trouble, or money issues all came her way via the coaches' recommendations for athletes to let her solve their problems. In solving them, she'd learned quite a lot about the CAU program. Maybe too much.

Caleb reappeared, snapping Anni out of her contemplation.

"Nice place," he said. She smiled and slid herself onto the edge of her desk.

"Thanks. So, what are you doing tonight?"

Caleb made a point of looking straight into her eyes. "Probably just studying a bit. You want to drop by the dorm and see me?" She opened her mouth to say something, then immediately closed it again. No football player had ever been so bold as to ask her to his dorm room.

"*Noooo*. Bad idea," she said cautiously. And just who do you think you are asking me such a question?

"Come on, call me and I'll try to sneak you up to my room."

She rolled her eyes. "You don't have to sneak me up anywhere. I'm on the football staff, remember? They won't say a word to me about anything."

Caleb walked up to the edge of the desk and confidently moved in between her legs, just inches from her face. She could feel his breath. He moved a stray hair off her cheek.

"Then drop by, and maybe we can go over some plays," he said as he lightly dragged his fingers up and down her arms.

Anni sighed and closed her eyes. She was trying so hard not to pounce on this man, but she managed to restrain herself. When she looked up, she saw Caleb turning and walking out the door.

"I know what kind of plays you want to go over," she purred. Caleb paused and half-turned, then left.

Anni sighed; she loved Rod, but she was around all these testosterone-driven hunks of young men all day, every day. Even though she was the ultimate professional, she did find it hard not to innocently flirt with them. She'd avoided any more than that until she saw Caleb. She had been mesmerized with him from the first time she saw him in the office. She had never seen such a gorgeous man in her life, and she couldn't get him off her mind. She knew sleeping with an athlete could bring her big trouble if someone found out. She was slow to move on something like this, but her fantasizing about Caleb was already getting out of hand. She had to get control of herself and start acting like a mature woman instead of some 18-year-old cheerleader. "I am not going to that apartment tonight," she whispered over and over again.

What Anni didn't know was that Caleb Lewis was a calculating, manipulating, dangerous man. Anni was about to get herself into a nightmare of the worst kind—getting to know Caleb Lewis in a sexual way.

Chapter 14

THE APARTMENT

It was about 10 that night when Caleb heard a tap on the door. He got up, his loose gym shorts with no underwear the only clothes he was wearing. He opened the door, and there stood Anni. She had on another mini skirt—she looked like a million bucks.

"I was still in the office and coach Axom had a few new plays he wanted to be sure you received, so…I just ran over here before I went home. Hope you don't mind," she added with a nervous laugh.

Caleb, waving her into his room, said, "No, I'm glad you're here. Come on in and stay for a few minutes."

"No, I really should go, but thanks," she said, scanning over his room as she backed away.

Caleb grabbed her by the hand. "Oh, come in and stay for a bit. I have some beer or coke, and we can talk about those plays you have there. It'll be fun."

"Well…okay, but just for a minute. Then I have to go." Her apprehension was tempered with giddiness at the magnificent hunk of man standing almost naked right in front of her. Her face flushed.

"Want a beer?" Caleb asked. The way that his muscles rippled when he moved excited something in her and she replied in a quiet monotone voice "Uh-huh." Anni was hypnotized looking at Caleb in his short, loose gym shorts. When he bent over in front of her to get a beer out of the fridge, she put her hands over her chest and gasped for breath. At that moment and without thought, a very primal urge compelled her to reach for his shorts.

"A few minutes later she got up quickly, brushed her disheveled hair out of her face, and hustled out the door.

Come back anytime! You still want your beer?" Caleb called after her.

She hustled right to her car, appalled by what just happened. "Oh my, I wasn't in there one minute and there I was …. ARGHH... What was I thinking? What is HE thinking?" But Anni could not get Caleb Lewis out of her mind.

Anni had never cheated on Rod and felt terribly guilty, but…*is oral sex REALLY cheating? It's not like we had intercourse or anything. I didn't even kiss him. He never even touched me.*

She sat behind her steering wheel smoothing her hair over and over again, as if to wipe away what had happened. "I'm…such a whore. What's *wrong* with me? Slut, slut, SLUT!" she snarled as she banged her fists on the steering wheel.

As she buried her head in her hands, she paused. Maybe this wasn't such a bad thing. Anni's sex life with Rod was pretty much on life support, and their marriage was close to flat-lining completely. "Maybe this would be a good thing to give our sex life a jump start," she mumbled. The encounter with Caleb had ignited energy in her that overcame the regret—if Rod wasn't in the mood when she got home, she would get him in the mood.

***

The next morning, Anni and Rod awoke at the same time, and he wrapped his arms around her and nuzzled into the back of her neck.

"Sheez, what happened to you last night?"

"I just got to thinking about how much I loved you," she said, taking his hand in hers, "and I felt like I haven't been a very good partner to you the last year. I just wanted you to know how much I love you."

Rod looked at her, then shrugged. "Well, keep thinking whatever you're thinking, because I like it!"

She giggled at him and said, "Don't get too used to it, but I'll try to do better."

CHAPTER 15

TORTURE

Caleb awoke, startled, sweat pouring down his face, screaming his mother's name. Oh how he wished this nightmare would stop, but how do you stop nightmares? Caleb got up from bed, snorted some coke, and went down to sit with Lavon for breakfast. He never thought twice about last night with Anni; it was pretty typical for him, after all.

He left his dorm and headed to CAU for football practice. As he walked down the hall of offices, he noticed Anni.

"Hi!" he nearly shouted. "How ya doing? That was a great BJ last night, thanks!" He could see that Anni was mortified—it looked like she wanted to crawl under a rock or pass out from embarrassment. She looked around quickly, then glared at him and mumbled something under her breath, turned around, and hustled to her office.

Caleb chuckled and kept going, finding his way to the coach's office.

"Go to the tape room and get taped up," Axom said. "We're going to work on some receiver routes today. Oh, and from now on, just show up at the locker room."

Caleb gave him a thumbs up and went to the taping room. Thankfully he remembered where it was. Inside was a guy doing all the mandatory taping on players' ankles, but apparently he'd do whatever else you wanted taped up too. Afterward, Caleb grabbed his helmet, slipped his practice jersey over his shoulder pads, and walked out to the practice field.

He had already met a few of the guys that were there; most of them were receivers, with a few linemen here and there.

"Caleb!" Coach Axom shouted, seemingly from out of nowhere. "Get under center and take a few snaps." Caleb nodded, watching the receivers as he jogged over to practice. Coach Hoenig, the receivers' coach, had them warming up their legs, and he'd throw a few lob passes to them as they ran up and down the field.

Caleb took a few snaps from Jason Briggs, a fellow from southern California who was also a freshman. As the ball rocketed into his hands from the snap, Caleb's eyes widened—this guy could pop the ball. He dropped a couple; he just wasn't used to a fellow of this size snapping the ball.

"Guess it'll just take some getting used to," Caleb mumbled, a little frustrated.

"That's why we're here, Caleb," Axom said. He apparently had the ears of a fox. "There's a bunch of stuff that you aren't used to, but it won't take you long. Don't get discouraged." Axom pointed further back on the field. "I want you to take the snap and drop back 3 1/2 steps, looking downfield the whole time for your spot." So Caleb took 10 or so snaps, practicing his footwork. He was setting up for another snap when Coach Axom blew his whistle. Everyone jogged over to him, so Caleb followed.

Coach Axom smiled and gave everyone a warm welcome. When all the sweaty players had rallied around, Axom said, "You're here because you play football. The only reason you have a place to sleep, food to eat, and a free college education is because you are football players. The university is making an investment in you, and we expect you to understand one thing and one thing only—your whole existence here is dependent on you being a football player. Yes, your education is crucial, and we expect you to go to class, study, and pass. We expect you to graduate from college and become productive citizens with a college degree from a great university. But first and foremost, we expect you to be football players; to live it, breathe it, and become the best player you can become. You aren't high school kids anymore; it's time to mature to the next level.

"I know all of you have hopes for the NFL. The truth is, out of this freshman class, we have maybe two or three that will even get a chance at that. If you aren't able to stand out on our football team, you darn sure aren't going to make the NFL. You are at the highest level of college football at CAU, and whether you make it to the next level only time will tell, but I can tell you this: the only players I have seen go on to the NFL are utterly obsessed with football. So, where do you want to be in 5 years? It's all up to you, and CAU will give you a pathway to make your dreams come true, whether it's in the NFL or the education you receive here. But ultimately, it's all you. Line up boys—your dreams start today!"

Needless to say, Caleb was pumped up and excited. He had only dreamed of the NFL, but now he realized it might be possible.

"All right," Coach Axom said, taking Caleb by the shoulder as the other players dispersed. "We're going to do some short button hook routes on either side. Throw the ball to a spot on the field 10 yards downfield to the sideline."

The first receiver lined up, and Caleb dropped back and waited for the receiver to get there. When his man was in place, he threw the ball—a good pass. Caleb smiled.

The sharp shriek or a whistle interrupted Caleb's satisfaction. "NO, NO, NO, CALEB!" Axom shouted. "You don't wait on the receiver! You drop back and throw the pass. It's the receiver's responsibility to be where the ball is going to go. Let's do it again."

Caleb squared his shoulders and crouched. He took the snap, dropped back, and fired the ball to the point he'd chosen; the receiver stumbled as the ball hit him right in the back. Coach Hoenig's voice carried across the field, shouting, "Boys, this ain't high school ball, and that's not a high school QB throwing! We didn't recruit slow receivers. You can all run, now quit lollygagging down the field and run, dang it!"

Caleb chuckled to himself at Hoenig's enthusiasm, then took the next snap and flung it to his spot. Receiver Lance Wood turned around just in time to catch it—it was a beautiful sight. In high school, he couldn't throw hard because his receivers complained he threw it *too* hard and it hurt them. Caleb was never positive where they might run anyway, but boy, this was a different level of football! He had to admit there was still a bunch to learn.

This set of drills went on for over two hours, the same route and the same four receivers. Caleb was the only QB, and his arm was starting to get tired and sore. The receivers were gasping for air, and poor Jason Briggs' back and shoulders were getting sore from all the snaps. Thankfully, Coach Axom finally blew his whistle and told everyone to come in.

Axom and Hoenig exchanged glances as the players gathered around. "Coach, these boys aren't in very good shape, are they?"

Hoenig huffed. "No sir, Coach Axom, it's about the worst I've ever seen."

Axom nodded. "What are we going to do about it?"

Coach Hoenig grinned. "We're going to run bleachers full-blown for the next 30 minutes."

"Let's go boys!" Hoenig shouted, and all the players groaned and headed for the bleachers. After about 20 minutes of bleachers, Caleb thought that Jason Biggs might have a heart attack—he was really struggling. Of course, he did weigh in at 280, so it took a lot of effort to move that body around. Lavon was doing okay; he just kept asking everyone, "When do we get to eat?" When those agonizing 30 minutes were over, Coach Axom told them to hit the showers and see the trainers before they left. They all jogged off the field plum worn out.

After Caleb had showered, he went in to see the trainer, John Duggar. Caleb hopped up on the table, where he got an ice pack wrapped around his shoulder. Duggar told him to leave it on for the next hour to help the swelling.

"And while you're at it," the trainer said, "go sit in the whirlpool for about 15 minutes, and come back and see me when it's time to take the ice off." Caleb took his time relaxing for that hour, and when John took off the ice pack, he said, "Go on over to the next room; you're going to get a massage."

Caleb had never had a massage before, so he was a bit uneasy about it. Soon enough, a big ol' boy named Janneral came lumbering in.

"Lay face down on the table," Janneral said. Caleb did as he was told, and the big guy started rubbing and pushing places on his neck, shoulders, and back. It was really hurting.

Amid the grunts and stings, Caleb managed, "Hey, back off a bit."

"Don't tell me how to do my job, boy," Janneral said. "You're a mess."

Man, this is torture, Caleb sighed inwardly. After 30 minutes of anguish, Janneral let him get up. "Go back home and get some lunch and rest. Your body needs to recover from practice today. Drink lots of water. Rest is the best medicine."

Caleb looked at Janneral and sighed, "With pleasure." He dragged himself to his feet and wandered back to his apartment.

CHAPTER 16

TEXAS SUCKS

After practice, all the freshmen were dragging themselves into the dorm, haggard and exhausted. Everyone went to the cafeteria and then straight back to their rooms. When Caleb got back, he went out on his little balcony, lit a joint, and sat there and smoked, looking out over the campus. It was a beautiful place; the weather here was unreal, nothing like the hot and windy conditions of Enapay. After he had finished his joint, he crashed on his bed and slept until 5.

Caleb got up and went downstairs to get some supper, most of the fellows were already down there playing games and watching television. Caleb went and ordered a steak and potatoes and sat down with Lavon, Lance and Jason. They were all discussing practice today and how tough it is. Lance Wood is telling everyone about the weather where he grew up in Nevada. All Jason Briggs wanted to talk about is how sore he is and all Lavon Jackson wanted to talk about is eating some more food. Caleb sat there listening for a bit and having a few laughs when another fellow freshman football player, Thad Crossland, came up to the table. Thad was an All-American running back from Dallas. About 6'1" and around 190, this kid was very strong and very fast, and it showed in his cocky walk. Caleb had heard about Thad's running ability since Enapay was fairly close to Dallas, but Caleb wasn't necessarily overjoyed when Thad sat down without even a greeting and started talking loudly—about himself. Echoes of how great he was and how he was going to be the next Heisman trophy winner at CAU resounded through the cafeteria. He went on to talk about how great the state of Texas was and blah, blah, blah, on and on about Texas. Caleb was a University of Oklahoma fan first, with Oklahoma State a close second. Oklahomans don't think much of Texas, and Texans don't think much of Oklahoma.

Caleb ignored Thad's bragging for a while, but after ten straight minutes of nothing but Thad's drawling voice, Caleb had finally stomached all he could. He looked Thad dead in the eyes and said, "Texas sucks, and only suckers live in Texas." The echo of Thad's loud voice in the cafeteria died immediately, and he clinched his teeth. Nobody in his life had talked to him or about his beloved Texas like that! The other guys at the table just looked at Caleb, startled by what he said; what happened to the quiet guy they thought he was?

"You say that again and I'm going to kick your Oklahoma-loving ass all the way back to Oklahoma," Thad snarled.

Caleb, without pause, looked right at Thad and said again, "Texas sucks, and only suckers live in Texas." Caleb Lewis wasn't scared of anyone, anywhere.

Thad stood up, shoving his chair backward with a shriek. "You and I are gonna take this outside and I'm gonna show you who's a sucker, white boy."

"I ain't going nowhere with no sucker from Texas." Everyone at the table got up and moved back a few steps.

The two stared at each other for a few moments, motionless. Then Thad suddenly threw a punch, but Caleb caught it and wouldn't let go. "You are about to get in over your head, sucker Texas boy." Thad threw another punch with his left hand but Caleb caught that one too, pinning both of Thad's hands in his. Thad tried to pull free, flailing more and more as he realized how strong Caleb really was. Then, Caleb head-butted him right in the nose, and Thad hit the ground. The other players stood in hushed silence. *This is one bad-ass QB*, Lance Wood thought to himself.

After Thad had hit the ground, Caleb looked around at his fellow players, who were hovering in a nervous circle off to the side. Caleb reached his hand out and helped Thad back up.

"I don't like Texas, and I would appreciate if you just don't talk about Texas when I'm around. And oh, sorry about your nose."

Thad looked at Caleb, continually wiping the blood dripping from his nose to no avail. "Uh, I'll try to be more careful next time." Poor Thad Crossland wasn't sure how to feel, to be honest—no one had ever treated him like that. Where he came from, he was the tough guy. He then wobbled off to his room, head down, without finishing his dinner.

Even after he'd gone, the other players standing there didn't move, but small smiles began to break out on their faces. "Caleb Lewis," Lance said, "you are a warrior, and I will follow you into battle anytime, anywhere, against anyone." Everyone clapped and laughed.

And so, in less than five minutes, Caleb had earned the respect of the entire freshman football class.

CHAPTER 17

FIGURING THE ANGLES

A week later, Caleb got up and headed over to the practice facilities to get taped up. The trainer stopped him as he walked through the door. "No tape today, Caleb; you guys are working with weight trainers."

This was how Caleb met Bobby Thompson, the weight coach who would be evaluating him based on individual exercises to see what could be done to help him be a better football player. They spent the morning together on evaluation exercises, and Caleb felt great.

When Caleb was packing up after the session, Bobby quietly approached Coach Axom. "Coach," he whispered, "I'm not sure how to tell you this, but Caleb Lewis is Superman. I can't find a single weakness on him."

"Well that's a nice problem to have, isn't it?" Coach Axom chuckled. "Just make sure he maintains what he has—you don't have to wear him out. A kid like this doesn't come around but once in a lifetime. Caleb is a thoroughbred, and we need to treat him as such. Be sure you don't hurt him."

Coach Thompson waved the comment away. "I think it'd be impossible to hurt him even if I tried."

After evaluation, Caleb made his way to the football offices—the place he really wanted to be today. He knew

Anni was a powerful person in this program, but he was still trying to find out exactly why. He hadn't figured all the angles yet, but at heart, Caleb was a predator, and he could smell blood. He knew immediately after meeting her that she was weak, so he just needed to get her alone for a night to pick her brain (among other things). As he walked into Anni's office, Beth smiled at him and he asked for Anni. She buzzed Anni to let her know who was out front, and after a bit of a seemingly heated conversation over the phone, Beth asked him to have a seat.

Caleb walked around and slid up onto the edge of the desk. "So Beth," he said, "we haven't really gotten to talk much. Have to admit I don't know much about you even though you're always helping me out around here. How old are you anyway?"

 "Twenty-two," she said a little shyly. "Just graduated college this last year, and this is my first job."

"Are you married?"

"No!" Beth exclaimed, amused. "I don't even have time for a boyfriend, let alone a husband. Been too busy going to college and finding a job."

"Yeah, it's tough when you're busy. Ever thought of going back home? Where you from?"

"Seattle. I came here to live with my aunt while I went to school."

"Ah. Your aunt sounds like a nice person. You still live with her?"

Beth puffed out her chest just a little. "Nope! I moved out last month and have an apartment about a mile from here." Caleb smiled as she is talking, but it was genuine—there was a light that seemed to radiate from her right before his eyes.

She had to admit that Caleb wasn't hard to look at. But Beth Owens grew up with very strict, Godly parents. She wasn't allowed to stay out late at night and was expected to be in church every time the doors were open. She was still a virgin and planned to be that way until she got married. She was a very spiritual woman, but to be honest, she was also frustrated that she couldn't keep a man in her life; she was starting to get a bit desperate. If she had learned one thing, it was that men wanted to have sex after the second or third date, and if they didn't get it, they'd move on to the next girl. All men want to marry virgins, they just don't have the patience to date them.

Caleb leaned in closer on her desk, a bit flirtatious. "Do you work out? You have an amazing body."

Beth blushed and smiled. "Yeah, I run 5 miles three times a week and take aerobic classes on the side."

He reached over, squeezed one of her biceps, and said, "I can tell. Your muscles are bigger than mine!"

The smile quickly vanished from her face and she jerked her arm away, looked him dead in the eyes, and said, "Don't touch me. I didn't say you could touch me." She paused, eyeing him. "You're the devil, aren't you?"

He laughed out loud. "No, I just appreciate a beautiful woman. And we should go out sometime."

Beth was taken aback. "Really?" She had never been asked out by such a gorgeous man in her life.

"Why not?" he said. "Just don't tell Anni; she probably wouldn't be happy with you dating a student. But I think you're a beautiful woman that I would be honored to take on a date."

Beth was just beside herself, but she put her hands on her lap and smoothed her skirt, keeping her composure. "Okay," she said a bit too enthusiastically, "but we can't tell *anyone*, or I could lose my job. You promise? Then again, I'm not really sure if there is a policy against a secretary dating a student."

"I promise," Caleb said, hand over his heart. She wrote down her phone number and told him to give her a call. When she handed it to him, her phone buzzed and Anni told her she would see Caleb now.

"Go on in," she said, giggling.

"Thanks. I'll call you."

Caleb walked in and made himself at home in Anni's office. "Hey, haven't seen you in a while. Where you been?"

Anni looked at him sternly, eyes furrowed, frowning. "Caleb, what I did is completely unprofessional and unlike anything I have ever done before. You and I are going to be working together for the next four years, and I wouldn't want you to think or feel awkward when you are around me. I am still just horrified by what happened, and I am ashamed of myself for letting my emotions get the best of me. I wanted to apologize to you and move on like that never happened."

"Are you talking about that BJ you gave me in my apartment?" He said, leaning in with his beautiful eyes and charming dimples. He knew she was very uncomfortable, and he couldn't lie—he liked tormenting her a little. "Why would you be embarrassed about that? I enjoyed it, and you must have felt like it was the right thing to do at the time." Then, Caleb's face got serious. "Anni, had you never given a BJ before?"

Anni was blushing so red she looked like she was sunburnt. "Yes, Caleb, I *have* given BJs before." She paused and made a disgusted sort of huff. "Why am I even telling you that? My sex life is none of your business! Just so you know, I have never been involved with a student and have not been with anyone but my husband since I was married! It wasn't the right thing to do no matter how I felt at the time."

Caleb got up and walked around her desk, putting his hands on her shoulders and massaging them gently. "Relax. You're beating yourself up way too much over this. Who did it hurt? Anything we do is private, and I wouldn't hurt you for the world." He bent over and started softly kissing her neck and rubbing her shoulders. She could feel those pleasant emotions rising again, and she turned her head to say something when he kissed her. It was the most passionate kiss she had ever had. Too soon, he stood up and pulled away.

"I've got some stuff at my apartment that'll help you relax. Come by tonight and I'll give you some."

"I just can't Caleb," she said, and it almost hurt her to admit it. "I just can't. You need to leave now."

Caleb turned to walk out the door and said, "I'll be at my apartment tonight, so if you change your mind, just pop on in."

Anni put her head in her hands. "Please go, Caleb."

On his way out, Caleb told Beth he would be calling her, and she replied, giggling, "Bye, Caleb!"

Caleb knew he would be seeing Anni tonight, but deep down inside he knew that there was something off about what he was doing—somebody always winds up getting hurt. He wanted to change his behavior, but how do you change a lifetime of habits in a few weeks?

CHAPTER 18

MAKING THE MOVE

Caleb went back to the dorm, ate with the guys, played some pool, then went upstairs to his apartment. He smoked a joint and then went to his desk to study the playbook. This was starting to become his typical day.

About 10:30, he heard a tap on the door. He already knew who it was. Before he'd barely opened it a crack, Anni came crashing through like a wild animal, wrapping her arms around him and smothering him in passionate kisses. She stepped back from him and let her dress fall to the floor—she had nothing on underneath. She was built like a brick house; Caleb was in awe of her 38 year old body, she looked like a girl his age. He was getting concerned, though; she is moaning and groaning so loudly he thought the guys next door would hear her. He covered her mouth, pulled her down to him, and started kissing her to shut her up.

When Caleb was done, Anni whispered, "I'd like to go again when you're ready."

He chuckled. "Sure, give me 20 or 30 minutes."

"Great," she said, snuggling into his big shoulders.

"Want a beer or a joint or anything else? It'll help you relax."

She looked at him, puzzled. "What exactly is 'anything else?'"

Caleb laughed a little. "Ever done any drugs besides marijuana?"

"Yeah, but not since I graduated college."

"What about heroin?"

Anni gasped. "NO! And you shouldn't either!"

"I do it only on very special occasions, and I feel like this is a special occasion, don't you?" he said, placing a hand tenderly on her hip. He knew Anni wasn't stupid like those high school girls he got hooked on heroin, and he had to take this very slowly and watch his words with her. She analyzed everything.

"That just sounds like a horrible idea to me. How about a beer or something else?"

"Well you smoke weed, don't you?" he said.

She felt a little pressured but gave in. "Well, it's been a while, but why not?"

He got up, went to the bathroom, and rolled a couple of joints—one for her and one for him. He had some PCP that he sprinkled on Anni's joint. Just a little. PCP, a powerful sedative, has trance-like anesthetic effects, and people are supposed to have a sort of "out-of-body," detached feeling when they take it. That would help her relax for sure.

They both lit up, and soon enough she was lying on the bed, naked and oblivious to anything going on around her. She was just mumbling to herself about the beautiful colors or something like that. As she giggled and hummed to herself, a dopey grin plastered all over her face, Caleb went to his desk, got out his Polaroid, and took shots of Anni naked in all kinds of positions, all very graphic. He kept snapping until he ran out of film. He hid the pictures, then laid down on the bed and fell asleep.

About an hour later, he felt a hand rubbing his chest. "Wow, that's some kind of weed you have there," Anni said.

"Only the best for you, Anni," he said with a smile.

She blushed. "Are you ready to go again?"

"I've been ready, just waiting for you to wake up." He rolled over on top of her, and they made love for the next hour.

It was almost 1 in the morning, and he asked her if she needed to call her husband. "No," she said proudly, "I called him earlier tonight and said I had a ton of work to do. Said I would be staying at the office, but I do need to get back and rest before tomorrow." She sighed, cupping Caleb's face in her soft hands. "Caleb, this was so much fun. Thank you so much. I'll see you soon."

"One thing before you leave," he interjected. "You think you could hook me up with my own apartment? I don't like rooming with other people, and it would be nice for you and me to have a place when we need it."

"I can do anything I want," she said with a swagger. "Consider it done." She got up, slipped on her dress, and floated out the door. Anni was on cloud nine.

Caleb could have cared less about the sex that night, but he *was* able to get some blackmail pictures that he could use later, if needed, not to mention his own apartment. He had learned that the only way to get to Anni was through her panties. It was her weak spot now, but over time he also knew that would wear off.

Caleb laid in bed, throwing his football to the ceiling and catching it like he had since he was a kid. He caught the ball and dropped it on the floor, rubbing his eyes. It has become a battle dealing with his demons from the past few years, and he considered, just for a second, throwing those pictures away. He knew nothing good would come from them, just pain for Anni. He turned over and went to sleep, hoping he wouldn't have that nightmare again.

CHAPTER 19

FALL FOOTBALL

It was early August, and Caleb had just turned 19. All the football players were starting to show up for full-time practice for the upcoming 1981-82 season. There were about 80 players on scholarships and some walk-ons. All of the juniors and seniors stayed in the athletic dorm next to Caleb's, and there was a big courtyard between the two dorms enclosed in a tall fence. Nobody from the outside could see in, and the players couldn't see out. Of course, it was planned that way—CAU didn't want the press photographing whatever went on behind those fences.

There were barbecue grills, a volleyball court, a basketball court, lots of tables and chairs, and all kinds of sporting stuff for the football players, but most of the players smoked weed and passed around whatever drugs they could get their hands on. There was no such thing as NCAA drug testing, so it was pretty much 'anything goes' in that courtyard.

Caleb had begun to meet the players, and football life was getting into full gear. Everything, it seemed, revolved around the game. Weight training in the mornings; lunch, film, and conditioning in the afternoon. In the evenings after supper, all the quarterbacks had football classroom study, which included film, plays, and formations. Extensive work on what and where receivers were going during any play or out of any formation. A ton of study on defensive schemes—being able to recognize different types of zone coverages and man-to-man coverages, different blitz packages, and on and on.

All of this was a bit overwhelming to Caleb, but freshman QB Billy Thompson from San Diego was *totally* lost. Even before the first day of real practice, Caleb overheard Coach Axom telling offensive coordinator John Coran and head coach Joe Richert that Billy was struggling with the terminology and schemes. They were thinking maybe they'd have to red-shirt him or move him to a different position. Caleb, on the other hand, was picking it up, but it was tough. He had never studied so hard for anything in his life, and it didn't leave much time for anything else. But Caleb was going to do everything in his power to be the starter at CAU as a freshman.

As for Anni, well, at this point he just didn't have much time; he was either studying or worn out every night. And she was busy too, helping with all the new move-ins. For now, things had cooled off a bit between them. He had called Beth a few times late at night, intrigued by her—maybe even falling for her. He hadn't ever loved or had a girlfriend, so he was confused by his feeling towards Beth. He hadn't told her how he felt—they hadn't even had a date yet, just talked on the phone—but he pushed it out of his mind. Right now, he just needed to focus on football.

On the first day of official practice, all the players on the roster showed up on the field. The coaches had been having position meetings and light workouts with the players for a couple of weeks, but this was the first time Caleb had been in full pads since he arrived in June, and he was anxious to get started. He saw his name listed on the depth chart as the third team QB, and he felt just a little insulted; he understood it, but he didn't like it.

Offensive coordinator John Coran called the entire offense over to him in preparation for a live scrimmage for the next hour. "No particular player schemes as far as 1st team and 2nd team are considered right now; we just need to get a feel for where we are." He would rotate players in and out of their respected positions, and he told everyone not to read anything into this scrimmage. He blew the whistle, and the offense huddled up, as did the defense.

Jason Allgood was the favorite to be the starting QB. Jason seemed like a nice guy, and Caleb really liked him. They had spent a bunch of time together in the last month, and he had put in his time and was prepared to be the starter. The starting running back was Luke Donaldson, a two-year starter from Meade, Pennsylvania. Big, fast, and tough as nails, he was already being touted as a Heisman trophy candidate on his way to becoming the leading rusher in CAU history. The second team QB was junior Henry Logano from South Dakota. He had some skills, but Caleb was sure he'd pass him over in no time; he just wasn't as good as Caleb, and that was that.

Coach Coran told them to huddle up, Jason as the QB. The first play they handed the ball to Luke, who went for ten yards before being tripped up. They ran about ten plays (looked a bit sloppy to Caleb), but Jason didn't make any mistakes and completed two of four passes. They put in Henry next and changed running backs. Henry dropped back for a pass on his first play and got sacked. Coach Coran went nuts, yelling at Henry about feeling the pressure and just standing there in the pocket, waiting for the receiver to get open. "You've got to make something happen! I've been watching you for two years just stand there and get sacked, and I'm sick of it!" Caleb thought it was a bit of a brutal outburst from coach; after all, it was Henry's first snap of the year in a live scrimmage. Henry, of course, was shaken up, and he fumbled the next snap from center. Both coaches started hollering at him. Henry, visibly shaken now, stayed in for ten snaps before Coach Axom screamed, "I can't take this anymore! Caleb, you can't be any worse than Henry. Get in there!"

Caleb took a deep breath and leaned in to the huddle. Coach called a 20-yard crossing route to Lance Wood. Caleb had worked for two months with Lance, who was really an unreal athlete. He took the snap, dropped back, threw a rope to the spot where Lance should be. *Pop.* Lance was there, caught the ball, made some fleet-footed moves, and scored. What a way to start! The next four plays were just routine handoffs with no particular success, and then Coach called for a down-and-out to Lance. Caleb took the snap, dropped back 5 yards, and the protection broke down. The defense was blitzing even though they were given explicit instructions not to run blitz packages. Caleb saw the linebacker bearing down on him, took a few steps to the left sideline, and saw the corner coming up fast on him. He took off across the field, turning and twisting, stiff-arming anyone he came in contact with. He ran 40 yards and scored. Everyone was a whooping and hollering, and the coaches were going nuts, screaming, "That's how you play football, boys!" The defensive coaches were shouting at their players, "A freshman is making you boys look like a bunch of pansies!"

Caleb took the next ten snaps, went four of five passing, and didn't make a single mistake. When the practice was done, Coach Axom pulled him aside and said, "Son, you aren't close to where you need to be yet, but that was a heck of a first scrimmage you just put on. Go in and let the trainers look you over and ice you down. You have the rest of the day off. I don't want you to study; just relax at your apartment for a night and get a good night's sleep. I'm proud of you."

For the first time in a very long time, Caleb felt happy. He couldn't wait to get home and call his dad to tell him about the scrimmage. And he might just give Anni a visit before he went home.

CHAPTER 20

THAT'S A BIG SAFE

After seeing the trainers, Caleb headed out of the locker room and upstairs to the administrative offices. "Hi Susan," he said as he walked in, "I need to see Anni."
"Sure, let me buzz her and make sure she's in. Beth, is Anni in her office? Caleb is here to see her."

"Sure, send him on back," Beth said, and Caleb could hear a smile on her face. "I'll let Anni know he's here."

When he walked in Anni's office, he was happy to see Beth's beautiful face, and she seemed excited to see him. He sat down on a chair and leaned toward her. "How you doing? I've been so busy the last few days we haven't had a chance to talk much. This football is crazy, and with classes starting up, whew! By the time I get home at night I'm pooped!"

"I understand," she said. "This is a very busy time of the year, but I've missed talking to you."
"Maybe it will slow down a bit in the next few weeks and we can go out sometime," he said with a smile.

"Actually, Caleb," Beth said, twiddling her thumbs, "I would love for you to go to church with me on Sunday."

Caleb paused. She hadn't mentioned anything about being a Christian or going to church or anything like that. "Hmm.

Well, we'll do something sometime for sure, just be patient. Anyway, is Anni busy? I need some help."

Beth buzzed her and told her, "Caleb Lewis is here to see you."

"Send him in," she said.

He walked into her office and shut the door, and she rushed over to greet him with a big kiss. "I'm really missing our playtime together," she said softly.

"Me too," Caleb said, hugging her tightly, "and that's why I came by to see if you wanted to drop by my new apartment after work tonight and see it."

She replied in a low, seductive voice, "Oh I want see it and much more. You can just plan on me being there at our usual time."

"Great! And one more thing…I'm running short on cash. What can I do to get some spending money?"

Truth be told, that was a complete lie. He still had most of the $30,000 he brought out to California. And his dad had sold all of Lillie's property, plus he got money for the apartment that burned down, *and* he claimed all of her life insurance and all the retirement she had built up over her life. Caleb got every bit of money from Lillie's estate. Jack had opened five CDs in his name for over $500,000, and put the money in five year CDs compounded daily at a 15% annual interest rate (which was common those days). Jack had told him not to touch that money, *ever*, and in five years he would have over a million in the bank. Jack was also sending him $400 a month so he could have spending money at college on top of paying the insurance on his Vette. Jack had been saving money for college, not only for Caleb but also for his deceased brother and sister too. He wanted to help him with that money so he could concentrate on his education and football.

If Caleb understood one thing in life, it was that money is power, and more importantly to him, freedom. He never spent much of his money, if ever. He extorted it from people and saved his own. He was pretty tight with his money and had become accustomed to other people giving him theirs.

"Well," Anni said, "you're talking to the CAU bank of football players. How much do you need?"

He elbowed her in good humor and said, "Well, I'm pretty special, so how about $10,000?"

"You ARE special," she laughed, walking over to her safe to open it. He quickly followed her, looking over her shoulder. Anni stood for a second, a little uncomfortable with Caleb seeing the contents of her safe—nobody had ever seen this money, but then again, nobody had ever wanted to see this money.

She turned around and said, "Caleb, please go to the other room. What's in this safe is private, and I've never shown it to anyone."

Caleb looked into her eyes, cocking his head to one side. "Well, I hope after all we have done that I'm not just *anyone*," he chuckled. "And I'm not going to knock you over the head and steal your money Anni, sheez." The two laughed quietly. "But it's okay. I guess you don't really trust me, and I was just curious what was in there anyway, so I'll go to the other room."

Deep down inside, Anni did want to show someone else this money. She was proud of it and what it represented—her power in the program. She waited for a minute, watching him leave, then pursed her lips. "Well, I guess it doesn't matter. You know I have money in the safe, and I do trust you. I guess there's no harm in it, just turn your head for a minute." Caleb did as he was told, and while he looked away she dialed in the combination. When she swung the door back, Caleb had to stifle whatever sound he was about to make. He had never seen so friggin' much money in his life! There were stacks and stacks of $100 bills and stacks and stacks of $10,000 wraps.

"Are you in charge of all this money?" he half-shrieked.

"Yes I am," she said proudly, "and you're the first person ever to see it. Pretty impressive, huh?"

"I'll say!" He shook his head. "Who decides what to do with all this money?"

"Only me, Caleb. It's only me. I'm the only person who even knows how much money is in here, and there's no accounting of this money whatsoever."

"Gosh. How much money do you have in that safe?"

"1.4 million right now, and it just keeps flowing in." Anni looked back at the money, smiled slightly, and then turned to Caleb. "You're the only person ever to see this money because I trust you enough not to tell any other football players or EVER mention this money to anyone. You could bring down the entire CAU football program if the NCAA ever found out about this. Caleb, *do you promise* on your mother's life never to tell ANYONE what you saw here today?"

He paused for a moment. "Sure, but you do know my mom is dead, don't you?"

He could immediately see the look of regret in her eyes. "Caleb…I didn't know. I'm sorry for using that expression. I…well, I just need you to know this money isn't something that's talked about to anyone, including players, coaches, or other administrators."

"I understand," Caleb said. "I won't say a word. I promise."

And Anni believed him. She was so wrapped up in her fantasy with Caleb that she believed he was perfect, that he loved her so much he would never do anything to hurt her. He was a straight-up knight in shining armor.

 "So, about that money I asked for…" Caleb ventured.

Anni reached in, grabbed a $10,000 wrap, and handed it to him. "Don't be silly with that money and go buy something expensive with it," she told him with a mock slap to his arm. "If you need something expensive, you come through me, and only me, and I will arrange for it. Do you understand?"

"Yes ma'am," he said, reaching over to kiss her. "I'll see you tonight."

On the way out, he told Beth he would try to call her, then he went right back to his apartment. As he left the building, those feelings of *this isn't right, Caleb* came rushing over him again. He wanted to turn over a new leaf in life, but man, how could anyone walk away from that much money? It was going to be easy pickings.

Caleb finally knew the power that Anni wielded and intended to milk that bank for all its worth in the next four years. He had her right where he wanted her, and she could do nothing stop it—the nude pictures of her in his bedroom meant he had proof of her infidelity, so he could destroy her marriage, her job, and even bring down the whole university with what he knew if she didn't cooperate with whatever he wanted.

Caleb had one thing left to do before he went home—stop by the department store and buy one of those new VHS camcorders.

CHAPTER 21

NO HARD FEELINGS

Finally, the football season was starting this week. CAU was opening with a very weak opponent—California University of Berkley; they were a Division II team just playing CAU for the money. Most Division I teams like CAU have a couple of walk-overs on their schedule, so this wasn't too much of a surprise. The first pre-season polls had come out, ranking CAU #4 in the country. Caleb had moved up to second team QB and was pressing Jason for the starting job. He figured that out of principle Jason would be the starter early on in the game. He was getting the feeling, though, that if Jason got hurt in the least or didn't play very well, he'd get booted and swapped for Caleb. It seemed like the coaches were looking for an excuse to make him the starter.

 Caleb was busy preparing, and a lot of his free time was being sucked up by the press. They were everywhere asking questions all the time. It was a time-waster, sure, but Caleb saw the manipulative merits in it. One thing all players had to do at CAU was take a "talking to the press" class taught by the PR people at the university. You never talk about anything or anyone that isn't obvious or known to everyone in the press. You could talk about the game, how you played—boring stuff like that. You should never talk about yourself too much, or the game you had, but always give credit for your success to everyone else on the team. Caleb learned a lot in the class about how to manipulate the press into believing what he wanted them to believe; the official term was apparently called "spinning your story."

Recently, there had been a guy named Don Phero from the Los Angeles Daily Leger that was always asking Caleb about his personal life back in Oklahoma. During the most recent interview, though, Phero may have crossed the line.

"Do you know a Jamie Johnson or Nia Campbell back at Enapay?" he'd asked.

Caleb replied, steely-eyed, "Yes, I know who they are."

"I heard they were your girlfriends," Phero said with a smile. "It's nice to have girlfriends, isn't it?" He just kept digging, and his too-big smile disgusted Caleb.

"You know, Don," Caleb said with a fake smile of his own, "I was lucky enough to have lots of girlfriends; do you have a problem with that?"

"No, no," Phero said. "Most high school quarterbacks have lots of girlfriends. It's just that these two seemed to be a bit more than that."

Caleb clenched his teeth, making sure to breathe slowly. His blood pressure was starting to make his head hurt. "Don, if you have a question about football, ask it. If not, I think we're done here."

Don paused. "Have you ever heard of a Daisy Belview?"

The look in Caleb's eyes could have burned a hole through a wall. He waved Phero over. "Come closer to me, Don." Once they were both off to the side, Caleb grabbed Phero by his shirt collar and yanked him over. "I'm not sure what you're fishing for, but let me tell you something. I'm not a guy that you should be messing with. Do we understand each other?"

The petite Don looked up at Caleb and smiled again. "I'm not scared of you, Caleb. There is a story much more interesting than you being a quarterback at Enapay. Either you can talk to me about it, or I'll continue to ask these questions until I get some answers. Do we understand each other?"

From then on, Caleb avoided Don at all costs, but the little guy was sneaky. Caleb knew that he was calling back home and asking questions, and he didn't like that. At all. For the next two weeks, he just kept pestering him about his life back home and asking questions about things that were making him very uncomfortable. He had always been afraid that his past may come back to haunt him, and this Don Phero was asking way too many questions.

Unfortunately, Caleb couldn't just threaten this guy or beat him up—that would be a story in and of itself, and he didn't need that kind of press. Caleb did, however, know some good ol' boys back in Oklahoma who were tough guys and could be hired to take care of someone. That night when he got home, he called one of his biggest hometown fans, Johnny Caldwell—that man could be trusted to keep his mouth shut. He was ten years older than Caleb, but they had become friends while he was in high school.

Johnny had a lot of respect for Caleb—a guy had hired him to muscle Caleb a couple of years ago, and Caleb almost beat him to death. Johnny liked a guy who could take care of himself. Caleb told Johnny about the sneaky workings of Don Phero and asked Johnny if he could personally handle the problem.

"Sure, Caleb, I'll take care of it. Don't worry about it," was Johnny's immediate, cheerful response. He was proud to know someone famous like Caleb, and on the other hand, he also knew Caleb's story; it wouldn't be good if people found out about the trouble he caused in his hometown.

"Johnny, you start spreading the word around Enapay that if anyone talks to the press, I will personally come back and take care of them myself. We have to *scare* these people Johnny. I don't know how else to handle it. I'm going to pay you $10,000 to handle Don Phero, and I'll mail you the money first thing in the morning. Is that fair?" Caleb didn't tell Johnny how to do the job; he didn't want to know. He just wanted Don Phero out of his hair.

***

After the phone call, he took a few deep breaths before heading downstairs for supper, and then he went back to his apartment to study his playbook. He had it down now. He knew every play, every formation, and what everyone did. He knew the defenses and how to check out of plays and into what plays depending on how the defenses set up. Caleb was a prepared man, anxious to show the world what he could do.

He went out to the courtyard and lit up a joint with the other players. Caleb, Lance, and Lavon were relaxing when some seniors came over and sat down with them—Randy Clearly, a linebacker from Indiana; Chris Kaplan, an offensive tackle from Kansas; and Josh Smith, a defensive back from California. The seniors for the most part didn't associate much with the freshmen, so this was a bit strange. They broke into small talk for a bit, but Caleb could tell that's not why they were here.

Chris Kaplan leaned in and said, "You think you're pretty hot stuff, don't you, pretty boy?"

Lance glanced over at Caleb, then at Chris. "You need to watch your tone. Caleb hasn't bothered any of you."

"Well we don't like the way he came in here and got all this attention from the press, and he hasn't even played a down of football yet!"

"You guys are just mad because the press don't want to talk to your sorry football-playing asses," Lance shot back.

Lavon slapped his knees and chuckled at that. "It ain't his fault. He didn't ask any of those press boys for attention."

"Shut up," Josh snarled at Lavon. "Ain't nobody talking to your big dumb ass."

A few more players had gathered around, hearing the conversation start to heighten. Caleb looked at the three of them and said quietly, "I don't reckon I asked for any attention from anyone, but I can't help it if I get it. Why don't you talk to the coaches about this instead of me?"

Randy poked Caleb in the chest. "Prove yourself before you start taking any glory, big boy."

Caleb looked Randy right in the eye and said, "You poke that finger of yours in my chest one more time and you're gonna have a broken finger." Randy was the bad-ass among the upperclassmen, but he chose the wrong guy to pick on.

Randy laughed and looked around, swinging his arms out. "There ain't no QB in the world that can kick my ass, freshman," he said with a laugh, then poked Caleb in the chest again.

SNAP! Caleb grabbed it and broke it like a dead stick. Randy hit the ground groaning.

The other guys stared at Caleb, horror-struck. He looked down at Randy and told him, "You had better go get that finger fixed before the game on Saturday."

Suddenly, from the side, Josh swung at Caleb and grazed him across the cheek. Caleb turned out of the way and threw a right that hit Josh square in the eye and decked him. Chris tried to grab Caleb, but he jumped out of the way and ran Chris's head hard into the brick wall behind him. Poor kid was knocked out before he knew what hit him. By now, there must have been 60 or 70 players that had flocked over to watch. The freshmen and sophomores were jumping up and down hollering, "Caleb, Caleb, Caleb!" Most of the juniors and seniors just turned around shaking their heads and went back to their dorms. Once again, Caleb had gotten the respect of the entire CAU football team in less than two minutes.

When the guys on the ground finally came to their senses, he stopped to help them up. "No hard feelings; let's just win some football games."

CHAPTER 22

SECOND THOUGHTS

Caleb went back to his apartment knowing that Anni would show up soon, and he wanted to fool around with his new camcorder first. His desk was right in front of his bed, so he got a gym bag, cut a hole in it, put the camera in, and pointed it towards the bed. He just had to remember to turn it on before Anni arrived.

At about 10:30, he heard a knock on the door. He made sure the blinking red *record* light was hidden, then welcomed her in.

Anni sighed as soon as she saw him. "Hey. I've been excited all day—I am so looking forward to this."

"Well, wait no longer. Here I am!" he said with a flourish. She dropped her dress, and like always, she didn't have anything on underneath it.

When they were done, they lay resting on the bed, talking.

"I'm hearing lots of good things about you as a football player from the coaches, Caleb."

"Oh yeah? That's nice. I'm working hard." He put his arm around her waist. "You want anything?"

She lay quietly for a moment. "I can't believe I'm saying this, but I think I want to try some of that heroin you talked about. I've been so stressed out, and I just need a good night's sleep."

"*Really?*" Caleb said, a little taken by surprise. "Okay, but just a little; I don't want you to like it too much."

"Oh Caleb, I just love the way you protect me." She nuzzled closer.

He had never had a woman ask him to take heroin for the first time. And it seemed so not like her.

He was starting to have second thoughts about this. He hadn't thought this all the way through yet, and he knew how dependent and unreliable a heroin addict could be. It could screw up his plan to get all that money out of that bank vault if Anni got fired. When he first offered it to her, he didn't know her whole story, and now that he did, this seemed like a bad idea.

Caleb got up and went to the bathroom. He rolled another joint and put some PCP on it. *This should knock her out for a few hours*, he thought.

"Well, sorry," he said as he reappeared in the bedroom. "I thought I had some in there, but I haven't looked in three months and there isn't any. Let's just smoke again and relax like that."

Anni looked disappointed, but she just shrugged and said, "Okay, that'll be just fine." She lit up, and within minutes, she was out like a light, babbling to herself about who knows what. Anni woke up 5 hours later, around 3 in the morning, and quietly left Caleb's apartment and went back to her office to sleep. He never heard her leave.

When he got up the next morning, he took out the tape, dated it 8/26/81 A., and put it up. He wanted the rest of that money from Anni, but he needed to be careful not to strong-arm her or try to blackmail her right now. She was very smart and would counter anything like that. Caleb knew he had the upper hand on her right now with the pictures, video, and her infatuation with him, but he also knew her passion would deteriorate over time. Anni would stop the affair at some point, or it would just slowly fade away. Caleb had to take his time and think this out. How was he going to get that money, and just how far and at what cost to Anni was he prepared to go? He figured he had four years to chart it out. Right now he just needed to get ready for the game on Saturday.

Caleb had changed since killing Lillie. It was as though all the anger he had built up over the first 18 years of his life came out of him when he murdered his mother. Since then, Caleb had acquired this new, strange thing called a conscience, in which he wasn't used to dealing with.

He was starting to actually care about how other people feel.

CHAPTER 23

PLAY BALL

CAU was kicking off at 2:00 P.M. today, and all the players were required to be in the locker room no later than 10:00 A.M.

"You think we'll get any playing time today?" Caleb said as he drove over to the stadium with Lance.

"I hope so," Lance replied, playing with buttons in Caleb's Corvette. "I never had to sit on the bench before, and I don't think I'm going to like it."

Caleb waved his hands. "CUB of Berkeley is terrible; I think we'll hang half a hundred on them by halftime."

"Is this too cool or what, dude!" Lance said, fiddling with more buttons. "We're going to be on national TV. If I see that camera on the side line, I'm going to be waving at my momma."

Lance pressed something on the dashboard, and Caleb's eye twitched. "You press one more button on my car and you're going to be walking." Lance quickly folded his hands on his lap. They drove in silence for a little while, and then Caleb sighed. "You think Luke has a chance at the Heisman this year? He's one bad dude on the field and is a pretty top-notch guy, I think."

Lance laughed. "I hope so! That way he can keep it warm till I win it." Caleb just chuckled and shook his head.

***

From 1:00 till 1:30, the team went out on the field to run some plays and warm up. The CAU Panthers band took over at 1:30 till game time. Jason Allgood & Kerry Wood, the offensive and defensive captains, went out to flip the coin right before the game started.

Caleb's heart was racing. He could hear the crowd cheering from inside the locker room as the team lined up to take the field right before game time. CAU has a long tunnel players go down, and at the end of it is a *big* panther head with smoke coming out of it.

Head Coach Joe Richert screamed, "Everyone hit the field!" and all 80 players came streaming out of that tunnel. The band was playing, the cheerleaders were jumping, and the crowd was going nuts. Caleb had never seen this many people in one place—it was pure craziness. He ran over to the sideline and picked up his headphones. His job was to relay the offensive play to Coach Axom, who would send someone in with the play.

Caleb was excited to finally be in the action, but he was also disappointed that he wasn't able to move into the starting job over Jason; there just wasn't time. This was the first time he had *not* started at QB in a game. Still, he perked up when he remembered what Coach Axom told him—"You're only one hurt QB away from being a starter, so you have to prepare like you're the starter every game."

***

"This is Joseph Jack, your play-by-play announcer for the CAU Panthers, on XKRT radio Los Angeles. The Panthers have won the toss and deferred to the second half as we get ready to kick off another exciting season for the #4 rated CAU.

"And there goes the kickoff for the 1981 CAU Panther season! Berkeley immediately goes three and out. The CAU defense is being touted as the #1 defense in the nation this year, and from that first series I can see why! Here comes the offense led by Heisman trophy candidate Luke Donaldson. Jason Allgood is the starting QB. This has been a long time coming for the 5th-year senior out of San Francisco, and he looks ready to lead this team to another Pac 10 championship!"

***

In the huddle, Rory comes in with the play, and Jason says, "42-formation red on 2."

Jason lines up the team, excited about the roar of the crowd and sweet smell of the grass. "Hut, hut!" he barks.

***

"Jason hands the ball off to Luke for a 15 yard gain down to the Berkeley 45," Joseph Jack shouted in his sing-song voice. "1ST DOWN PANTHERS! Jason lines up under center and drops back to pass…ohhhh he overthrew a wide open Rory Lomas at the 10."

Rory jogged back to the huddle and swatted at Jason. "Dude, that was 7 points you just overthrew! You got this, man. Settle down."

Joseph Jack had barely paused to breathe. "2nd and 10 Jason hands off to Luke, he crushes a linebacker at the 40, runs through a huge gap in the secondary, he is going to score! Panthers 6 Berkeley 0! The p.a.t. is up and good. That was an impressive drive and Luke Donaldson looks to be all that he's cracked up to be."

That was a pretty imposing drive, Caleb thought, crossing his arms. The rest of the half hovered with CAU in the lead 7 to 0, but the offense looked absolutely awful. Jason was 2 for 12 throwing and didn't look very sharp.

"This doesn't look like a #4 team in the country should look!" Joseph Jack boomed into his microphone. "Jason Allgood is really struggling out there, and the offense can't seem to get out of the way of each other. The Panthers are going to have to make some adjustments at halftime and figure out what's wrong, folks."

***

The coaches were going nuts in the locker room.

Coach Swerving, the offensive line coach, was screaming at the players until his voice started to crack. "Are you guys wearing panties? I'm fixing to open me up a can of whip-ass and pour it all over you boys if you don't start knocking some people around out there! I swear to all mighty God as I'm standing here, when this game is over we will go to the practice field and run ropes until midnight if you don't start hitting someone!"

Coach Richert rubbed his face, mumbling through his hand, "I don't think I've ever been this embarrassed before." He crowded himself right in with his players, intimidating in his closeness. "We're making some changes, and if you want to keep your job on this team, you better suck 'em up and show me something this half!"

Coach Axom walked up to Caleb and grabbed him by the shoulder. "Get ready, kid, you're starting the 3rd quarter."

Caleb was surprised, but he thought, *Well, I know I can't do worse than Jason just did.*

Jason approached Caleb before the start of the 3rd quarter and said, "Good luck. I know you got this, buddy. Go get us the win."

Caleb looked at him, immediately seeing the disappointment on his face, and said, "Thanks, Jason. You got us the lead, and I'll see if I can hold it."

***

"This is Joseph Jack back for the third quarter, and Berkeley is preparing to kick off to a struggling Panther team that looks confused about how to play this game of football. There goes the kick out of the end zone, so the Panthers will be lining up on their own 20. Wow! This is a major change in the lineup—the #1 high school QB recruit in the nation, Caleb Lewis, is making his debut in a CAU football game. Caleb came from Enapay, Oklahoma and from all accounts is the best QB to come out of high school in a long time, but this ain't high school football, and I'm anxious to see how he reacts under pressure."

Caleb trotted out to the huddle. "Boys, I ain't ever lost a football game, and we ain't gonna lose this one. Let's crush these guys."

Joseph Jack leaned into his mic. "Caleb lines up under center, hands the ball off to Luke off tackle, OH NO, Luke fumbles the ball and it popped out behind him!" Joseph Jack's voice kept rising. "Lewis picks up the football, scoots around the right defensive end, knocks down a linebacker, cuts left, stops, cuts right. HE HAS DAYLIGHT. He's at the 40, 45, 50, look at that speed! There isn't anyone going to catch this kid! UNBELIVABLE, 80 yards on his first play from scrimmage as a CAU Panther! The stadium is going crazy!"

Caleb handed the ball to the official and was mobbed by the rest of team in the end zone. Caleb trotted off the field thinking, *I can't wait to get back in there.* Caleb's heart was still beating fast, smiling from ear to ear, and he was so excited that he wasn't paying any attention while CAU kicked off to Berkeley and went three and out again.

***

Joseph Jack continued, "Freshman QB Caleb Lewis and the rest of the Panthers are heading back onto the field and are huddled up on their own 25."

133

Caleb laughed in the huddle. "These guys aren't any tougher than some high school teams I played. Okay, here we go. 33 right, motion left-cross."

"Halfback is in motion," Joseph Jack continued, "Caleb drops back for a pass—a rope to Danny Boings to the Berkeley 45, a 30 yard gain. 1ST DOWN PANTHERS! Luke Donaldson gets the handoff and gets 10 tough yards. Caleb drops back, a screen pass to flanker Larry Fitszer for 20 yards.1ST DOWN PANTHERS! Folks, this looks like a completely different team than we saw in the first half.

"And Caleb takes the snap, drops back, Rory Lomas is open in the end zone…a beautiful pass from Caleb in the corner of the end zone! TOUCHDOWN CAU! Caleb Lewis looks like a 5th year senior out there folks, such composure and full of confidence. Panthers 21, Berkeley 0."

The game continued like this until the final whistle, with Caleb raking in the points. He felt like he was walking on air, feeding off the adrenaline and the roar of the crowd. When the clock ran out in the 4th quarter, Caleb was so happy he wanted to just yell at the top of his lungs.

***

"This is Joseph Jack back for the post-game roundup. This was an incredible performance today by true freshman Caleb Lewis. In his first game and only one half of play, Caleb threw 10 passes, no incompletions, for 285 yards, and rushed for 168 yards. This kid is all and more than he was cracked up to be. Get ready Los Angeles, Caleb Lewis has arrived, and I have a feeling Panther football is going to be something special to watch this year. This is Joseph Jack signing off, and your final score—CAU Panthers 49, Berkeley 0.”

The TV reporters were all over Caleb after the game, and he gave them a rehearsed statement, just like he’d practiced in that interview class. “If it weren't for my teammates I wouldn’t have done this well. My linemen gave me great protection, my receivers caught the ball, and the defense was unreal. This is a team win, and I am just a small part of the team.”

Back in the locker room, the team was celebrating and whooping and hollering like they had just won the national championship game. Head Coach Joe Richert shouted at the team to gather around him, and the rowdy players settled down and crowded in.

“Congratulations, boys. But remember—this wasn’t a very good ball club we just played, and we SHOULD have won by 49. This is just one game in a very long season, so get ready to strap your helmets on next week, boys—we play Notre Dame. It will take intense study and great practices for us to beat them, but we *can* beat them. It will be a battle like you have never been in, so enjoy the win today. But starting Sunday, we prepare for the Irish.”

***

Caleb talked with reporters for another hour or so, and as he was leaving the locker room, it occurred to him that there was no Don Phero to be found. *Man, that Johnny works quickly.*

As he was walking back to his car, Coach Axom ran out after him.

"Caleb!" Axom shouted. Caleb paused and waited for the coach to catch up. "I'm very proud of the way you played today," Axom said, giving Caleb a friendly punch to the shoulder. "I couldn't find anything wrong with your game, and I'm an expert on pointing out mistakes. But don't let this game go to your head—you have four more years of this ahead of you, and they won't all be this easy, trust me."

"Yes sir, coach," Caleb said with a nod.

"I also want you to be aware that for right now, you are off limits to the press, and we have told the press that. The reason for that is you have enough to worry about without those weasels all over you all the time asking you the same questions over and over. I also can't guarantee that you will be the starter on Saturday against Notre Dame. As good as you were today, Jason has played against the kind of pressure, speed, and size that Notre Dame brings to the table, and I'm not sure you're prepared for that yet. I will tell you one thing, though—like today, if Jason is struggling, you will get your chance."

Coach Axom looked at him seriously and spoke softly. "Caleb, I know about the problems you had back in Enapay, Oklahoma, and I took that into great consideration before we offered you a scholarship. I haven't shared that information with anyone else. I took a big risk on you.

What happened to you at such a young age would have made any young man unstable. I get it. I do want you to know that I haven't seen anything like that young man described to me in Enapay since you've been out here. You've been a hard worker and you study hard. You do what we ask of you and don't ask why. I'm so proud of you."

Caleb smiled, but he felt a bit uneasy. "Uhh, what *do* you know about me in Oklahoma?"

"A lot," Axom said, "and I think it's a sad, sad story, and I feel bad for you. But may I tell you one thing I've learned in life, Caleb, it's that God doesn't give us more than we can handle. Sometimes God tests us with life's difficulties because he knows if you endure it, then you will come out stronger on the other side. Ah, Caleb, I meant to ask—do you have a Bible?"

He replied, uneasy with this conversation, "No, not here."

"Well, I will make sure you get one. I want you to read the book of Job; I think it will help you understand some things. I think God was testing you growing up, and he has great plans for you. I think all the heartache, pain, and suffering you have endured AND caused yourself have made you a smarter, stronger person than you would have been without it. God doesn't make mistakes, Caleb, and God loves us like no one else and only wants the best for us."

Caleb looked at Axom with tears in his eyes. "Thank you, coach, I needed to hear that. Let's go beat Notre Dame next week."

When Coach Axom left, tears were rolling down Caleb's cheeks. But he wasn't entirely sure what he was feeling. Pride in Coach Axom's words of praise? Sure. But if there was a God, he was still pissed at him no matter what Coach Axom said.

It had been a good day, and he wished Lillie could have been here to see it—she would have been so proud.

CHAPTER 24

SPANK IT

Late in the afternoon, and Caleb and Lance were heading back to the dorm to get something to eat. From the moment Caleb walked into the dorm, everyone started applauding and hollering. The noise was almost deafening. He was embarrassed by all the attention and waved his hand as if to say the praise wasn't necessary, but what could he do about it? He hung out with the guys for a couple of hours, relaxed, and called his dad. After speaking with Jack for thirty minutes or so, he hung up and stretched out on the bed. A thought occurred to him: *I haven't done any heroin in quite a while, and I don't have to get up in the morning.* He opened a pack and sprinkled it on a spoon, heated it up, shot up, and laid down for the evening.

Around 10:30, he heard a tap on the door and thought to himself, *I hope that's not who I think it is.* He walked over and turned on the VHS camera, then opened the door. Anni, like always, walked in kissed him, dropped her drawers, and stood there posing for him. Caleb was still full of heroin and sore from the game. He rubbed his face.

"Anni, I'm a little too worn out for sex tonight, but you wanna do something else? Maybe we can just relax and chill out tonight."

"Really?" she said incredulously. "You don't want some of this?" swinging her arms out like a model, and the curves of her body were beautiful. Caleb just looked at her with those intense eyes, but when he didn't sweep her into his arms, she sighed. "I've been looking forward to this all day, especially after watching that magnificent performance this afternoon on the football field."

"Not tonight, Anni," Caleb said again. "I just don't have it in me and I'm not in the mood. If you want to get high, I'll fix you up. If not, you need to leave now."

Anni was puzzled. "I'm throwing myself at you, Caleb, and you're treating me like some desperate high school slut and with a lack of respect that I don't appreciate." She stood and marched toward him until their noses were almost touching. "Caleb, I didn't want to say this ever, but you know I can cause you a bunch of trouble with this football program, and I can also cut off your money resources in a second. You need to think about these things before you tell ME no."

Caleb's blood pressure was rising fast. *Is this woman trying to strong-arm me?* Anni stepped backward again and sat down proudly, confident that she had put this young buck right where she wanted him. She was about to learn a few things.

He just stared intensely at her as she went on and on about how powerful she is. How he should be grateful that she was allowing him to have sexual relations with her. How special she is and blah, blah, blah, on and on. His irritation continued to build. And then it hit a breaking point.

Caleb reached down, grabbed Anni, and picked her up by the throat with one hand. Holding her above his head, he swung her like a puppet and said, "Don't you EVER threaten me again, woman." She was choking from the grip around her neck, red-faced. She clawed at his hand to try to break out of his grip, but he didn't stop. "I can hurt you so bad—don't you EVER, EVER threaten me again!" Caleb threw her hard on the bed.

Anni gasped for air, shocked by his temper. When she could breathe again, she screamed back at him, "NOBODY is going to treat ME like that, Caleb, and you don't scare me one little bit." She slapped him as hard as she could across his cheek, and the sharp hit echoed through the apartment. "I will ruin you," she said. "I hate you and I wish I had never met you."

Caleb didn't flinch when Anni slapped him. All he said was, "You crazy, spoiled rotten witch." He suddenly reached out, grabbed Anni, and bent her over his lap. She went down screaming and kicking, and he started spanking her hard. "If you're going to act like a spoiled little brat," he said between hits, "then I'll treat you like a spoiled little brat." By the time Caleb was done, her little bare butt was beet red and swollen, covered in hand prints.

Anni didn't move for a while after that, and in the quiet, Caleb got control of himself again. He went to the bathroom, rubbed some water on his face, and tried to figure out how to fix this. He got out some heroin and waited on her to calm down. He could hear her crying hysterically. *I have to fix this. This is bad. Don't screw up the bank.*

Caleb got a wet towel and started dabbing her face with it. After what seemed like forever, she stopped crying. He gently threaded his arm around her.

"Anni, I'm sorry. I'm just so tired. What happened tonight will never happen again, I promise. Are you okay?"

She looked up at him, tears streaming down her face, totally defeated. "I have to go."

"No, don't leave," Caleb said, making sure his arm was still gently around her. "I got you some of the heroin you wanted to try; it'll help you relax and have a good night's sleep. How does that sound?"

"You spanked me like a child!" Anni whimpered, tears starting up again. I feel so humiliated and degraded….How anyone can do that is beyond me. I feel so violated. I don't even know what to say. Why did you do that?" Anni had never known about Caleb and his quick temper, and now that she did, she was thinking this whole affair thing was more trouble than it's worth.

"I was tired and asleep when you knocked on the door. I had no idea you were coming over. That's a poor excuse for spanking you, I know, but I hope you know it won't happen again. Now let me see your arm—you'll feel great in few seconds."

"I don't know, Caleb. You scared me tonight. I think I just want to end this whole thing."

"It'll be okay," Caleb said and took Anni's arm. She didn't seem happy, but she didn't fight either. He stuck the needle in and drained it. Caleb didn't want to play the heroin card, but he was backed into a corner and couldn't let her leave like that. He didn't have much choice but to knock her out until she had time to calm down and get herself together. She could feel the warm heroin coursing through her veins, and she looked at Caleb and started to say something, but she tumbled back on the bed and closed her eyes. She woke up the next day around 11:00 AM.

Anni's butt was sore and covered in red welts, but other than that, she felt incredible. She had never felt so rested. Still naked, she crawled up between his legs and woke Caleb up. He looked down at her, groggy, and said, "What a nice way to wake up in the morning." Anni smiled, scooted up on him, and finally got the sex she came for.

After they were done, he apologized again for spanking her and she apologized for popping in, especially after a game. "Next time I'll call before I come over. Again, I apologize. I am so sorry I treated you like that and acted so childish."

"I accept," he said, "and let's put this behind us and move on."

She smiled, satisfied. "Caleb, I have never rested that well before—that heroin is unreal. I'd like to do that again soon."

Caleb took her by the hand and said, "Anni, you have to be real careful with the white stuff; you can become dependent on it fast, and I wouldn't want that to happen to you. Plus it's very expensive and hard to come by."

Anni slid out of bed, went to her purse, and proudly pulled out a $10,000 wrap. She handed it to him and said, "Well, I have lots of money, so I think I can afford it. I will be very careful."

"Okay," he said, "but we aren't doing heroin every time you come over, you just need to know that. Maybe once a week, after a WIN, we can do it. Okay?"

"Great plan!" Anni said, beaming. "Let's count on it."

"Oh, and by the way, why don't we ever have sex at your office? The guys here are starting to notice that you come and go here late at night. We may need to change locations occasionally, you know? What do you think?"

"Hmm. Well, let me think about it, okay?"

Caleb nodded; he had been formulating a plan for a couple of weeks, and this was the first step to putting the plan into action.

Anni left to go back to her office, and Caleb got up, turned off the recorder, dated it, and went down and had some lunch with the guys. Now that he had Anni under control again, all he could think about was preparing for the next game versus Notre Dame. He was pumped up and ready to go.

CHAPTER 25

GAME WEEK

The team started watching films of Notre Dame late Sunday afternoon, and the coaches were formulating their game plan. Notre Dame was rated #5 in the country and CAU #4, so this was the game of the week on national TV. Head Coach Joe Richert was already getting bombarded with questions about who he was going to start this week at QB.

"Now boys, as good as Caleb was last Saturday, I'm just not sure he's ready for a team like Notre Dame. I'm not saying he won't start, and I'm not saying he will. You'll find out on Saturday." It's not like Coach was actually going to give them any info—he wanted ND to have to prepare for both QBs. That would take more time for the defense and give CAU an advantage.

The practices this week had been the most intense that Caleb had ever seen. Everyone was on-point about their assignments and responsibilities. Head Coach Richert didn't seem too worried—if CAU executed offense and defense like they had practiced all week, they should come out on top. Vegas had the point spread at CAU minus 2.

The game was Saturday at 2:00 pm at Notre Dame, so the team would be flying out to South Bend on Thursday. On Friday, they had a very light workout to get used to the field conditions and the stadium.

Caleb was pumped up about being in the stadium with such an impressive history and tradition—this place had been around for a while, and it was an important landmark in Indiana. In his free time this week, Caleb had gone to the campus library to read up on Notre Dame and its football teams.

There was barely any down time, though, and the team did their special drills, ran some plays, and threw a few passes, just getting used to the field. Caleb looked up to see Touchdown Jesus hanging high above the stadium—the huge mosaic wall of Jesus loomed over the end zone, mirroring the raised arms of a referee signifying a touchdown. *That's silly*, Caleb thought.

After the team had finished, they dressed and took a bus back to their hotel. The rest of the night was about rest and mentally preparing for the big game. Caleb was rooming with Lance, and after they had supper, they went to their rooms to just watch some TV and relax.

***

Once at the stadium on the big day, things got serious. Coach Axom popped in to the locker room and stopped Caleb as he was suiting up. "Jason will be the starter, but like always, you need to be prepared mentally to go in at any given moment."

Caleb wasn't surprised, but he hoped he would get in the game; he believed the coaches knew he was the best QB,

146

and Jason knew it too. It seemed like they had Jason on a short leash, which didn't leave him much room for mistakes.

After all the pre-game hoopla, the teams ran out and to their sideline. Caleb picked up his headphones to relay the offensive calls to Coach Axom. Notre Dame won the toss and deferred to the second half. Notre Dame would be kicking off to CAU.

***

"This is Joseph Jack, your play-by-play announcer for the CAU Panthers, on XKRT radio Los Angeles. CAU Panthers vs The Notre Dame Fighting Irish, the national TV game of the week. The Panthers held on to the #4 spot this week after an incredible performance by freshman QB Caleb Lewis last week. Coach Richert has kept quiet on whether Jason Allgood or Caleb Lewis would be the starter today. Notre Dame comes in rated #5 in the country and breezed by a normally strong Penn State in their opener."

"Notre Dame has won the toss and deferred to the second half as both teams line up for the kickoff. There goes the whistle and there goes the kick. Thad Thompson catches the ball at the 10-yard line and cuts left to the 20, 25, he has some daylight. Ohhh brought down by a shoelace at the 40 by the Notre Dame kicker. Well, we know who the starter is as Jason Allgood trots onto the field and huddles up the team."

Jason crouched in with the team and shook his head quickly to clear his mind. "Ok guys, I apologize for last week—I

147

had the jitters, I guess. We're going to win this game, though. 41, Holla formation, jack back in motion on 3, don't jump offside. It's a three count."

Joseph Jack continued, "And Jason takes the snap and hands off to Luke Donaldson, who makes a tough run for 15 yards to the Notre Dame 45. 1st DOWN PANTHERS! Jason under center drops back, throws the ball to Rory Lomas over the middle—the ball is tipped—interception Notre Dame—Oscar Velvet is at the 15 looks like he is going to score for Notre Dame—Luke Donaldson makes an incredible save at the ten yard line of CAU!"

Jason charged off the field cursing at Rory for tipping the ball. The other players just looked at Jason blandly—they know he overthrew the ball. It wasn't Rory's fault.

"Notre Dame lines up in a power set, snaps the ball and goes right in the center of the CAU defense and scores! The P.A.T. is good and it's Notre Dame 7, Panthers 0."

Coach Richert threw his clipboard to the ground so hard the corner stuck in the turf like a knife. He rushed in to meet the defense coming off the field. "Dang it boys, you have to play tougher than that! All I want to see out there are assholes and elbows! Get your heads up and dig in!"

***

"Notre Dame lines up for the kick," Joseph Jack warbled on, "and Thad Thompson catches the ball at the 10, cuts to his left, ahhh Notre Dame strips the ball and recovers the fumble at the Panthers' 15. Notre Dame lines up, tries to go up the middle again and is stuffed for a 3 yard loss. Patrick under center takes the snap, goes right, tosses the ball to the flanker on a reverse—he's all alone and will walk in for the touchdown—PAT good, Notre Dame 14, Panthers 0."

Coach Hoening was screaming at Thad, "HEY! What kind of rookie crap was that! YOUR primary responsibility on a return is to PROTECT THE BALL!" Thad just walked on over to the sideline, ignoring him.

***

"Heading into halftime your score is Notre Dame 17, Panthers 3. Once again, Jason Allgood is really struggling out there. Luke Donaldson has been carrying most of the load for the Panthers, which is a problem for CAU. At this level if you are one dimensional it can get ugly; Notre Dame is piling up nine in the box, just daring Jason Allgood to throw the football, which he has struggled with today, going 3 for 15 in the first half. It makes me wonder if we'll see Caleb Lewis starting the second half."

***

"You're starting the second half," a voice behind Caleb said. Caleb turned around in time to see Coach Axom walk over to Jason. "Son, I know you're trying, but it's just not working today. Caleb is starting the second half."

"I don't blame you coach," Jason said, disappointed but still classy as ever. "I just can't get it together."

***

"This is Joseph Jack, your play-by-play announcer for the CAU Panthers, on XKRT radio Los Angeles getting ready for the second half kickoff. The Irish won the toss to begin the game and deferred to the second half, so CAU is lining up to kick the ball, and there it goes! Walker catches the ball at the five, gets hit hard but spins off the tackle, heads toward the center of the field, hit again but keeps his feet, he is going to score. A 95 yard touchdown return for Notre Dame! Not exactly a great start for a struggling CAU team this half. Notre Dame 24, CAU 3."

Caleb looked around at the sideline. *Man, everyone's head is down. I hope they haven't given up.*

"And Notre Dame kicks off to CAU out of the end zone. CAU will be starting at their own 20. Ah, I thought this might happen—Caleb Lewis, the true freshman from Oklahoma, is trotting onto the field for the second half."

Caleb came in at QB and huddled with his teammates. "You guys ready to beat these pansies?" Everyone smiled, and the adrenaline started to flow again.

"And Caleb takes the snap, a straight handoff to Luke for a 5 yard gain. Caleb lines up under center for a 2nd and 5 play. Lewis takes the snap, drops back looking for Rory—he's covered like a blanket. Caleb's getting pressure; he moves to the right side of the field, Lance is open. Caleb throws the ball, a long pass. Lance catches it in the end zone! Touchdown Panthers! This kid from Oklahoma is something special folks!"

Caleb ran down to the end zone and grabbed Lance. "We got this, brother, we got this! Let's show our teammates how to win. Never give up!"

For the first time that day, Notre Dame went three and out, and Thad fair caught the punt on the 33.

Back in the huddle, Caleb said, "There's no way we're losing this game, boys. Hey, don't the grass smell sweet?" The guys chuckled, and Lavon said, "It sure do Caleb, It sure do."

***

"Caleb takes the snap, drops back to pass, Notre Dame has a full blitz coming. Lewis steps up in the pocket, is hit, spins around, hit again, puts his hand down on the turf to keep his balance, takes off to the corner, cross cuts across the field, he has daylight, he's at the 40, 45, 50, 45, 35, 25, TOUCHDOWN! HOT DIGITY DOG LOS ANGELES, we have something special at quarterback! Caleb Lewis is the highlight reel of the week. I don't know what to say—this kid is like superman. There is no way that CAU can keep playing Jason Allgood; Caleb Lewis is just too good. He has so many moves, and the accuracy of his arm is uncanny. We're still behind, but we're starting to take control of this game. Notre Dame 24, CAU 17."

***

"We're in deep in the fourth quarter now, and your score is Notre Dame 24, CAU 20. The CAU defense has been impressive this half and have virtually shut down Notre Dame. The Notre Dame defense is getting tired; their players are walking around with their heads down and hands on their hips. They have been on the field almost the entire second half."

Caleb huddled up the team. "This is the drive we win this game. Everything you have on every play, boys, and we walk out of here with the WIN."

"Three minutes to go in the game and Caleb takes the snap, hand-off to Luke, a gain of 10. 1st DOWN PANTHERS! Again a hand-off to Luke for a gain of 15. Luke Donaldson is having a heck of a game. The Panthers are on the 50 yard line with 2:10 on the clock. Caleb takes the snap, drops back, Rory Lomas is streaking down the sideline, he has three steps on the defender, Caleb slings the ball, HE HITS RORY IN FULL STRIDE, TOUCHDOWN CAU! TOUCHDOWN PANTHERS! CAU has the lead for the first time in this game, and time is running out. Notre Dame 24, CAU 27.

"CAU kicks off with 1:30 left in the game. No punt's now for Notre Dame, it's all or nothing. Notre Dame goes 4 and out so all Caleb has to do now is take a knee."

"And there goes the whistle! CAU has a win for the ages."

***

When the game was over, ABC grabbed Caleb and started asking him questions about the game. Caleb said all the right things, praising his coaches, teammates, and the administration at CAU. Caleb wouldn't talk about his own accomplishments; he just praised everyone else. Caleb was becoming very adept at the art of spinning stories.

Coach Axom grabbed Caleb and off they went to the locker room. "Well, Caleb, looks like you're the starting QB for CAU, congratulations. Keep this up, and you should be for a long time. You still have a bunch of stuff to learn, but hopefully, your athleticism will get you over the rough spots that'll come." Caleb was excited and felt fortunate to be the starting QB for CAU as a freshman; he knew it was a rare thing for a freshman to start at this level. Determined to work harder than ever before to show the coaches they had made the right decision, he walked out of the stadium and back to his hotel room with his head held high. He was really happy that his dad could watch the game on TV, and he couldn't wait to call him. Jack was the only family he had left, and without him, Caleb would be totally lost.

CHAPTER 26

A DATE

Back in L.A., Caleb was still having problems with his hometown of Enapay. The more famous he became, the more these people would talk about him. ESPN, a new cable network that had launched in 1979, asked Caleb if they could do a hometown story about him. They wanted his story, a story about a young man from a small town in Oklahoma who had gone through heartache and pain at a young age. His parents getting divorced, his brother killed in Vietnam, his sister dying in an accident, and his mom dying in that explosion. Caleb couldn't stop ESPN from doing a story, but the coaches did step in and asked them to hold off on that. "There will be plenty of time to do that," Coach Richert told them. "He hasn't even started a game yet; you guys are doing this way too early in his career. Let's see how this turns out before we start delving into his early life, please."

Caleb, of course, was not happy about any of this. He didn't want to talk about it and had no plans to ever go back to Enapay. Even though he had never been arrested for anything or even been questioned about any crime, he knew there was stuff out there that could not only ruin his career but put him in prison for a long time. Caleb had way too many skeletons in his closet, and he had to gather them up before they started stepping out of that closet.

Caleb called Johnny Caldwell that afternoon and talked to him about the whole situation.

"It is hard to control because of all the rumors about you in high school," Johnny told him. "I've gone to a number of people that I heard were talking and asked them to keep their mouth shut or I would shut it for 'em, but for everyone I shut up, two more come out of the woodwork. It's like trying to step on cockroaches—there are way too many of them. What pisses me off is most of these people never had any dealing with you one way or the other. They just heard the stories and can't keep their mouths shut because everyone wants their moment of fame, I guess."

"Well, do you have any ideas on how to shut 'em up?"

"Caleb," Johnny said with a sigh, "short of me killing a couple of them and showing folks what would happen if they talked, I have no idea."

"Johnny, I don't want to kill people. There has to be a better way."

"Well, you figure it out and I'll do what you want."

***

Caleb was lying in his bed that afternoon thinking about the people he'd hurt in Enapay. Now, he understood why he was like that at that time—he had read every psychiatric book he could get his hands on since he had been at CAU. In fact, he was so fascinated by psychology that he was considering majoring in it. Thanks to the change of his environment and his growing enjoyment in

155

psychoanalyzing himself, he felt like he was starting to get a grip on who he was, for the most part. He considered just going back to Enapay and apologizing to many of the girls that he hurt, but he couldn't wrap his mind around that. *Would that bring on more trouble? Those girls are really angry; no telling what would happen if I showed up at their doorsteps. They might have a heart attack or just shoot me.*

Caleb knew somewhere down the line, all the sex, pain, and drug addiction was going to come flooding out from some of these girls. He looked over at the Bible that Coach Axom had given him and actually picked it up. He figured he'd skim through it and see if it had anything promising like those psychology books. The havoc he caused in Enapay wasn't normal, and he knew it. He was going to keep working on these really complex problems himself, and if he couldn't figure it out, he might go talk with Coach Axom about it. Caleb trusted him.

Caleb meandered around for a while, lost in thought. He ate lunch and chatted with the guys for a while, then decided lying on his bed and reading a book was pretty nice and went back to his apartment to do just that. He was relieved that he hadn't received a call from Anni and from her sore butt the last time, he didn't figure she would just pop in to see him. He lounged in bed for a while, then picked up the phone and called Beth. "Whatcha doing?"

"I'm not doing anything," Beth said, and Caleb could hear the smile on her face. "Just got home from church about 6, and I'm just watching TV and getting ready for bed."

"Well, I was thinking maybe I could drive over there and we could go get something to eat and go see 'Raiders of the Lost Ark,'" Caleb said. "I heard it's really good."

"Yes!" Beth said. "I'd love to do that. I live in the Paradise Apartments right down highway 60 from you. It'll be a big complex on the left, and I live in building 4, apartment 10."

"I'll be there in 10 minutes," Caleb said, swinging out of bed.

Beth cut in, "Give me 30 minutes—I need to get prettied up for you. I was getting ready for bed."

Caleb chuckled. "See you in 30 minutes then."

"See you soon!"

Caleb hung up the phone and hopped in the shower to wash, shave, and blow-dry his hair. He put on his clothes and some cologne, then went down and jumped in his Vette. He had never been on a *real* date before, so this was new ground for him. Thinking about being with a girl one-on-one was still a little nerve-wracking, but Beth talked so much it would probably be fine.

When Caleb knocked on the door, Beth came springing out in a cute, modest dress with frills. She smiled at him coyly. *Mother Mary, this is one handsome man.* She jumped up and hugged Caleb and said, "Thanks for calling! This will be fun."

Beth made Caleb feel good—she was so pure and had a joy about her that was contagious. Caleb looked down at her and smiled. "You look fantastic tonight."

The first thing she did when she slid into the Corvette was fiddle with the buttons. "I've never ridden in a Corvette before. How fun!"

Caleb was nervous watching her toying with everything. "I hadn't either until I got this one. I'm kinda tall for it, but I'm getting used to it. So, where would you like to eat?"

 "I don't care, I'm not all that hungry," she said as she rolled the windows up and down repeatedly.

Caleb sighed and reached over and slapped her hand away from the window buttons. "Me either, but the movie doesn't start for a couple of hours. What should we do?"

Beth looked down at her hand, confused. *Why did he just slap my hand?* But when she looked up at Caleb again, she couldn't help but smile. "Let's go down to the beach and walk around," she said.

"Great idea! I haven't been to the ocean before; I haven't had time since I've been here. How do I get there?"

Beth pointed and said, "Go west, young man," and giggled at herself.

***

After about half an hour of pleasant talk on the way, they hopped out of the car and made their way down the beach. "That's one bunch of water there; I haven't ever seen so much water!" Caleb said with a smile. "And look at those big waves crashing in…WOW!"

Beth reached over and took Caleb's large hand in her little small one and they walked along the beach for an hour, just talking about anything and everything. Beth was so easy to talk to; Caleb's words just poured out of his mouth and she laughed and giggled the whole time. The sun was setting over the Pacific, and it was just spectacular—he had never seen anything like it. Beth put her hands around Caleb's waist and stood on her tiptoes to reach up for his face. He lifted her up to him and gave her a very soft, loving kiss. It was easily the best kiss he had ever had, and Beth said with a soft sigh, "Best kiss ever."

Caleb smiled.

***

When they arrived at the movies later that night, it didn't take more than a few minutes of them standing out front before people started recognizing Caleb. He signed a couple of autographs, and before he quite knew what happened, there were twenty or thirty people lined up. People were taking pictures and wanting autographs. He hated all this attention, and it made him uncomfortable. Thankfully, the manager of the theater shoved himself through the crowd, snagged their arms, and led them inside.

"I have a private suite upstairs that's really nice for celebrities like you, if you'd like to use it," he said. "I'll send a waiter up to get your drinks and snack orders. How does that sound?"

Caleb looked at Beth, and Beth looked at Caleb, and they both grinned. "Sounds good to us!"

Caleb sank into the chair next to Beth, head back in a deep sigh. "That's the first time that has happened, but then again I don't leave the campus much. Sorry."

"I thought it was kind of exciting," Beth giggled. "I felt like I was with a Hollywood star."

Caleb laughed. "You're with a country boy from Oklahoma who ain't no Hollywood star. I just play football."

She playfully jabbed him, grabbing his hand. She didn't let go for the rest of the movie. And he was okay with that.

***

When it was over, they made a quick exit out the front and got in the car. "It's late and I have class and football tomorrow, so I'd better get some shut-eye and would you PLEASE quit playing with the buttons in my car?"

Beth chuckled and folded her hands in her lap.

As Caleb walked Beth up to her apartment, she reached up and put her hands around Caleb's neck. "This is the best date I've ever had. Thank you so much for asking me out."

Caleb, relieved, replied, "You aren't going to believe this, but it's my first date ever. I just wasn't too interested in girls until I met you. You're special. Thanks for going out; we will do it again soon, okay?" Caleb reached down, gave her a kiss, saw her into her apartment, and went home.

160

Chapter 27

BAD HEART

CAU was playing Fresno State this week and was heavily favored. The coaches hadn't announced who the starting QB was going to be, but it was common knowledge among the press. Caleb had prepared all week long, watching tons of film and studying defensive formations and the game plan. One thing Caleb was happy about was that the game was going to be in Panther Stadium, so no traveling this week.

Thursday night, Caleb decided to call up his dad to see how things were going in Enapay. Mary, Jack's wife, answered the phone, and Caleb tried to spark up some chit chat for a few minutes, but Mary was unusually quiet. Caleb asked if he could talk to Jack, but he was just speaking into a long silence on the phone. Finally, Mary said, "Caleb, Jack asked me not to say anything to you, but I think you have the right to know." Her voice was quivering. "Jack had a bad heart attack on Tuesday at the hardware store."

Caleb's heart plummeted. "Where is he? Is he okay? Please tell me he's okay."

"They took him to Oklahoma City and did four bypasses, and he's in stable condition right now. I think he's going to be fine, but it'll be a long recovery." Mary sighed deeply.

"I had just come home from OKC to get some things to take back, and I'm fixing to head back up there tomorrow."

"But, he's okay, right?" Caleb said. He was sweating.

"Well, Caleb, it's a major surgery, but yes, the doctors think he's over the hump."

Caleb stood up. "I'm on my way. I have to see my dad."

Mary huffed, frustrated. "Oh Caleb, your dad wouldn't want you to come home and miss your first start at CAU! That's why he didn't want me to tell you."

Caleb said simply, "Do you need anything? I have plenty of money, and with Dad not working you're going to need some to get by."

"No, Caleb. Your dad is a very frugal person. We have plenty of money, but thank you for offering."

Caleb said, "I'll see you tonight" and hung up.

The first thing that Caleb did was call Head Coach Joe Richert "Coach, I'm sorry about this, but I'm heading back to Oklahoma tonight. My father had a bad heart attack on Tuesday, and if I don't go see him and he dies, I'll never forgive myself."

"Caleb, I am so sorry about your father," Richert said. "I want you to drive over to my office—I'm going to take care of all this for you." Coach Richert has been a college coach for a long time, and he knew he wasn't going to stop Caleb from going to OKC—all he could do was try to control the situation, and he was an expert at that.

Coach Richert called in Anni, and when she arrived, he told her what had happened. "Either you or Beth are going to Oklahoma with Caleb; I don't care which. You just be DARN sure Caleb Lewis is back in L.A. early Saturday. Don't you let him out of your sight! We're paying for all the expenses. Now get on the phone and make all the arrangements and reservations you're going to need." Coach Richert's next move was to call Axom, who rushed down to his office.

The only thing Coach Axom could say was, "Dang it, dang it, dang it! It's always something." He thought back to the stories he'd heard of Caleb in Enapay. "If Caleb loses Jack, we'll lose Caleb; there's NO way emotionally he can handle that." Coach Richert nodded. He knew it too. Axom waited for a moment, then said, "Well, do I tell Jason he's starting on Saturday?"

"Heck no!" Richert said, a little louder than he'd meant to. "I'll have Caleb back in uniform on Saturday if I have to drive him home myself. I hope after Caleb sees Jack, and IF Jack is doing okay, Caleb will be back here by Saturday. If I know Jack as I think, he'll tell Caleb to go back to L.A. and win that game."

***

Anni walked into the office and said, "If his father dies, it will destroy Caleb, his father is the only family he has left you know?"

Coach looked at Anni and said, "Don't you think I know that? Do you think I got to where I am today not knowing stuff like that?" Coach Richert then got on the phone and called the best Heart Surgeon in L.A. (and also an Alumni of CAU) and asked him to call Jack's heart Dr. in Oklahoma and get an up to date report on Jack's health. Coach Richert wanted to know what the diagnosis was and what he needed to prepare for with Caleb.

"There's no way I can leave the office two days before a game," Anni told Richert. She called Beth. "Pack a bag for two nights—you're going on a trip."

***

Caleb walked in about that time, and Coach Richert told Caleb how sorry he is about Jack. "Caleb," Richert said, patting him on the shoulder, "we've booked you and Beth a flight to OKC, so you should be there by 1 A.M. We also booked you two hotel rooms at a nice hotel close to Baptist Hospital and got you a car rental. Beth should be here soon, and I'm going to have a short meeting with her and then you two will be on your way." Everyone there hugged Caleb and told them they would be praying for Jack and if he needed anything to give them a call.

Beth busted through the doors a moment later. "What's going on?" She saw Caleb standing by himself in a corner with tears in his eyes, and rushed to him and hugged him; she knew that something terrible must have happened. Caleb grabbed Beth and broke down, crumpling to his knees—he was trying to hold it together, but the thought of losing his dad was just too much. Beth rubbed his back gently, squeezing him tight and telling him everything was going to be okay.

"Beth," Coach Richert said, hating to interrupt, "come in my office for a second and I'll get you up to speed." Beth sat, hand over her mouth, as she heard the story. Coach Richert leaned in. "I want you to take care of everything with Caleb and to keep me informed of his mindset during this time. Anni will give you some money; you are to pay for everything. I even want you to find out what the surgery and hospital costs are going to be and if Jack has health insurance. If he has health insurance, we'll pay all the deductibles and percentages that he owes—be sure Caleb knows CAU is doing this." Richert sighed, running a hand through his hair. "Beth, this is against NCAA rules— everything we're doing here could get us in trouble—but to heck with the NCAA! I feel like it's the right thing to do. I want you to babysit Caleb the whole time; don't let him out of your sight. You are to convince him to be back here on Saturday morning because that is what his dad would want, and that IS what his dad would want. Short of Jack dying before Saturday, you are to have Caleb Lewis back in L.A. Saturday morning. Do you understand?"

Beth nodded and left the office, heading straight down to Anni. Anni gave her $10,000 and told her to pay cash for everything. "Don't use the CAU name on anything or give any clues. If the press in Oklahoma picks up on this, don't answer any questions about anything. Just move on, ignore them. You call me when you get there and keep me informed of what's going on at all times."

***

"Yes, we've got two first-class roundtrip tickets on hold, please."

165

"And what are the names on these tickets going to be?" the attendant asked.

"Tom Farhaw and Amanda Jones." The receptionist typed away on her keyboard for a minute or two.

"That'll be $3,000 for two round-trip first-class tickets." Beth reached in her purse and paid her in cash. They boarded immediately—the flight was scheduled to head out in just a few minutes. As they settled into their seats, Caleb was very quiet. Beth reached over, grabbed his hand, and asked if he would like to pray with her.

Caleb smirked. "God don't much listen to what I say, but you go ahead." Beth prayed and asked God for healing for Jack if that is in his will and to give Caleb peace and God's grace as he goes through this difficult time.

When she said amen, Caleb said, "Thank you. I don't get prayed for anymore since my mom died."

Beth squeezed his hand a little tighter. "Yes you do. I pray for you every day, and I will continue to."

Caleb smiled for the first time in a while. "Thank you. I need all the help I can get."

***

"Hello. I'm Caleb Lewis. Can I see my dad, please?"

It was nearly two in the morning, but the nurse could tell that Caleb was anxious. "Sure," she said, "but don't wake him up if he's asleep, please."

"I won't."

He walked quietly into the room where Jack was resting and pulled up a chair next to his bed. He gently wrapped his hands around Jack's, careful not to wake him. Jack wasn't intubated, which was a good sign. After all, he's still young—only 46 years old and still strong as an ox. Caleb sat there holding his father's hand, and without much of a thought, he lowered his head and started praying for the first time since he was a child. Tears welled up in his eyes, and his lips quivered.

"God, I know you and I haven't gotten along very well the last few years. You did some bad things to me, and I did some bad things to people, but I sure would appreciate it if you would not let my daddy die. Dad is all I have left. Can't you let me have my dad? Anyway, I would be thankful if you would heal my dad. And I'm gonna try to do better, God. Amen."

Almost immediately, Caleb felt a peace come over him that he had never felt before. He just knew Jack was going to be okay.

While Caleb sat with his father, Beth checked into their hotel. When she returned, Caleb said, "I want to talk to the doctor in the morning, and then I might come get some shuteye. But for now, I'm going to stay here. You go ahead." Beth smiled and kissed Caleb on the cheek, gave him her room number and phone number, and went back to the hotel to sleep.

About 6 that morning, the doctor came in to check on Jack. Caleb got up and introduced himself, asking the doctor to fill him in.

"Jack had a massive cardiac arrest due to blockage of four arteries. We put in new arteries, and from the looks of the numbers here, your dad is going to be better than ever—he'll feel better and have more energy. It will take about six or so weeks to recover enough to be on his own, and he should be able to go back to work in about 12 weeks."

Caleb let out a sigh of relief. "Thanks, doctor. I appreciate all you've done. This guy is pretty special to me, and I only want the best for him."

The doctor smiled. "Well, you're pretty special to your dad; you're all he talks about, and his eyes just light up when someone mentions your name. You stay the rest of the day, then get back to L.A. to help your teammates win on Saturday. Your dad is going to be fine."

The doctor walked over the nurse's desk and whispered, "Can you please hand me that football I left here yesterday"? He walked over to Caleb and said, "This probably isn't appropriate right now, but my son is your biggest fan, and he would be so excited if I got your autograph on this football."

Caleb looked at him and said, "I'll sign your butt with a pen in my mouth if you promise to give my daddy the best you have to give!" and signed the football.

The doctor laughed and said, "I promise."

About that time, Caleb heard a grunt from behind him and then an exasperated, "I told Mary not to tell you about this!"

Caleb turned around, looked at his dad, and reached down to give him a very gentle hug. "Did you really think I wouldn't come here to see you?"

"You need to be back with your teammates!" Jack said. "I don't need a babysitter. If I could get out of this bed, I'd whoop you."

Caleb laughed and proudly looked around the room. "My daddy could probably do it, too." About then Beth walked into the room, relieved to see that everyone was talking.

Caleb grabbed Beth by the hand and pulled her over to the bedside. "Dad, I want you to meet Beth Owens. She's my girlfriend, and she came out with me to see you."

His girlfriend? Beth thought. *Why am I always the last to know anything?* She greeted Jack with a smile and told him that she and Caleb had been praying for him, and it looked like those prayers were being answered.

"Well, we can't get too many prayers," Jack said, "and our God is a GREAT God. I just pray that his will be done, and I will be fine here or in heaven, so I'm not too worried about it."

"Let's not rush that heaven thing yet, Dad," Caleb said. "You have a lot of football to watch me play before you take off."

Jack chuckled. "I'll do my best to hang around. Caleb, you get on back to L.A. and get us a win on Saturday. I don't think they're going to let me watch because they don't want my blood pressure to get too high, but I'll read about you in the papers. I love you, son, and Beth, you have your hands full with this one! You keep him on the right path for me, okay?"

Beth giggled. "He's a handful, but I can be pretty feisty myself!" she said with a fake punch. Jack just laughed.

Jack wrapped Caleb in a warm, tender hug. "Thank you. Now you go win that game, son. Show them coaches they made the right decision naming you the starter!"

On the way out the building, Beth stopped by the billing office and talked with the account receivables manager. She told him she would be paying whatever the insurance didn't pay. She gave them a non-CAU address where they could send the bill.

As they plopped down into their plane seats, Beth said to Caleb, "So I'm your girlfriend now? How exciting!" Caleb just laughed and grabbed her hand, giving it a squeeze.

Beth and Caleb were on their way back to L.A.

BREAKING IN

Saturday had arrived quickly, and the pre-game routine was well on its way to kick-off. Caleb was full of confidence and as determined to win as he had ever been in his life. CAU had moved up one spot in the rankings to #3 in the country, and the press was humming about Caleb and his exploits on the field.

The game itself went as others had before. Fresno kicked off to CAU and Thad returned it to the 35 yard line. On the first play from scrimmage, Luke took the handoff and went 65 yards untouched for a touchdown. Nobody except Luke had broken a sweat yet and CAU was up 7-0, 45 seconds into the game. Caleb had never seen a running back like Luke Donaldson, either on the field or off. A nice guy, real humble and quiet, just went about his business on the field without being cocky about it. After CAU had kicked off, Fresno went three and out and punted. Thad returned the punt 57 yards for a touchdown! CAU 14, Fresno 0. Caleb had played one offensive play and within the first two minutes was killing these guys.

CAU won the game 70 to 0, and even by the end of the first half, CAU was up 49 to 0. Luke had rushed for 213 yards in the game and never played in the 4th quarter, and Caleb threw one touchdown pass to Rory and ran for one of 12 yards. CAU was dominating so bad that the coaches quit throwing the ball after the first quarter, so Caleb's stats weren't so great, but Caleb didn't care—a win is a win. Caleb never went on the field in the second half, but Jason and Henry got some game time, as did the whole 2nd team, and Caleb was happy about that.

After Caleb showered and the trainers looked him over, he dressed and went back to his apartment. First thing he did is call Mary and ask how his dad is doing.

"Everything was really good and he feels much better today. I think they're going to let him go home on Monday if his blood work looks good. He's happy with your win today, Caleb. He's so proud of you."

"That's great news. I'll call you guys on Monday and see how it's going. Tell Dad I called, and thanks for taking care of him. Bye-bye."

As he lay sprawled out on the bed, his phone rang—Anni. She congratulated him on the win and asked if he would like to come by her office around 11 tonight. Caleb smiled. "Sounds good. I'll be there."

"Do you think you could bring some of that white powder too? I need a good night's rest."

"Sure," he said. "I'll see you later tonight."

Around 11:00, Caleb opened his gym bag, popped a new tape in the recorder, and put his drug paraphernalia in the bag. Almost nothing could beat a tape of Anni in her office having sex with a student and doing drugs. Caleb was building his case. He had a plan, and this was just one more step to cleaning out that safe.

Caleb walked into Anni's office about 11:15, and Anni jumped up from her desk and said "Hi. Let me lock that door behind you." She led Caleb back to her small bedroom, gave him a key, and said, "This key opens the back door to my office, so from now on, come up the fire escape stairs and into the back door. I know your dorm is about a mile from my office, but I would prefer you walk here when we meet. Coaches work really late, and your car sticks out like a sore thumb."

"Okay, I like walking anyway," Caleb said as he put his gym bag down.

"Anyway, I'll be right back," Anni giggled and went to the bathroom. Caleb placed his gym bag in a good recording position, turned on the recorder, got his drug bag out, and put it on the end table next to her bed.

Anni walked out of the bathroom already naked and ready to go. They had sex for about twenty minutes and were lying there relaxed on the bed, just talking about things. Anni asked Caleb about his dad and how he was doing and a bunch of small talk. Finally, she rolled over and said, "Well, I'm ready to rest now. Show me how you do this stuff. Last time you just jammed the needle in me, but I would like to see how you prepare it."

Caleb replied, "Sure. It's fairly simple, but you need to be careful that you don't get too much. I have mine in packs of 1/10th of a gram, and I add about 10cc of water to the syringe. Get your spoon out and put the powder on the spoon and squirt the water onto the powder. Heat it up a little bit, but be careful not to burn it. Stir it up until all of the powder is dissolved, and then put a small bit of cotton from a q-tip in the mixture. Put the tip of the needle in the cotton and draw up the mixture with the syringe. Then turn the needle facing up, and if there's any air in the mixture, tap it to get the air on the top and push the plunger to get the air out before you use it.

Anni looked at him, perplexed. "Caleb, I find it extremely disturbing that you know how to do all of this."

Caleb laughed and said, "I rarely do heroin, *and* if you're not careful you'll end up dependent on it, and that's a BAD place to be, Anni. I can't stress that enough to you."

She waved a hand dismissively. "I'm a very strong woman, Caleb. I can control anything. Don't worry about me."

He just looked at her with a smirk on his face and said, "Okay, don't say I didn't warn you." He took her arm and found a vein. "When you've found a vein, some blood will rush into the syringe—that's how you know you're good to inject it." He paused. "You wanna do it?"

"I'll give it a shot, no pun intended," she giggled. She took the syringe and stuck it slowly into her arm. When she saw blood, she pushed down the plunger and just fell back on the bed.

Caleb sat there and watched her for a minute to be sure she was okay, then got up and got dressed. The syringe was still dangling in Anni's arm. He got his camcorder out of the bag and took video of Anni lying there naked in her office with a needle in her arm. When he was through with the tape, he reached over and pulled the syringe out of Anni's arm, then ran some hot water through it to clean it.

While she was off in whatever world she was in, Caleb went to Anni's office to see if that safe was open—it wasn't. He pulled out her office drawers, looked in the bookcases, looked through papers, everything. He turned that office upside down looking for the combination, but no luck. He went back to Anni's bedroom to check on her—she was out like a light. He noticed her purse in the bathroom. *Well, I haven't looked there yet.* He opened the bag, and inside was a daily planner. On the last page were three numbers: 1-26-79. Caleb wrote the numbers on the palm of his hand and went back to the safe.

After a few skillful turns of the knob, he heard it click. He opened the safe and just stood there looking at all that frigging cash; there was more in there than the last time he saw it. He went back to the bedroom and turned off his camcorder, picked up his gym bag, and proceeded to take out $80,000 in wraps and $20,000 in loose hundred dollar bills and stuffed it all in his gym bag. He arranged the money in the safe so it looked exactly like it did when he opened it. Caleb knew you can shear a sheep many, many times, but you can only skin it once. He wasn't about to skin that sheep yet. He doubted that Anni would notice it was missing; the accounting was just too loose, and to his knowledge, she didn't write down the amount of money in there, she just tried to remember it. If she did see some is missing, who was she going to tell? The coach? The athletic director? The police? The A.D. and coaches didn't want to know anything about that money in any way, shape, or form, and she sure couldn't tell the police about it.

Caleb checked on Anni one more time, took his gym bag, and walked out the back exit, whistling a tune.

CHAPTER 29

CHURCH

Caleb's phone rang about 8:30 Sunday morning—it was Beth. "Caleb, will you please, please, *please* go to church with me at 11 today?" Caleb begrudgingly replied, "Okay."

Beth went to the Calvary Hill Baptist Church in L.A. It was a Southern Baptist Church like the one Caleb went to as a child in Enapay. As they pulled into the parking lot, Caleb said, "Man this is one big church! My church in Enapay is the biggest in town, and about 1,000 people a week attended. How many people go to this church?"

Beth replied, "Well the bulletin they hand out every week says about 5,000, but it doesn't seem that large to me."

As they walked into the church, ushers welcomed them. "We're so glad you've joined us today. If you have any questions about our church or our beliefs, we would gladly answer them. God bless you." The ushers immediately recognized Caleb and were excited that the QB for CAU was a Christian man going to their church.

A number of people came up to Caleb and shook his hand, welcoming him to Calvary Baptist (and also just wanting to shake his hand). Caleb's instincts told him this was going to get out of hand pretty quickly.

"Thank you for the warm welcome," he said to the usher.
"Could you make sure that nobody bothers us during
worship? I don't want to put up with that during church,
please."

"Absolutely!" the usher said. "God bless you, and no one
will bother you, I promise." Beth held Caleb's hand and
proudly walked into the sanctuary.

Caleb looked around and said, "Man, this place is amazing;
I've never seen a church like this." They sat towards the
back of the church and listened to the praise band playing
music until church started.

The preacher's name was Dr. Jonathon Braxston. He came
out and welcomed everyone to church and said a very
powerful traditional prayer asking God to pour out his holy
spirit on this place of worship today.

"Father,

Make me an instrument of your peace. Where there is
hatred, let me show love. Where there is injury, let me give
pardon. Where there is doubt, let me have faith. Where
there is darkness, let me spread light. Where there is
sadness, help me find joy! I pray Father today that you help
those who are hurting, depressed, addicted to drugs and
alcohol. To comfort those who grieve, to help the lost. To
let those who don't know of your saving grace know that
there is hope for them through the redemption of the cross.
To convict those who have drifted away from you and
bring them back to the joy of the Lord. Amen."

Caleb felt a wave of discomfort wash over him suddenly. *I hate church and all these hypocrites. They all think they're better than me…well, they are probably better than me, but that's not the point. I shouldn't be here, what am I doing?* He looked over at Beth and whispered, "Beth, I don't feel well. I'm going to the bathroom."

She looked at him, concerned. "Do we need to go?"

"Maybe."

He walked to the bathroom and washed his face, then made his way outside and stood in front of the church for some fresh air. *If there is a God, he won't forgive me for what I've done. Why would he?* He stood outside, taking deep, calming breaths when a man approached him quietly.

"Are you doing all right?" the man asked.

"I'm fine," Caleb said. "I just started feeling ill and came outside to get some fresh air."

The man looked at him closely for a moment and said, "You're Caleb Lewis, aren't you?"

"Yes sir, I am."

The man put his hand out to him and said, "My name is Don Woodlake. I'm a deacon here, and I'm very excited about your future at CAU. You've been spectacular so far this year."

"Thanks, but we have a long way to go and lots of games left to play."

Don looked at him and said without a hint of judgment, "Caleb, are you a Christian?"

 "Yes sir, I sure am," he lied. The last thing he wanted was this guy explaining Christianity to him. He had heard that from too many fanatics and didn't want to hear it again.

"That's good," Don said, "because from my experiences in my life, without Christ in us we are like a boat without a rudder just drifting in the ocean with no direction. Christ gives our lives a foundation and purpose, and without that relationship things can go pretty bad, I've found."

Caleb replied, "Yes sir, thank you for those words."

"Caleb, if you ever need to talk about anything at all, I would love to visit with you. I'm sure your life is getting ready to be pretty crazy, and you need to have that love and guidance that only the Bible and Christ's love can give."

"Yes sir," Caleb said. "Well, I think I'm feeling better. I'm going to go sit back down." *This is the most uncomfortable place I have ever been in. I've got to get out of here.*

He returned to the sanctuary and slunk back down next to Beth. They listened to the singing, which was actually really good, and the sermon from Dr. Braxston wasn't too bad. Dr. Braxston spoke of God's love for us no matter how bad we are. Caleb just wondered why he always felt bad after hearing God's words—everyone else seemed so happy. He always felt worse leaving church than when he came.

After church was over, he nearly bolted from the place and they went back to her apartment. He told her he would call her later. "I have to go to the film room this afternoon and start preparing for the Washington Huskies this week. It's our first Pac 10 conference game of the season."

"Okay," Beth said. "I had so much fun with you today!" Caleb gave her a kiss and said he would call her later tonight.

"Thanks for going to church with me," she called out as he left.

Man, she's so sweet. I think I am falling in love with her.

And so he was on his way to meet with Coach Axom and the other QBs to start preparing for the Washington Huskies.

CHAPTER 30

REDEMPTION

The Washington Huskies had cracked the top 25 last week for the first time in 5 years and, they were undefeated, just like CAU. They weren't a big defense, but they were very quick and ran lots of different blitz packages and defensive schemes to utilize that speed. The game plan was to just run the ball at them and "out-big" them and wear them down. By the time practice was over on Thursday, Caleb had the game plan down pat and was ready to play. They'd be flying out to Washington early Friday, have a light practice there, then go to a movie for a bit of relaxation.

Caleb made sure that the first thing he did when he got back to his apartment was to call his dad. They'd released Jack the past Monday, and he was home resting. The game wouldn't be televised, so Jack said he'd keep up with it in the papers.

"Call if you need anything," Jack said once again. "I love you."

 "Love you, Dad," Caleb said. "Take care of yourself."

He hung up and sighed—thank goodness his father had pulled through the worst of it. He sat thinking quietly for a few minutes, then a sudden ring from his phone made him jump.

"Hello, this is Julie Tatum. Do you remember me from Enapay?"

He paused, wracking his brain for a memory of her face. "Uh, hi! How are you doing? It's been a long time."

"Not long enough," she said with a huff.

"What do you mean?"

Caleb could hear her voice quavering. "Do you remember the date we had when we were sophomores in high school?"

Caleb's eyes narrowed and he scowled. "Uh, I'm not sure. Why do you ask?" He did know who this girl was and where this was going, and he wasn't going to incriminate himself on a phone call; he didn't know if it was being taped.

"Well, let me remind you of it," Julie said. "You took me to the lake, and we were walking on the beach, and you were drunk and high on something. I was so proud and excited that I was going out with Caleb Lewis, the best-looking guy in Enapay High School, not to mention the quarterback! As we walked, you convinced me to lay down with you in some dense coverage by some trees and told me you wanted to make out with me. I wanted so badly to be one of the cool girls, so I said okay. Do you remember kissing me, your hands all over my body? I told you to slow down. I told you I was a virgin and didn't want to go all the way, I just wanted to kiss. I still remember so vividly you looking at me with those terrible, evil eyes of yours—I'll never forget them. You were so messed up, and you turned crazy all of a sudden, like someone flipped a switch. Out of nowhere you threatened to beat me up and said you would kill me if I didn't do what you wanted."

Julie stopped for a minute as her voice cut out in a fit of sobbing. When she'd regained her composure, she said, "You grabbed me by the throat and started choking me and started making a weird noise deep in your throat. You were staring at me with those vile blue eyes. You were just glaring at me as if you were getting pleasure from watching me die. After I almost passed out, you let go of my throat and I got my breath back. You were so big and strong and I was so small, I felt so helpless. I *told you over and over again* that I wanted to go home. I've never felt so powerless. I just wanted to be at home safe with my mom and dad. You took off your clothes, and I tried to get up and run, but you grabbed my leg and dragged me back. I started screaming as loud as I could for help and then you hit me hard, three times in my stomach."

Julie was sobbing uncontrollably now. She could hardly get the words out of her mouth. "Then you told me to take my clothes off, and I was screaming 'NO, NO, NO' and you told me, 'Don't worry, you won't be a virgin much longer.' I stood there looking at you, so scared and ashamed that I just took off all my clothes. I had never been naked in front of a man, but there I was, standing there in front of you. I felt so dirty, so degraded, but I didn't want you to hurt me anymore. I didn't know what else I could do. Then you grabbed me, threw me to the ground, and turned me over on my stomach. I have never felt so much pain in my life, and you just kept *going*! I felt like you were ripping my guts apart! When you'd finished, I lay there on that beach in total shock, feeling totally degraded and bleeding badly. Then you got up, put on your clothes, and told me to 'get dressed and quit crying, you sound like a little girl.' You said if I ever told anyone anywhere about this you would do the same thing to my little sister." She paused. "You said something I'll never forget. You said, 'Julie, you should thank me; you're no longer a virgin. You won't have that burden to carry around anymore.' I should *thank you*? You just raped me and I should *thank you*? I have *never* been so traumatized, so terrified in my life since that night! I've had nightmares about that night over and over again since it happened. I've never spoken of this to anyone for fear you would hurt my little sister." Caleb could hear Julie's voice coming out in short, angry puffs. "I want redemption, Caleb. I want $25,000. You ruined my life. I haven't been on a date since that night because I'm terrified of men and what they might do to me. Caleb? Caleb? Are you there? Are you listening to me?"

Caleb just sat there silently. Finally, he said in a soft, comforting voice, almost a whisper, "Julie, where do you live now?"

"In a town called Sallisaw, Oklahoma."

"Is your name still Julie Tatum?"

Julie snarled. "I just told you, you psycho, I haven't had a date since I was with you."

"Julie," Caleb said quietly, "I want to help you. What's your address in Sallisaw?" Julie told Caleb which address to send the money to, and Caleb sat silently for a minute. Then he smirked.

"Julie, I think you may be drunk or on drugs, and you may have mental problems. You certainly have a big imagination! The only thing I can remember about our date is we went out to eat and to a movie and then I took you home. You're not by any chance in a mental institution, are you?"

Caleb held the phone away from his face as she screamed, "YOU MAKE ME SO SICK, I want $25,000 or I'm going to the police and the press about this!"

"I want to help you because I'm concerned about you as a friend of mine, Julie. Can I call you on Monday and talk to you some more? Could I have your phone number?"

Julie gave Caleb her phone number and then said confidently, "You have until Tuesday morning. If I don't hear from you by then, I'm going to the police about this."

Caleb said, "You need to rest this weekend and get yourself together. I'll call you Monday evening," and hung up the phone.

Caleb sat there on the edge of his bed, staring at the floor. *Ugh, I knew this stuff was going to come back and haunt me someday.* All the true crime books he had read in his life kept popping up in his mind. His brain was like a computer, searching files to come up with an answer. He thought and thought about how to handle this. *If I just give her the money, what will happen when she spends all of it? She will just keep coming back for more and more, and where will it end? But man, I can't just keep killing people I've hurt. It's not her fault.* He thought and thought, but only one solution kept coming back to him. He then did something he didn't really want to do, but try as he might, he couldn't come up with anything else. Caleb reluctantly called Johnny back in Enapay. He asked Johnny if he would be interested in another $10,000 job and gave all the details.

"Monday at the latest," Caleb said.

"I remember Julie. I asked her on a date once after she graduated high school and she said no."

"I bet she said no," Caleb said. "Anyway, I'm not sure if she lives with anyone, so you'll need to do a bit of surveillance. She's trying to blackmail me for money and has threatened to go to the police if I don't pay her." He paused, then said, "Johnny, I know I don't have to tell you this, but I feel I need to so we don't have a misunderstanding. You are the only one I've ever spoken to about any of this, and I'm putting a bunch of trust in you. If you were to get caught, I would still take care of the money you need until you get out of prison. But you can NEVER mention my name or what you do for me to ANYONE. You do understand this, don't you?"

Johnny replied with a bit of panic, "Caleb, all I want to know from you is when all this is over, you won't come back and kill *me*."

Caleb chuckled. "I promise you'll be safe as long as you keep your mouth shut."

"Okay, buddy," Johnny said, "consider it a deal."

"Thanks," Caleb said. "And we don't ever have to mention this trust thing again—my word is my bond, and your word is your bond, okay?"

"Okay," Johnny said. "I'll get this done before Monday."

Johnny knew that Caleb was smart and felt like he must have other people working for him, so he'd better watch his step or he'd be the next one on his list. Johnny never knew Caleb to be a liar, and as long as he just did his job and shut up about it, he would be okay.

Caleb went to his closet to see how much money he still had. After counting, it turned out to be over $150,000 stuck in a gym bag. He took out $10,000 to mail to Johnny first thing on Friday morning before the plane left.

As he lay in bed, he felt terrible for what he did to Julie Tatum. He knew that in his high school years he was out of control, and he knew why, but what could he do about it now but get rid of her and put her out of her misery? *Maybe I'm doing her a favor.*

CHAPTER 31

THE HUSKIES

Early Friday morning, Caleb put $10,000 in a thick envelope and mailed it to Johnny, making sure to be back well in time for the two-hour flight to Seattle. When the team arrived in Washington, they ate a quick lunch and had a very light workout, mainly just to get a feel for the turf. Around 6, they had supper at the hotel and then loaded into the bus to go see the movie "The Road Warrior." Movies seemed to be a great way to relax them before a game, and the guys really enjoyed it—the rest of the season, when they played out of town, they called themselves The Road Warriors.

Saturday morning, everyone was at the stadium by 10 to start all their pre-game rituals.

Caleb knew everything there was to know about the Huskies' defense. The coaches were concerned about their right defensive tackle, Larry Birdshot. He was a big guy— around 6'7", 280 pounds, and very quick and strong. He was a projected All-American and a first-round draft pick for the NFL. CAU had worked numerous schemes to block him and slow him down, but he would be a hand full to deal with during the game.

***

"This is Joseph Jack from XKRT radio Los Angeles. The #2 rated CAU Panthers are going to have a tough one today. The Washington Huskies are undefeated for the first time in five years and ranked #25 in the country. They have a true first team All-American defensive tackle, Larry Birdshot, who is a force to be reckoned with. True freshman offensive tackle Lavon Jackson will have his hands full trying to stop him. The Huskies have won the toss and deferred to the second half."

"Here goes the kick; Thad Thompson catches the ball in the end zone and comes out down the left sideline. Makes a sweet move, cuts to the middle of the field and is brought down at the 30. Caleb Lewis huddles up the team."

"Ok boys, you know the game plan," Caleb said. "Lavon, just keep hitting that guy until he can't take it anymore. We're going to try and rattle him. NO MERCY."

Joseph Jack continued, "Caleb hands the ball off to Luke, right at Larry Birdshot, Luke goes for 15 yards. 1ST DOWN PANTHERS! Caleb drops back, it looks like a screen to Rory, right over the outreached hands of Larry. Rory makes some moves and gains 20 yards on the play. 1ST DOWN PANTHERS! CAU is down to the Huskies' 35, and Lewis huddles up the team. Every play has been right at Larry Birdshot. Caleb makes the handoff to Luke, no… Caleb bootlegs the ball, turns the corner, 30, 25, 20, ain't nobody going to catch him! HOT DIGITY DOG, Lewis scores on a 35 yard scamper to put CAU up!"

Coach Axom grabbed Caleb on the sideline, yanking him close. "That'a boy, just keep the pressure on them, Caleb. Good job."

"There goes the kick," Jack shouted, "and CAU kicks the ball out of the end zone so the Huskies will be starting on their own 20. The Huskies just can't get their offense on track and have to punt the ball. Lewis is trotting out to gather up the team."

"Lavon, keep that monster in check and these guys can't beat us."

Lavon looks at Caleb with a grin. "I ain't scared of nobody, Caleb, but this guy is tough. But I promise you I ain't gonna quit on ya, buddy!"

"Lewis drops back deep for a pass, looking at a streaking Lance Wood. Lewis plants his foot…. OHHHHHH! Larry Birdshot just slammed Lewis in the back for a sack."

Lying on top of Caleb, Larry said, "You better get used to lying on your back, boy; it's going to be like this all day long. All day long."

Caleb was sprawled on the ground with the breath knocked out of him. He got up slowly, thinking, *I ain't ever been hit that hard before.*

Caleb stood and told the guys to huddle up. Coach Axom sent in the play, but Caleb was pissed and didn't like it. It was just running play to Luke, and he wanted revenge for that last play. He ignored the play from the coach and called the exact play as before—the one he got hurt on.

Caleb told Lavon in the huddle, "I have faith in you, Lavon. You get that block and we score." He took the snap, stepped back five yards, turned, set his foot, and threw the ball 60 yards to Lance; nobody was even close to him. CAU 14, Huskies 0.

The next series, CAU had the ball and Caleb tried to run that bootleg again. Larry just blasted him again, hit him square in the chest full speed, and all 280 pounds of Larry came down on Caleb's chest. He just lay there with Larry looking right in his eyes talking smack. Caleb grimaced and said, "I *will* get you before this game is over, punk. You better be looking for me."

He was getting angry now and maybe a bit out of control. He didn't really care what play the coaches sent in, he was going after Larry Birdshot. Caleb called a 33 draw left shotgun formation and told Luke, "You just follow me; I'm going to be the lead blocker. Hut, Hut," Caleb dropped back 6 yards like he was going to pass, then handed the ball to Luke. He was looking right at Larry Birdshot, and Larry was looking at Luke. Caleb hit Larry with everything he had and Larry literally came off his feet, falling backwards and slamming into the turf. He then hit the linebacker, came off of that block, and just destroyed the safety. The corner had a good angle on Luke and tackled him. The next play, Caleb just made up his own play like a sandlot football game. He told the right guard to pull and knock the crap out of Larry. That's what happened. Lavon just brushed blocked Larry to slow him down and the guard pulled, coming right down the line of scrimmage to just lambast Larry and send him to the turf. Caleb handed the ball to Luke, who went 38 yards before getting tripped up.

Caleb stood over Larry and said, "All day long, punk, all day long."

The next play was a passing play—a crossing route to Rory, but Caleb had no intention of throwing the ball; he was going to embarrass Larry. They snapped the ball, and he stepped back 3 yards and just waited for Larry to get loose from Lavon. When Larry broke free, he charged like a bull at Caleb, who just circled to the left, put his foot out, and tripped Larry. Larry looked really clumsy on the play, and the officials didn't notice the trip. Caleb took off around the left defensive end and ran 23 yards to score. CAU 21, Huskies 0.

When Caleb got to the sideline, the players were just looking at him like he was God. Coach Axom walked over and used a firm hand to whirl Caleb toward him. "I don't remember putting in a couple of those plays. Any ideas where they came from?"

He just looked at Axom and said, "Crazy things can happen in a football game, Coach." Coach Axom just turned and walked away shaking his head.

***

"It's the middle of the second quarter and Caleb is trotting back on the field," Joseph Jack said. "He's huddling up the team and…. *What the heck was that!* Well folks, I guess if you live long enough you'll see everything. Larry Birdshot just blindsided Caleb with his back turned in the huddle in between plays! I've never seen anything like that before. Larry's helmet went right to Caleb's kidney. It's a flagrant foul, and Caleb Lewis has hit the ground hard. It looks like he's trying to get his breath back.

"The CAU team is going nuts! The fight is on. Both teams have cleared the benches, and helmets and fists are flying everywhere. Caleb Lewis is still lying on the ground trying to get his breath. Whistles are blowing; yellow flags are flying in every direction. It's mayhem out there!"

Caleb slowly wobbled to his feet, looked around, and saw three of the Panthers on top of Larry. Larry's helmet had come off. He went over to them and shouted, "Get off of him!" They slid back to their feet, and Caleb reached down and grabbed Larry's hand, helping him up. "Good hit, big guy," Caleb said, and he threw a right hook that would have knocked out Muhammad Ali and totally KO'd Larry Birdshot.

Joseph Jack was screaming in the mic, "The officials have stopped the game! They have ejected Larry and sent everyone in for halftime to cool off a bit. Larry is still unconscious as the teams go into the locker rooms."

Coach Richert got everyone together and said, "Boys I like your fight in this game, but what I *don't* like is the lack of sportsmanship I see on the field. I understand that Caleb took a very cheap shot from Larry, and I'm sure Larry will be suspended for a few games, but I don't want to *ever* see our bench clear again! Let the officials handle it. We have to keep our composure and act like *somebody*, not just a bunch of ruffians. We're up 21 - 0, now let's go back out there and add some more, but with more class than we showed in that first half."

The trainers took Caleb to the medical room and x-rayed him. There was a big bruise on the right side of his chest, but it didn't look like anything was broken. The trainers put a rib protector on him and told him, "We'll look at it again after the game." Caleb wanted to beat these guys so bad. He wanted to embarrass them, and he planned to do just that.

Before kickoff, the officials went to both benches and told them they would be suspending players if this game continued to get out of hand.

CAU kicked off to the Huskies, and the CAU defense was playing great. The Huskies went three and out and punted to CAU. Without Larry Birdshot in the game, it got out of hand quickly. CAU wound up winning 56-0, and Caleb had a spectacular game—he rushed for over 160 yards and threw for 416 yards and five touchdowns.

The next day in the papers, all that was talked about was Caleb Lewis. The press had never, *never* seen a quarterback like Caleb. He was first in the nation as a rushing QB and third in passing, and CAU had just finished their fourth game. Caleb Lewis was becoming a national sensation.

CHAPTER 32

ROD VOHEM

The plane was landing in LAX around 9 that evening, and to say that Caleb was sore would be an understatement. He had never taken so many hits in a game before, and he was definitely feeling it. His ribs were just killing him, and moving in any direction was painful. When Caleb got back to his dorm, he called his dad and told him stories of the game. Jack, of course, was just eating up every word. Jack told Caleb he needed to listen to his coaches and not let his emotions get the best of him during the game, to learn and calm down and let his teammates carry their share of the load. "You don't have to do everything. That's why it's called a team."

"Yes sir, I'll try to do better," Caleb said.

After he said his goodbyes to his father for the night, Caleb called Beth. He repeated the same story to her, then said he would try to see her on Sunday.

"We're going to church in the morning, aren't we?" she said hopefully.

Caleb just sighed and said, "I don't know, it depends on how I feel in the morning. Right now I just need to rest, Beth. Do we have to go to church?"

She replied impatiently, "Caleb, we never *have* to go to church, we *get* to go to church. We don't go to church based on how we feel the day of church; we go to church to worship and give thanks and to learn more of God's word!"

He grudgingly replied, "Okay, okay, OKAY, I'll pick you up in the morning. Sheez." *Ugh, this church thing is killing me. This could be a deal breaker for us. I don't know how long I can keep this up.*

He gingerly stretched out on the bed, and not a moment after he'd closed his eyes, the phone rang again. It was Anni. She wanted him to come over to her office.

"I'll be there in a bit," he said with a deep sigh. "But listen to me—I'm so sore and hurting from the game today that I may just have to lie there. Is that okay with you?"

"I can do that, but I need some white powder. Be sure and bring some. I'll call Rod and tell him I won't be home tonight. He's used to me having to work on Saturday nights, and he's also on-call all night, so he won't be home much, if at all."

"Well then, I'll see you soon," Caleb said, stifling a grunt as he got up. Anni hung up the phone, got in her car, and headed back to her office. She needed some powder badly.

Caleb got his gym bag and put the heroin and drug kit in it. He decided to walk over to the offices; it was about a mile from the dorms, and it's a beautiful night. It might loosen him up a bit, he thought.

When he got to the office, he went up the fire exit and let himself in the back door. Anni was already lying on the bed ready to go. "I heard you played another spectacular game again today," she said.

"I don't know about that," he said with a dismissive wave, "but I've never been so beat up after a game before." He took off his shirt and Anni put her hands over her mouth and gasped. The right side of his rib cage was black and blue, and he had scrapes and cuts all over his body.

"Oh, you poor thing! Can I do anything to help you?"

"Yes, actually you can. Do you remember how I taught you to fix the powder? That might help more than anything right now."

"I think so," she said uneasily, "but can you watch me to be sure?" He nodded, and she went to work. A few minutes later, as she tapped the air out of the syringe, Caleb asked if she could shoot him up. "I'll try," she said. When she saw blood, she pushed the plunger down. Caleb laid back, and Anni went to get her fix ready. Soon, they were both passed out on the bed, naked.

 At around midnight, Caleb thought he heard something, but he was so high he just laid back down. A few minutes later, he heard a man say, "I can't believe what I'm looking at. My wife passed out naked on the bed with the CAU QB." Caleb looked up to meet eyes with Rod Vohem, Anni's husband. His face turned white, and he looked over at Anni, passed out on the bed. He jumped up and put on his gym shorts, but he couldn't get any words out. "I bet

Coach Richert would be interested in this," Rod said, brushing off the scrubs he was still wearing from work. "What do you think, Caleb?" Caleb didn't know what to say. Rod smirked. "You know what I want to do?" He had this weird look on his face, and he was sweating profusely.

"What?" Caleb said, taking a half-step back.

Rod walked over to the bed and started shaking Anni. "Get up, get up!" She wasn't moving, so he went to the bathroom and filled up a cup of water and threw it on her.

Anni gasped for breath and yelled at Caleb, "What are you doing?" Then she glanced over and saw Rod. "You have got to be kidding me, how did you get in here?" Her words came out in a half-intelligible slur.

"Don't you remember that time you forgot your keys to the office and asked me to bring the one you had at home?" Rod said. "Well, this is the same one," he said, holding up the key. "I was off work and thought I would be nice and come by your office and sleep with you tonight, and lo and behold what did I find? Caleb Lewis naked in bed with my wife. Tell me about that, honey. I'm curious. Do you sleep with all the football players, or is Caleb just the lucky one? Can you also explain to me how a 38-year-old woman goes about seducing a 19-year-old kid? Oh, and when you're finished with that, I'd like to know what Coach Richert would think about this. I bet there might just be a policy against the Vice President of Football Operations sleeping with the football players. I think I'll call him and find out."

Anni, still high as a kite and slurring her words, said, "Now you just wait a minute, mister! This isn't what you think it is."

He laughed loudly. "Really? It's midnight and you're naked in bed with the CAU QB! And I also noticed you're doing heroin now. WOW! So tell me, Anni, what is this then? I'm really anxious to hear how I'm seeing this wrong."

Anni, feeling overwhelmed and confused, said, "Rod, our marriage has been nothing but a convenience for both of us the last 15 years. You don't love me anymore; we rarely see each other. All you do is work, and all I do is work— we just share a home together. That's it."

"What you say may be true, but deep down I always felt you were a modern day Jezebel, and now I have proof of it!"

Anni, insulted by his statement, screamed back at him "I have NEVER cheated on you until Caleb, and I'm no JEZEBEL! I'm a LADY!" she yelled, laying on the bed naked and full of heroin. She stopped and thought for a moment about what he just said, and she wasn't sure what a Jezebel was, but it didn't sound like a good thing.

Rod just shook his head, then walked over and picked up the phone. "I'm calling Coach Richert, and then I'm calling the press. After that, I'm calling Caleb's dad to let him know what his sorry son has been up to at CAU."

Rod had just made a terrible mistake in bringing Caleb's dad into this. Caleb was trying to keep from pouncing on this little egotistical prick of a man. But as he watched those nimble fingers start dialing numbers, he snarled.

Caleb snapped and grabbed Rod, lifted him up, and threw him against the wall. Caleb wrapped his hands around his throat, too tight. "Listen, you little sissy prick! If you ever tell anyone about this, about *any* of this, I swear to God I will kill you."

Anni saw what was going on and ran over quickly, grabbing Caleb by the head. "Caleb, CALEB! Look at me, baby. Focus on me, Caleb." Anni wasn't laughing now— she knew Caleb could kill Rod, so she pulled Caleb's head down to look him in the eyes. Caleb continued to choke the life out of him, and she continued to talk to him. "Caleb, let him go baby. It is going to be okay. Please let him go."

Caleb looked at her, and then at Rod, and reluctantly dropped him to the floor. Rod was gasping for air. "This isn't over, Anni," he snarled.

Caleb reached down, grabbed him by the hair, pulled him up, and said, "Which hand do you use with your scalpel?"

He looked at Caleb and said, "What?"

Caleb slapped him hard and said, "Which hand do you use with your scalpel!"

He replied angrily, "My right hand! Why do you want to know?"

Caleb slapped him again and grabbed his left hand, gripped his left pinky finger, and pulled it as hard as he could, bending it back to the top of his hand.

"You broke my finger, you MAD MAN Rod shrieked, bent over and clutching his hand to his stomach.

Caleb reached down again, grabbed him by the hair, pulled him up, slapped him again, and said, "If you ever tell anyone, *anywhere* about any of this, next time I'll break every finger on both hands. Do you understand me?" Rod just fell back to the ground, trembling and shaking his head yes. He had never seen such rage before.

Caleb eyed him, then smirked. He reached down, pulled the shaking man up again, and said, "You're a rich guy, aren't you?"

He said, "Yes, I g-guess so."

Caleb looked him right in the eye and said, "Well I'm not, and you're going to mail me $3,000 a month in cash until the day I graduate college."

Rod made a derisive noise. "No, I'm *not* going to give you money."

"What did you just say to me?" Slap! "What did you just say to me?" Slap! "What did you just say to me?" Slap.

Meanwhile, Anni was standing there watching, frightened by Caleb, and Rod was crying and screaming like a baby. He was running all over the room trying to get away from this madman.

"Okay, okay!" Rod yelped after getting pinned into a corner by the fridge. "Quit hitting me! I'll send you the money every month. Can I go home now?"

Anni just couldn't take any more of this and was so tired from the heroin, she laid down on the floor and went back to sleep.

"No!" Caleb shouted. "You can go home when I tell you you can go home. I want you to repeat to me all that I just said."

He replied, his voice stammering, "I am not to tell anyone, anywhere about any of this. And I'm going to mail you $3,000 a month until you graduate."

"That's correct. And what will happen if you cause us any problems?"

He replied, crying, "You will break my fingers."

"Yes," Caleb said, beginning to pace. "And if that doesn't work, I swear to God almighty as I'm standing here, I *will* kill you." He pulled Rod in close. "Now, let me fix that finger," Caleb said and grabbed it and pulled it hard, snapping it back in place. Rod screamed and hit the floor again. "Now go to your car and wait for me—I'll be out in a few minutes. I need a ride back to my dorm."

"Okay," he said, scurrying out of the office.

Caleb cleaned up the bedroom and picked up Anni off the floor. She was like a limp noodle, passed out after all of that excitement. He put her back in bed and told her to rest.

"Everything is going to be fine," he said, covering her up. He got his gym bag, walked into her office, and grabbed ten wraps of $10,000 from the safe before he left.

Once in the parking lot, Caleb swung into Rod's car and said, "Take me to my dorm, sissy boy, and you sure better treat Anni with respect from now on or you're going to answer to me."

As Caleb walked back into the dorm to the screech of Rod's tires fleeing as fast as he could, Caleb was hurting. His side was killing him, and he just needed to rest. It seemed like his whole life was nothing but trouble, just one bad thing after another. *How and when is this going to stop, and what do I have to do to change it?*

CHAPTER 33

SOMETHING IS BLOODY WRONG

Caleb woke up, startled, sweat pouring down his face, screaming his mother's name; rattled by the images of the same nightmare for months now, all he could manage to think was *when will this end?* He lay in bed for a few minutes, sweating and hurting so bad. It was 6 A.M., and he went to the bathroom to pee and it was full of blood. Unable to sleep and unwilling to be alone for a while, he put on his church clothes and headed to Beth's apartment. She was surprised to see him so early.

"Come in and have a seat," she said with a smile, rubbing her sleepy eyes.

"Thanks. Can I just lie down on your bed until church time?"

"Sure, are you okay?"

"I'm not sure," he said. "I feel like I was hit by a truck." She led Caleb into the bedroom and helped him take off his clothes. When she slipped off his shirt, she was frightened at how bruised and beat up he was. "Caleb, do I need to take you to the hospital? That looks awful."

"No, the trainers looked at it and said it is just a bruise. I'll be okay, I just need to rest."

Beth frowned. "Well, pull off your own pants and climb in bed, I don't think it's appropriate for me to help you with that." She bustled off to get him some Ibuprofen to help with the pain.

After about three hours, he got out of bed and walked to the bathroom. Beth was standing in front of the mirror putting on her makeup when he walked over and started peeing right in front of her. She curiously looked down. *That thing looks really big, but maybe that's normal?* She didn't know—she had never seen a real one. Trying her best to hold her composure, she rolled her eyes and said, "Caleb, *gross*! I don't want to watch you pee, good Lord." She glanced down at him peeing again and saw that it was blood red. She sucked in a breath. "You get dressed right now. We're going to the hospital!"

"I'm not going to any hospital," he said, exasperated, "and if we did, how are you going to explain to everyone what I was doing in your apartment at 6 in the morning?"

"Well, it's 9:30 now, and I don't care what anyone thinks!" she shot back. She wasn't just Caleb's girlfriend—she also had responsibilities to the CAU football team. Caleb Lewis being sick, and her knowing and not doing something, would be bad. "Get dressed and get in my car."

When they arrived at the hospital, Beth marched through the crowd of people in the ER and made a bee-line for registration. She said, "I have Caleb Lewis, and he's bleeding internally. He needs help NOW!" The lady knew who Caleb was and got him in immediately.

Beth went to the payphones and called Coach Richert, who in turn called Anni at home. Rod answered the phone. "Is there a problem I can help you with?"

Coach knew Rod was a general surgeon and told him that Caleb was bleeding internally, and that he was at Grace and Mercy hospital. Rod paused. "I'll be right there."

"Good," Richert said. "I want to keep this in the family; we don't want the press catching wind of this until we know what we're dealing with." He then called Coach Axom and the head trainer and told them to get to the hospital.

After everyone had arrived at the hospital, Coach Richert, the ER physician, and Rod Vohem had all congregated into a little gaggle of discussion. Caleb was just staring at Rod, then motioned for him to come over.

"You better watch what you say, or I'll come off this table and slap you all over this hospital," Caleb whispered.

"I'll never say anything about what happened last night," Rod said. "My word is good, Caleb. Right now we need to see what's wrong with you, and that's what I do best."

They took Caleb into radiology and shot him full of radioactive dye and started taking pictures of it. After about an hour, they had a diagnosis. He had a badly bruised kidney, which was causing the blood in the urine. Caleb asked if there was anything that could be done about it, but the doctor said, "It just needs time to heal. I think you'll be fine in a few days—"

"Doctor," Rod interrupted, "I think you may be wrong. I would suggest that I do exploratory surgery to be sure the bleeding is coming from the kidney and not somewhere else."

Coach Richert cast a sidelong glance at him, brows furrowed. "Now you wait a minute, Rod. The last thing I want is to put Caleb in any danger, but you two doctors seem to have a difference of opinion on this kidney damage. Doing surgery would take him out the rest of the season, and if there's a chance a little rest is all he needs, I think we need to take that chance."

Beth was standing there quietly listening, then said, "My father is a urologist in Seattle, Coach Richert. Would you like me to call him and see what he says?"

"Absolutely, Beth! Can you give him a call right now and let him talk to these two doctors for me?"

Rod gave her a dirty look and said, "So, we're taking advice from a secretary now? You guys can do what you want, but just remember one thing—Caleb is bleeding internally as we speak. I just want to go in there and see what it is." Of course, if Rod Vohem did that surgery, he was going to be sure Caleb lost that kidney and would never be able to play football again. A chance to ruin Caleb had been presented to him on a silver platter, and he wasn't going to ignore it.

The ER doctor looked at Rod like he was crazy. He'd seen hundreds of injuries like this, and not once had they ever done exploratory surgery. Beth came back a few minutes later and took Coach Richert aside.

"Something stinks here, coach. My dad said—and he qualified what he said by saying that he hasn't seen the results of the x-rays or blood tests—but it would be highly unusual to do the type of surgery Dr. Vohem is talking about this early in the injury. He said if in a week it hasn't gotten any better or if it gets worse during the week, exploratory surgery is a possibility, but it's way too early right now."

Rod and the ER doctor were bickering as Beth looked on, but the last straw for her was when Dr. Vohem screamed at Coach Richert and the ER doctor, "If Caleb dies, the blood is on your hands, not mine! You've been warned!"

Beth knew something was fishy here, and she had a very uneasy feeling. Her instincts were telling her something else was going on with Rod Vohem. As she was prone to do in these sorts of confusing situations, Beth went to a small chapel by the ER and asked God for guidance and courage right now and to heal Caleb.

As Beth was leaving the chapel, she felt a very strong intuition—an urging in her gut. She walked into the ER, looked at everyone assembled there, and said, "This surgery isn't the right thing to do for Caleb. I know I'm just a secretary, and I'm out of my place here, but I *refuse* to let you perform this operation." She glared at Rod, unblinking.

Rod huffed. "Why don't you go answer the phones, little girl, and leave the medical advice to me."

She looked at Rod with daggers coming out her eyes and said, "Caleb, get up off that table. I'm taking you home."

He looked at her and said, "Yes ma'am." He knew she was a strong woman, and she had become very protective of him.

Coach Richert and the others paused for a moment, a little surprised at Beth's strong words, but Richert just shook his head and asked the doctor, "Do you think Caleb can play ball this week?"

"He probably shouldn't, but let's take a urine test every day and re-evaluate it on Thursday. If there's still blood in his urine, I recommend he doesn't play. He doesn't need to practice this week for sure, but he can attend all the meetings and preparations for the game."

Coach nodded, then looked at Beth. "Good job, Beth. And where in the world did all that spunk come from? You always seemed so quiet and reserved in the office."

She smiled. "From God, Coach. The Bible teaches us, 'for God hath not given us the spirit of fear, but of power, and of love, and of a sound mind. AND," she took a deep breath and said very quickly, "Caleb is my boyfriend, and I don't care if you fire me for it. I love him, and he loves me."

Coach Richert paused for a moment, then smiled. "I can't think of anyone better for him than you, Beth. Can you get him back to his dorm and make sure he's comfortable?"

"Sure thing," she said.

They drove back to the dorms, and she helped him back to his apartment. She had never been in his apartment before, and she always wondered why he got to room alone; that never happens with freshmen. Once inside the apartment, she helped him undress, got him some water, and tucked him into bed. Caleb looked at her and said, "Did you just tell Coach Richert that you and I were boyfriend and girlfriend?"

She giggled. "Yes I did, and I'm telling Anni about it too. I don't care if I get fired."

"Beth," he whispered, "except for my dad, nobody has ever stood up for me like you did tonight. Thank you. I love you." That was the first time in his life he had ever told a woman he loved her, and it felt good. "I'm not sure about telling Anni about this right now, but you do what your heart tells you to do. But I don't think she'll take it well."

Beth reached over and kissed him and said, "Caleb, don't you ever be afraid to go where God leads or to speak when God speaks to you. When God is on our side, we can't be wrong." She sat down with him for a bit, just to make sure he was okay. They had given him pain pills at the hospital, and he fell asleep. Beth kneeled beside Caleb's bed and said a prayer. "Lord, I ask that you heal Caleb and soften his heart. Lord, he needs you so much and I pray that you give me the words and the wisdom to help Caleb come to know you. Amen."

After a while of watching over him, she wanted to let him rest in peace, so she got up. Without anything else to do until he woke again, she started looking around the dorm.

She opened a cabinet, saw a bunch of VHS tapes, and wondered what movies were on those. She picked one up and looked at it—it was labeled 8/26/81/A. She looked at another, and it said 8/31/81/A. She went and looked around for a VHS tape player, but Caleb didn't have one; he just had a TV. *This is odd; all these tapes and nothing to watch them on. Oh well.*

She went into his bathroom and snooped around, looked in his closet. *I need to buy him some clothes; these are really outdated.* What Beth just barely missed in her snooping were the pictures Caleb had of Anni naked. They were in the drawer next to his bed, and she didn't think to look in there. After she'd satisfied her curiosity about his apartment, she went and gently laid down next to Caleb— he was out like a light. She put her head on his chest and went to sleep with him.

At 4pm, she woke up and looked over to check on Caleb. He was still sleeping, but the trainers wanted him at the field house at 5. She started kissing him on his ears, whispering, "Get up, you have to go see the trainers." Caleb opened one eye and started laughing. He thought she was just the cutest girl in the world. "Caleb, you have to get up now, you have to go to the field house."

What a weekend, one thing after another, Caleb thought. Wobbling to his feet, he made his way over to the stadium to see the trainers. UCLA would be the next game.

CHAPTER 34

ADDICTED

Caleb awoke the next morning, startled, sweat pouring down his face, screaming his mother's name. *Again. Arghh I wish this nightmare would stop.* He got up, snorted some coke, ate breakfast with his friends, and headed to class. It was early October, and the CAU campus was in full swing. He didn't know how many students attended CAU, but it was a *bunch*. He had taken 12 hours the first semester because that's what the coaches advised, but it was all pretty easy, basic stuff—English, college algebra, American history, the standards. Caleb had no problems with his classes. He went to class Monday through Wednesday from 8 till 2, then went to the stadium to start football from 2 till around 5:30. Everything was busy, and there wasn't any extra time to do much.

The football team had been pretty excited recently; CAU had moved up to #2 in the country, behind Alabama. CAU would be playing UCLA—their chief rival in the nation— this week, and everyone was preparing like it was the National Championship. The trainers had been taking a urine sample from every day since Saturday, and the blood was getting lighter and lighter each time. Caleb didn't suit up for practice that day; he just studied the game plan and watched film.

Caleb got back to his apartment around 6 that evening, had supper with his friends, and went upstairs to study. An hour or so later, Lavon and Lance were knocking on his door.

"What do you bums want?" Caleb asked with a mock frown.

"Yo man, just hang out a bit. Do you mind?" Lance asked

"Nah, come on in." Caleb waved for them.

They were sitting around telling lies for a bit when Caleb asked Lavon "So, what do want to do for a living big guy?"

Lavon sat back and thought for a moment, staring at no particular place, and then said, "When I was a kid back in Bossier City, I would just sit on a hill behind my house on Hollywood Street and watch them big trains go a-roaring down the track. I could watch them all day long. Boy, I just loved hearing those loud whistles and the bells on the crossroads clanging. I used to run out there to them tracks before the trains showed up and lay things on the them, like pennies or rocks—whatever I could find—and just laugh and laugh when them trains squished 'em. Now, I wouldn't put pennies on the track very much. I mean, a penny is a penny and when you is poor as I was, well, that's just a waste of money. Did you know that you can put your ear to the track and actually hear them trains comin'? I got so good at it, I could tell you how far away they were and how long it would take 'em to get there; what ya think about that? I'ma thinkin' I might want to be one of them train drivers someday. My uncle Josh used to be a train porter and man, he traveled all over the place. I just used to love hearing those stories about where he'd been and stuff like that. Yup, just driving them trains down the track sounds pretty good to ol' Lavon."

Lance asked him "Don't you want to play in the NFL someday, Lavon?"

"Well, I reckon if I'm lucky enough for that to happen I would do it. I hear them NFL boys make a lot of money, but you can only do that for so long. If I get to play pro ball I reckon I will, but when I'm done I would like to be a train driver, I think. That just sounds like the best job in the world to me. Heck, it don't even sound like a job. But what about you, Lance?"

"Man, that's easy. First I want to play in the NFL. If that doesn't work out for whatever reason, I think I would like to go into sports announcing. I mean, look at me, putting his hands out, I'm the prettiest guy in the world, don't you think? I speak well also—I'm taking journalism classes and majoring in it. After I make the hall of fame in the NFL, those television stations are going to be begging me to come to work for them. Caleb, what are you going to do?"

Caleb, laughing, said, "You *are* one handsome man, Lance. But I don't know, dude. Like you guys, I hope to play in the NFL, but I just kinda take things one day at a time. I try not to make too many plans, but I'm going to major in psychology and if the football thing doesn't work out, I think I would like to be a psychiatrist."

Lance looked at Caleb and said, "My brother, that just sounds awful to me!" and started laughing.

***

After his friends left, Caleb picked up the phone to call Jack and see how he was doing. Jack, being Jack, was more concerned about Caleb's bruised kidney than his own heart and advised him, "Just sit out this week and let that heal; that isn't something you want to fool around with, son."

"Well, the coaches and doctors will make that call on Thursday, but I hope I can play," Caleb said. "So how are you feeling, Dad?"

"Oh, about as fine as I'll ever be!"

Caleb smiled. "That's great. Anyway, I'll let you go and I'm going to go get some rest myself."

Just as Caleb was about to hang up, Jack said, "Oh, one more thing, son." Caleb perked up. "Didn't you go out with a girl by the name of Julie Tatum when you were in high school?"

Caleb paused. "Yes sir, we had one date when I was a sophomore."

Jack sighed. "Well, I have some sad news, son. I heard Julie overdosed on drugs on Sunday. She was living in Sallisaw, and Mary told me she'd always had a drug problem since high school. They're having a funeral for her here on Tuesday. Mary and I sent the family some flowers and added your name to the card. I just thought you might like to know."

“That is sad; she was a nice girl,” Caleb said. “Thanks for telling me, Dad. I have to go now. I’ll call you on Thursday, and I’ll let you know the coaches’ decision. I love you, bye now.”

He hung up the phone and just fell back on his bed, staring at the ceiling. *How many people am I going to have to kill before I clear everything up? Is it even worth it?* He just laid on the bed and closed his eyes. He felt awful. Before killing his mother, Caleb had developed a wall around himself that protected him from his conscience, but now that wall was crumbling.

***

About 9 that night, his phone rang—Anni. She was beside herself, asking him to come to her office, and *please* bring some powder.

“Anni,” Caleb said warily, “what have I told you over and over again about that heroin? It’s nothing to be toying around with. I would truly hate to see you get addicted to it, and it’s so easy to do. Please don’t ask me to do that.”

“Addicted?” She laughed. “I’m not addicted to it, silly, I just like the way it helps me rest.”

“That’s exactly what it does, Anni—it gives you a feeling of euphoria, but as time goes on you need more and more of it to get the same results.”

“Caleb please, please, *please*, I promise I won’t ask for any more this week. I PROMISE.”

He just sighed and said, "Okay, I'll be over in a minute."

She replied, "I love you Caleb." He got off the phone, grabbed his bag, and put five packs of heroin in it. He knew from experience with other girls that Anni was already a heroin addict. Caleb just shook his head. *How many friggin' more people's lives can I ruin in a week? I've killed one, humiliated and beat up a man (and probably ruined his marriage), and now I have Anni addicted to heroin. What's* wrong *with me? I'm just a horrible person. Why can't I stop hurting people?"*

He pulled into the stadium, went up the back stairs, and let himself in. There she was in all her glory, lying on the bed naked. He looked at her in disgust and said, "No way, Anni! You just put those panties back on. I'm tired and sore, and it just ain't happening tonight."

She looked up and said, "Okay. I don't care. I just thought you might want to, and I wanted you to know I'm here for you anywhere, anytime."

He looked over at Anni and asked how Rod was.

"Caleb," she said with a sigh, "our marriage was pretty much over anyway. I married Rod when I was only eighteen years old. Looking back on it, I'm not sure I was ever in love with him. I liked him a lot, but I think I married him because he was going to be a doctor and I wanted that security. He's the only man I have ever been with until I met you." She ran her fingers through her hair, tousling it as if frustrated. "What's weird, though, is since you slapped him around Saturday night, he's been just the kindest man. I can promise you, he had NEVER been treated like that before. I was so messed up Saturday night, and I was so scared about going home on Sunday. When I got home, Rod told me everything was just fine—you and I can do whatever we want. The only thing he asked of me is that we didn't embarrass him in public; as long as it's private, he didn't care. Oh yeah, I almost forgot." Anni went to her purse and pulled out an envelope. "Rod said to give you this $36,000 and he would pay you again in October of next year, if that's alright with you. He didn't want to mess with mailing you money every month, so he just wants to pay you once a year."

Caleb said reluctantly, "Give him his money back. I don't want it." Caleb was slapping himself mentally—why does doing the right thing feel so wrong?

Caleb took out five packets of heroin and tossed them to Anni. "I think you're becoming addicted to the powder already, and that makes me sick, Anni. Here are five packs; you NEVER take more than one packet in a day. Do you understand?" She nodded. "They say if you can only do one pack a week then you aren't addicted to it. I am giving you five to see how long it takes you before you ask for more. If you call me on Saturday wanting more, then you have a problem. I'm also giving you my drug kit; I rarely do this stuff anymore. One more thing—heroin isn't a cheap drug. If you want to use it, you're going to need to keep the money coming. I'm not using my money to supply your drug habit."

Anni went to her purse gave Caleb a $10,000 wrap and said, "Okay. I have lots of money—that's the least of my problems. And I DON'T have a drug addiction."

He gave her the drug kit and watched Anni as she put the poison in her veins. She fell back on the bed and went to sleep. Caleb watched her for a few minutes, then thought to himself, *What the heck*, and went to her office to take another $100,000 out of the safe. He had now stolen $300,000 from that safe, amassing over $420,000 since he arrived at CAU, not counting the money Lillie left him.

This is the easiest money I've ever made.

CHAPTER 35

SQUEEZED BY

Early Tuesday morning, Beth arrived at the office at her usual time, 8 in the morning. She went into Anni's office to see what work she needed to do that day, but Anni wasn't at her desk. *Odd,* she thought, *she's always there early in the morning. Maybe she had to go run an errand. She'll probably be back soon.*

Beth went back to her desk and puttered through her day, answering phones and dealing with regular paperwork. At noon, she still hadn't seen Anni. She had called Anni's house, but the maid simply said, "She hasn't been here all morning" and hung up.

Beth walked back into Anni's office and reluctantly walked back to the bedroom. Anni's bedroom was off-limits to anyone, but she just had to know. She opened the bedroom door, and there was Anni, sprawled out naked on the bed, still asleep. Beth walked in and saw the syringe, spoon, and lighter laying on the end table next to her bed. *What in the world?* She shook her gently and said softly, "Anni? Anni, it's time to get up."

Anni opened one eye, looked at her groggily, and said, "What are you doing in my bedroom? What time is it?"

"It's noon on Tuesday." Anni's eyes widened a little. "I was worried to death about you."

She jumped up out of bed and wrapped a sheet around her. "I'm *so* sorry—I must have been really tired! I'm going to shower and get ready, and I'll be back at my desk in an hour."

"Okay," Beth said. "Is there anything I can do for you?"

"No, but thanks," said Anni. "Just keep this to yourself, please." Beth returned to work, totally perplexed by what she just saw. *Is Anni on drugs?* She sat there for a second, pondering, then said a silent prayer for Anni, asking God for a spirit of love and not judgment to help her help Anni.

Around 2 that afternoon, Caleb was heading over to the locker room to meet with the trainers and prepare for the game on Saturday. When he went in, the trainers handed him a cup and said, "You know what to do with this." He peed and then went to his locker and started putting on his practice stuff.

Coach Axom cleared his throat. "What are you doing?"

"Getting ready for practice."

"You just put on shorts and your jersey. You aren't getting any reps today, just observing practice."

Caleb huffed. "I feel fine, Coach! There's nothing wrong."

Coach's eyes narrowed. "Did I stutter? You are *not* practicing until we get approval from the doctor, and that is that!"

Caleb wasn't happy. As much as he liked Jason Allgood, he didn't want to give him a chance to get his 1st team job back. He watched the whole practice from the sideline, sulking. *This sucks.*

On Friday, Coach Axom went to the locker room before practice and told Caleb that Jason would be the starter on Saturday. Caleb wasn't a happy camper, and for the first time since he had been at CAU, he questioned the coaches and their decision. When he brought it up to Coach Axom, Axom listened to him for a bit and finally said to Caleb sternly, "The decision is made. Even if Jason gets hurt in the game, you won't get in—we'll put in Henry. Caleb, I'm sorry but you aren't even suiting up for the game. When the doctors tell us that your kidney is 100%, you'll be the starter again. We aren't taking any risks on you damaging that kidney. Do you understand me, young man?"

"I understand," said Caleb, frowning, "but I think it's BS."

"Caleb, you are a smart kid. You've already sat out this week, and next week we don't have a game. That gives you another week to heal. Let's not take any chances, okay?"

Caleb sighed. "Okay, coach, okay."

In the locker room before game time, Caleb went up to Jason and wished him luck. "Don't let them rattle you, because that's going to be their game plan."

"Thanks, Caleb. I just appreciate getting another opportunity to play before I graduate."

Caleb shook his hand and told him, "Go win the game, buddy."

Caleb was standing on the sideline as the team came out of the tunnel. He felt uneasy and isolated, and he didn't like it one bit. UCLA kicked off to CAU and Thad returned the ball 25 yards to the 45. Jason went in, but the coaches just kept handing the ball to Luke. The game plan was for the defense to shut down UCLA and win the game; CAU had the #1 defense in the country, so it was a reasonable plan. The coaches just hoped the offense could manage at least three points and win. Luke Donaldson was going to carry the load for the offense and was expected to get 50 or more carries this game.

The first half came and went with the score still 0-0. Jason hadn't made any mistakes, and Luke had rushed for over 160 yards. But the field goal kicker, sophomore Randy James, had missed two reasonably short field goals and was rattled by the pressure. Field goal kickers are a quirky bunch of people. Confidence is everything, so if they come out and make the first one, they're usually pretty reliable. But if they miss the first one or two, they get all in a panic. Caleb decided to stay out on the field during halftime. He didn't ever get to do that, and CAU had a great marching band. He just figured, *What the heck, I'll stay and watch them and enjoy the show.*

When the teams came back on the field, CAU kicked off to UCLA. They had a good return, drove the ball down and kicked a field goal. Now CAU was down by 3, and Caleb was getting anxious—as were the fans. Going late into the 4th quarter with 2:00 to go, CAU was still losing. Caleb was getting pissed; he just knew he could have won this game if it were *him* out there. UCLA punted the ball, and

Thad Crossland caught the punt on CAU's 10-yard line. Thad started down the sideline, cut across the field, and finally ran 90 yards for a touchdown. Caleb was going nuts, jumping up and down and screaming at Thad—so was the whole team. Thad had lived up to his hype and won the game. CAU was still undefeated and had a bye week, which was excellent timing for everyone. There were lots of nagging injuries, and it gave everyone time to heal a bit.

***

When Caleb got back to his dorm, he called Beth to see if she wanted to go out to eat and watch a movie. Beth just replied, "Oh good, I was hoping you would call. Let's go."

After the movies, they went to Beth's apartment and were having a grand old time when out of nowhere, Beth nonchalantly asked Caleb if he had ever accepted Jesus Christ as his savior. This was who Beth was, and she had been around this man long enough and needed to know a few things. Caleb hem-hawed around a bit, trying to change the question. Beth would have none of that and looked Caleb straight in the eye.

"Have you ever accepted Christ as your savior? It's a simple question Caleb, yes or no."

Caleb didn't want to get into this conversation. At all. "Well, I went to church till I was about twelve or thirteen, so does that count?" he said with a dismissive laugh. "My mom was a Christian woman and so is my dad, and my brother was debating whether to go in the ministry when he got home."

Beth grabbed Caleb's hand tenderly. "Well, do you understand how to accept Christ? And is that something you'd like to do?"

Caleb was feeling pressured and tired of these questions. He wanted the fun Beth back. "Beth, I know you have something special because I can see it and I can feel it when I'm around you, but I'm not you." His frustration was building. "You have no idea of my life and what I've been through or what I've done. You grew up a little rich girl with two parents who watched your every move. I didn't. It's so hard for me to understand why you, or any other Christians for that matter, believe in this fantasy called Christianity. There's a big guy in the sky looking down on us and judging us? Seriously? If we're good we go to heaven, and if we're bad we go to hell. I know it works for you and millions of other people, but I just don't get it!"

Beth sat there quietly holding his hand, letting him talk.

"What's the point of life, anyway? You read a book that's thousands of years old and believe God wrote it and we're supposed to live our lives by it? It all seems so stupid to me, but hey, if it works for you I'm glad, but for me I just don't have the kind of blind faith to believe in something I can't see. And while I'm at it, you know what else bugs me?" Caleb stood up and started pacing, and though Beth wished he'd change his mind, she couldn't help but smile at just how excitable all this made him. "Christian people seem to have this superiority complex, that they're somehow better than everyone else!"

Beth leaned forward but didn't stand to follow Caleb. "Being a Christian doesn't mean I'm somehow superior to you. One reason people misunderstand Christians is because we want you to have what we have—"

"What business is it of Christians to think that I want what they have? Maybe I want *you* to have what *I* have—have you ever thought about that? But I don't try to force my beliefs down other people's throats like Christians do."

"Caleb, don't you want a peace in your heart and a life with a purpose? I believe the meaning of life and the reason God put us on Earth is so we can prepare ourselves to go to heaven. You told me you've done terrible things in your life. You probably believe you were so bad that why would God forgive you of your sins. I understand that, but the bible IS God's word for us. In the book of John it says that if we confess our sins, he is faithful and just and will forgive us our sins and purify us from all unrighteousness."

Caleb just rolled his eyes and threw his hands up. "I don't need your God's help; I don't need anyone's help, and I don't want to discuss this anymore. You're making me uncomfortable and pressuring me to do something I'm not ready to do right now and probably never *will* do. I am going home now."

Beth, calm as always, said, "I'm not making you uncomfortable, Caleb—that's God. All of us have something inside of us that guides us and gives us strength and hope. That feeling we have in our heart of right and wrong and a deep, penetrating knowledge that there's to be something more to life than just this. That's God reaching out to you, Caleb."

Caleb had heard enough of this. He reached over and gave her a kiss and said, "That's enough of this nonsense. I'm going home." Beth wrapped her arms around him, hoping he could feel how much she wanted him to understand. As he went to close the door behind him, he mumbled, "I'll think about what you said."

Caleb got in his Vette and headed back to the dorms. On the way back he was thinking to himself, *How can she be so sure of herself about all this? How can anyone believe that stuff? Of all the girls at CAU, I had to get involved with someone like Beth. Jeez.*

CHAPTER 36

TOO LATE

Caleb got back to his dorm after his date and thought he would try to sleep in on Sunday morning (that is, if Beth didn't call him about church; she didn't mention it on their date). He lay down around 11 that evening, and the phone rang at 1 A.M. He jolted awake; it had to be one of two things—something bad had happened to Dad, or Anni was calling.

"Hello?"

"Hi!" Anni's cheerful voice resounded in his ear. "What are you doing?"

He replied groggily, "It's 1 in the morning. What do you think I'm doing?"

"Well, you just aren't going to believe what happened."

He said suspiciously, "I can't imagine."

"I must have lost that powder you gave me. I just can't find it anywhere!"

Caleb huffed. "I bet you can't, because you used all of it this week."

"Well, I didn't use it, Mr. know-it-all. And anyway, I paid for it," she said irritably.

"No, Anni, *you* didn't pay for it. The CAU boosters are paying for it."

"Well, whatever," she said dismissively. "I wanted to use some tonight so I could sleep in the morning."

"Anni, I told you this was going to happen!" Caleb grumbled. "Why didn't you listen to me? Now you're in a terrible way and you have no idea what a mess you're fixing to get into."

"CALEB," Anni growled back, "you're exaggerating this and blowing it way out of proportion. I DON'T have a problem. I just want to sleep, and that stuff is really good for sleeping. Why don't you bring me 30 packets this time and I'll be more careful with them? That way I won't have to bother you anymore about it."

He knew how bad she needed it. He had seen it over and over again with the girls he got hooked on it in Enapay. He sighed. "I'll be over in a minute." He truly didn't want this to happen to Anni, and he also knew it wasn't going to turn out well. All drug addicts think they don't have a problem and can quit anytime they want, but Caleb knew better.

He got out six packs instead of the thirty that she asked for. He wanted her to have to ask for it, plus, it gave him a reason to get to that safe. Maybe just six packs would make her realize how much she was using. He hopped in the Vette and headed over to the stadium. When he walked in, she was at her desk working and still had her clothes on. He was just happy to see her dressed; that was unusual. He wanted to give her the powder, go back home, and go to sleep. It had been just one thing after another the past two weeks.

Anni looked up at Caleb, trying to be strong, but she was sweating and shaking a tiny bit. Her condition didn't go unnoticed by Caleb. "When's the last time you shot up?"

"Yesterday morning," she said, looking away. "It's been almost 36 hours. I was trying so hard not to take any today, Caleb, but I can't help it."

He had seen this so many times, and if he just refused to give her any, she could go and do something stupid. She could try to find her own, but as naïve as she was, that would be very dangerous. She could get robbed, raped, or possibly murdered. A girl like Anni in the type of neighborhoods they sell heroin in would stick out like a duck out of water. She could also commit suicide, which Caleb had seen also, or she could become very sick. He sighed. "Come on. I brought six packs for you, but it'll be gone in six days if you don't get yourself under control, and quick."

She got up from her desk, went in her bedroom, stripped down to her panties and bra, and got out her needle. He noticed there were already red spots where she had been using the same vein to shoot up.

"Anni, you have to start using different veins or you're going to collapse the vein you're using. And it's already leaving marks on your arm that any doctor—including Rod—is going to see. Can we take a minute and let me

show you different places you can shoot up?" She nodded,
trying not to be impatient.

***

Anni asked him if he wanted to have sex after she shot up.
She told Caleb she would do *anything* he wanted to do.
Caleb just sighed and said, "No thanks." He waited for a
moment, running his eyes over her sad form, then said,
"Anni, you need help right now. I'll pay for you to go to a
drug rehab center and will give you all the support I
possibly can. I've seen this before, and you're in much
deeper than you know. If you don't get help right now,
your life is fixing to turn out badly. There's still time, Anni.
I'm begging you, please let me help you!"

Anni refused to look at him and said simply, "Do you mind
if I go ahead and take my powder now?" Caleb let out a
sigh and shook his head, so she hastily fixed the powder
and shot up. "Thank you, Caleb. I'm going to do better—I
promise." She fell back and went to sleep.

He stayed to be sure she was okay and then got his gym
bag and went to the safe. He couldn't believe it. He had
taken over $400,000 from that safe, and there was more in
there today than last time. He was starting to think the safe
was printing its own money! He knew he had to start taking
more, because Anni was going to get worse and worse. It
would be just a matter of time now before she lost her job.
He wanted to take that safe down to about $500,000 before
the new person took Anni's job. All the rumors were that
she kept $500,000 in that safe, and that's what was going to
be in there if she lost her job—he'd see to that. He figured

he needed to take about a million to get it to that amount, and that was if it didn't keep growing. Caleb took $400,000 and shuffled the money around in the safe. He went over and kissed Anni on the forehead and left. As he closed the door, he felt a ping of that darn conscience of his rising up in him again. He looked down at the bag and thought, *When is enough enough?*

CHAPTER 37

REGRETS

Caleb woke up at noon on Sunday. He was so glad Beth didn't call him to go to church, but now he was wondering why. *She's probably mad at me because of our discussion about Christianity.*

He had to go to the stadium at 1 to pee again, and then he had the rest of the day off. With nothing better to do, he thought to himself, *You know, I'd like to go to Disneyland.* So he decided to phone up Beth. "Let's go to Disneyland."

Beth giggled. "You've got to be kidding me? The big tough football player wants to go to Disneyland?"

He laughed and said, "Why not? I've wanted to go since I was a kid, and it's pretty close, I think. Let's go—it'll be fun."

"Okay, superstar," she said with a smile, "let's go to Disneyland!" He was like a kid at Christmas time and told her he would be right over.

Caleb rushed up to his room and grabbed a thousand dollars out of his money bag before heading over to Beth's. When she opened the door, the first thing he said was, "I'm sorry about last night; I shouldn't have spoken to you or about your faith that way."

Beth took his hand. "It will take care of itself in time; don't worry about it."

Beth had never seen him this excited. "Ahhhh, you're just so stinking cute!" she said, giving him a pat on the arm. "Let's go to Disneyland! What rides are we going to ride?"

"Every single one of them!" Caleb said as he ducked into his car. "We're going to see and do everything in there!"

She laughed as she too plopped down in the Vette. "Do you need any money? I hear Disneyland is expensive."

"Nah, I have lots of money."

"Okay, Mr. Moneybags," she chuckled.

When they pulled into the parking lot, there were so many cars that they had to park what seemed like miles from the entrance. They parked, hopped on a shuttle bus, and took off towards the entrance. Caleb paid the lady and in they went.

Caleb and Beth had more fun than they could have imagined. They rode the big rides and the little rides; if it could be ridden, they rode it. They both ran, and laughed, and talked. It was the best day ever for Caleb, and that wasn't really an exaggeration. He did sign lots of autographs, but he was getting used to that. They had their pictures taken with every Disney Character they saw. They ate more junk food, drank pops, and went to shows. When they announced it was time to close the park, Caleb's shoulders slumped. "Dog gone it, I wish they were open all night!"

Beth smiled, then suddenly jumped up on him, wrapped her legs around him, and gave him a big kiss. "Caleb, I love you so much. I'm so happy you're in my life."

He just grinned and said, "Well, you're a lucky girl." Beth bopped him in the chest and started laughing.

***

Later that night, he walked her to the door and she asked him to come in and rest a bit. He said, "Sure, but don't try to take advantage of me, okay?" Beth rolled her eyes and went to put on her PJs. They laid on the couch, watching TV and talking.

He decided he'd be a bit of a tease. "You sure got some nice boobies under those PJs. They've been squishing on me since you laid down, and I think your nipples are hard too."

She blushed badly and said, "CALEB! I can't believe you said that! You just try to embarrass me, don't you?" She bopped him in the chest again.

She snuggled up to Caleb and asked him softly, "Caleb, how many girls have you had sex with?"

He knew this was a loaded question—any answer would be the wrong one. "Well, uh…why do you ask?"

She replied softly, "I'm just curious, I guess. I know you've been with plenty. You're the best-looking man in the universe and the QB and all. I bet all the girls were just throwing themselves at you."

"Do you really want to know?"

"The past is the past," said Beth, "but I have to know."

He sighed and said lovingly, "I've been with so many girls, Beth, I don't even know the answer to the question." He looked at her with his big dimples and beautiful eyes and said, "All those girls mean nothing to me, Beth. I've never in my life felt about another girl the way I feel about you. You're the best thing that has ever happened to me."

"Ahhh, Caleb you're going to make me cry. I don't care about those other girls. I just want you to be faithful to me as long as we're dating, okay?"

He replied firmly, "OKAY."

Caleb surprised her and told her he had been reading the Bible a lot since they had their argument. "It's quite the story."

"That's nice, Caleb; I hope it gives you encouragement." She stopped for a moment, as if thinking, then said, "Focus mainly on the New Testament. The Old Testament has a lot of valuable lessons, but it can be hard to understand." Caleb figured she would go on and on, but Beth didn't say anything else about it. Beth knew she had planted the seed the night they had their rant, and she had faith that God would take care of the rest.

They sat in silence for a while, enjoying each other's company. Then Beth whispered, "Tell me about your mother, Caleb. What happened?"

He laid there quietly, reflecting for a moment; he hadn't talked about his mom to anyone before. "My mom was a good woman who loved me very much. She made some bad decisions in her life, so she and dad got a divorce. Mom died in an explosion at our house just six months ago." He swallowed hard, focusing on getting the words out. "My mother was a gorgeous woman, half white and half Indian, with the silkiest long black hair. I can still remember as a child snuggling with her, and she used to read me books every night. She was a very loving mother; I was lucky to have her. You know, I have my mother's eyes and skin, and I have my dad's size and his big old dimples."

His voice started to crack. "I wasn't very kind to my mother the last four years of her life, and I just wish so, *so* much that I could take it back." Tears were starting to trickle out of his eyes. "I miss her a bunch. I read somewhere that we never appreciate what we have until we don't have it anymore. That is so true. I just wish I would have been more gentle and kind towards her."

"My dad divorced Mom when I was eight years old. My brother got killed in Vietnam, and my sister died of a drug overdose. This all happened within a five-year span. It was all so sad, and my mother held her head high during all that grief." He grinned a little and said, "Mother just loved going to church. Every Sunday she would try to get me up for church and I would just chastise her and threaten her. She was such a Godly woman and I was like the devil, but it didn't matter; to Mom, I was always her little baby boy. Beth, I was all she had left in this world and I treated her like trash. I have quite a few regrets in my life, but none greater than the way I treated my mother. My mother was nothing but loving and kind to me. She loved me no matter how bad I was or how badly I treated her. Man, I wish she was still here."

Beth reached up, wiped Caleb's tears, and said, "That's such a sad story, Caleb. I…just don't know what to say." They just sat there silently, and she hugged him tightly. They were both so tired, and they eventually fell asleep on the couch together. He woke up around 3 A.M., he picked her up and tucked her in her bed and told her he loved her.

As the months passed by, Caleb continued to read the Bible almost non-stop. He was consumed by it—it was just his nature with books.

CHAPTER 38

DOLLARS & DEATH

Regular-season football was nearing its end, and Caleb had just been incredible. He'd been on the cover of every sports magazine in the country, and everyone was calling him the prototype quarterback of the future. In his last six games, he had thrown for over 2,400 yards and rushed for over 800 yards. He was number three in the country throwing, and the number one quarterback in rushing. CAU had inched into the #1 spot in the country, and Miami had moved into the second spot. CAU is averaging 43 points a game and the CAU defense is #1 in the country in rush and pass defense. This CAU team was a juggernaut.

The CAU media relations office was inundated with requests for interviews with Caleb. The coaches were trying their best to bounce most of the attention to Luke's bid for the Heisman, but the press was relentless. The boosters all want to meet Caleb and have their pictures taken with him. CAU had hired a press agent just to take all of the requests and to protect him. And don't even mention all the men's fashion magazines that wanted him on their cover—he was handsome, after all. Even Playgirl has offered CAU a million dollars if Caleb would do a centerfold shot. CAU declined all these offers. He had to get a private line in his dorm because so many sports writers and fans were calling all hours of the day and night.

The money was steamrolling into the CAU Athletic Department. The A.D. John Westinghouse reported that since game two this year, CAU had sold out every game. Every season ticket had been sold out for the next four years. CAU had increased the ticket sales by 30,000 people a game. Even though John didn't say it, everyone knew who is solely responsible for bringing in millions of dollars to the CAU athletic program. CAU had never had a sellout since building the new stadium, now, there weren't enough seats. Every major T.V. network was re-working their scheduled lineups and trying to get CAU football and Caleb Lewis on national T.V. every week.

It was late November, and CAU had already won the Pac 10 conference, leaving one game. If they beat Stanford, they would be in the National Championship game in January at the New Orleans Superdome. They would have the whole month of December to study for college finals and work on their game plan for what looked now to be Miami University.

***

Meanwhile, Anni was totally addicted to heroin. She was going through two packs a day, sometimes three. Caleb scrambled to keep up with her addiction, but it was out of hand. Beth had been doing Anni's job, plus trying to juggle her own work. Anni just slept at the office all the time now. Beth would come in every morning and try to wake her up. Sometimes she would get up, other times she would just stay in bed. The money was just piling up every day—Beth had never seen so much. The boosters would just drop by and give her money every day. They wanted to be a part of this program and had plenty of money

Anni was beginning to isolate herself from everyone. Rod had talked with Beth numerous times about Anni, but he dared not mention Caleb's name. Rod tried to talk to her about going to rehab to get help, but as always, she remained adamant that she didn't have a problem and for everyone to just mind their own business. The coaches and John Westinghouse were also noticing Anni wasn't in the office as much.

One day, John Westinghouse came into the office, plopped a piece of paper down on Beth's desk, and said, "This is what I want you to do." It was a time sheet. He wanted her to start keeping a time sheet on Anni, and he also wanted to know about the money in that safe—for the first time ever.

"I'll keep the time sheet, but I have no idea about that safe, John." He tightened his lips but didn't argue.

"I'm also going to send you some more help," he said. "You can't do two jobs."

Beth breathed a sigh of relief. "Thank you, I need it."

John motioned as if to say "no problem," and the two stood in silence for a moment. Finally, he asked, "What in the world is wrong with Anni? Is there anything we can do to help her?"

Beth opened her mouth to speak, then closed it again. She didn't want to talk about it, but she couldn't lie. She took a deep breath. "John, this is the saddest thing I've ever seen. Anni's become addicted to heroin."

John sat there for a minute with a look of disbelief, and said, "Are you absolutely positive? "There's no doubt whatsoever in your mind about this?"

Beth fought back the tears prickling in the corners of her eyes. "Yes, I see her every morning, I've seen the needles she uses and the packets they put the heroin in."

"And how have you felt lately, doing Anni's job?" John asked.

"It's been fine, if a bit stressful."

John got up and said, "Beth, I want you to take over Anni's job immediately. I guess I should ask you, is that something you want to do?"

She replied, "I guess so; I just hate the circumstances, John. It makes me sick to my stomach, but you can depend on me."

John nodded. "Well then. Anni is immediately relieved of her duties at CAU, and you are now the Vice President of Football Operations. You'll have a large salary adjustment also coming. In the morning, there will be a locksmith here to open that safe. I want *you* to pull the door open; I don't want the locksmith to even see what's in there. I also want you to tell the locksmith to change the locks on all the doors and change the combination to that safe to whatever you want. I want you to take care of business here on out, okay?" Beth nodded mutely; she didn't know what else to say. John took a step closer. "Beth, I've been told by everyone who has ever met you that you're an honest Christian woman. I know this is not what you wanted, and I'm sorry for the circumstances surrounding this."

She looked at John and said nervously, "John, I do hope that *you* are going to tell her she lost her job. I don't want to do that."

" I have to talk to the president of the university about this and tie up some loose ends, then I'll go inform Anni." Beth watched John leave, and there was nothing she could do. All she knew to do was pray for Anni.

***

That night around midnight, Rod came bursting into Anni's office; he wanted to know a few things. She was going to talk, or he's going to court to get control of her. He unlocked her door and walked into her office. Anni is sitting at her desk starting to pack up her personal items. He figured she had dropped below a hundred pounds, and she just looked awful. Her hair was a rat's nest, and mascara was dripping down on her face and she had obviously been crying. She'd tried to put some rouge on her cheeks and got way too much.

"Anni," he said almost tenderly, "I know we haven't gotten along recently, and I've accepted that. I'm going to have divorce papers drawn up and send them to you. I'll be fair in the settlement. I just wanted you to know."

"Sure, whatever you want to do. I understand."

"Anni, can I ask you a question?"

"I guess," she said with a shrug and kept on packing up like she could care less what he had to say.

"Where are you getting the heroin?" Anni didn't reply. "Is Caleb giving you these drugs?" Anni said nothing. Rod frowned. "I've looked at all our bank records, and I can't find any that show where you could be spending the kind of money it would take to supply your habit." Again, Anni didn't reply. "Are you embezzling this money from the CAU booster program?"

Anni, finally exasperated, looked up and said, "I get the heroin downtown; Caleb has absolutely nothing to do with it. The only thing Caleb and I have ever had together is sex, and that's it. And since you're asking, I haven't had sex or seen Caleb in over a month—he called it off." She shook her head. "I'm tired of talking with you. Please leave, Rod."

Rod then made a fatal mistake. "If I find out you're embezzling money and that Caleb Lewis is supplying your habit," he said, "I'll go to John Westinghouse and the police and tell them everything I know."

She looked up again and said calmly, "I haven't done anything wrong, so there's nothing to tell. Please leave now."

As soon as he left the building, Anni started panicking. She called Caleb and told him exactly what Rod said and exactly what she said.

"I'm on my way over, Anni."

When he arrived, he rushed into Anni's bedroom and sat by her bed. She was crying hysterically. "I've messed things up for us, Caleb. You told me what would happen if I didn't listen to you, and now it's all going to come crumbling down for both of us," she whimpered. "Caleb, they fired me today!

He took her hand, softly cradled it in his, and said tenderly, "Anni, I'm sorry you lost your job but it's not going to crumble. It will be better soon, Anni, I promise." Anni looked like an old lady lying there on her bed. Even he had never seen such an alteration in a person's appearance from drugs.

"I'm out of my powder, Caleb; did you bring any with you?" she said meekly. Anni looked and sounded as hopeless and confused as he had ever seen—she was like a wounded animal. She motioned for him to come to her for sex. She was trying so hard to make Caleb happy, and sex was all she had left for him. It was the single saddest thing Caleb had ever seen.

Caleb was sick to his stomach, crushed. He'd ruined this woman, just as he had ruined so many women before her. He laid the heroin next to her nightstand and said, "Let me fix you a wet rag and let's get that makeup off of you, okay?" He fought back tears as he wetted a washcloth. Looking up, his eyes connected with his reflection in the mirror, eyes red and glossy from tears. He snarled, slammed his fist into the glass, and broke it.

"I'm *sick* of you and sick of the way you ruin people's lives!" he growled at the pieces of himself reflected in the glass.

When he returned to the bedroom, Anni was staring at him with a peaceful, odd look. "I love you Caleb," she murmured with a smile. "This isn't your fault," she said, suddenly plunging the syringe down. Caleb instinctively leaped to get it out of her hand, but it was too late. 8 packets of heroin lay open on the nightstand.

Anni had killed herself.

Caleb, in anguish, dropped to his knees and let out a long, silent scream. Screaming with all he had from the bottom of his soul. He sat on the floor and sobbed for another thirty minutes. He had never felt this bad about something since he killed Lillie.

He had come into Anni's life and in a matter of months had turned this absolutely beautiful, smart, funny woman into a desperate heroin addict and watched her snuff out her life.

After an hour or so, he wobbled to his feet and went to the safe. He'd brought three gym bags with him this time. But the money didn't look so good to him all of a sudden. He kept staring at it and thinking, *I can walk out of here with 1.5 million in the bags and still leave $800,000 in that safe.* He grabbed a bundle and stared at it in his hand, and all he could see was Anni's face and what he did to Anni to get it. It just wasn't worth the price it cost anymore. He closed the safe and locked it, walked in and kissed Anni on the forehead one more time, and left the building.

In his apartment, he dug out every tape he had of Anni and destroyed them all, along with the pictures. He put his head down on his bed and laid there; he was so uneasy—he just tossed and turned. He couldn't take it anymore. His mind numb, he slid out of bed and knelt down on his knees, just like he and Lillie used to do, and he prayed.

"God, I'm *so* tired of living this way. I so desperately need and want your help. I accept your son Jesus as my savior. I know he's your son and died on the cross for me, so that when I die I can be with you. Please forgive me of all the terrible, terrible things I've done in my life. I really *am* going to try to do better. Thank you, and amen."

This simple prayer changed Caleb Lewis forever.

Caleb got up from his knees and closed his eyes, and immediately the comfort of the Holy Spirit flooded into his life. Caleb felt a peace that he knew only the grace of God could give.

That night alone in his dorm room and full of despair, Caleb Jack Lewis finally made the most important decision of his life, accepting Jesus Christ as his savior.

The energy returned to Caleb's body. He was so excited, he just had to call Beth…he had to tell someone about this! He wanted to shout it to the hilltops, and he contemplated running out of the dorm and doing just that even though it was 2:30 in the morning.

Beth answered the phone in a panic, but Caleb cut in before she could even speak. "Beth, I have some wonderful, wonderful news!"

"You better at this time of the morning," she grumbled.

"I just accepted Jesus!" he yelled.

She dropped the phone and screamed, then pumped her fists in the air "YES, YES, YES!" She picked up the phone and just started sobbing. She couldn't catch her breath.

"Oh Caleb, I've been praying so hard for you since I met you! I'm so happy for you! Didn't you feel great after you prayed?"

He replied, almost in awe, "I've never felt anything like this before, Beth."

"Do you know why, Caleb?"

"No, not really," he said.

"It's because you've been reborn, Caleb! All things are new, all things are fresh, and all your sins have been forgiven. It's the greatest, most awesome thing in the world to experience the love that God has for us. I'M SO EXCITED I JUST PEED MYSELF!"

Caleb laughed, and he'd never felt lighter. "Go back to bed, honey," he giggled. "I'll talk to you tomorrow."

"Okay. I have some big, big, news, but I'll tell you tomorrow, okay?"

"Okay," he said with a smile. "Love you. Good night."

CHAPTER 39

DÉJÀ VU

Beth came into the office the next morning exhausted. She had prayed herself to sleep last night asking God to help Anni overcome her addiction. Naturally, she had asked Anni soon after she started working there if she was a Christian. Anni had said, "Thanks for asking—I accepted Christ as my savior at 13." (If you're around Beth very long, she *will* ask if you're a Christian. Never fails.) She also prayed so hard for Caleb, thanking God for softening his heart.

Beth walked in and knew it was going to be a stressful day. She opened Anni's bedroom door to check on her. Immediately, an uneasy sense washed over her. *Something's not right here.* Beth shook Anni and asked her to say something. No response. She reached over, grabbed Anni's shoulder, and turned her over on her back. Anni's eyes were wide open, and her face had turned a shade of blue. Beth sucked in a breath and stepped back, shaken, and bolted for the phone. The ambulance would be there soon, but it could never be soon enough for Beth. She stumbled back in and looked at Anni but just fell to the floor; her legs wouldn't hold her up. She tried to be strong, but she couldn't hold in the sobs.

Soon all the coaches and the secretaries were congregated outside Anni's office, trying to figure out what on earth was the matter with Beth. They could hear her crying from all over the building. Coach Richert walked in and examined the scene when he arrived. Westinghouse had already told him about Anni, and that Beth was the new VP, so he had an idea of what may have happened here. He knelt down on the floor with Beth and tried to calm her, but her body was trembling so harshly she couldn't stand up. She was curled up, arms wrapped around herself, rocking lightly back and forth.

Coach Richert motioned for the other coaches, who helped her up off the ground and put her in her office chair. The Medical Examiner soon came by to investigate Anni's death, and after about an hour, their preliminary ruling came up as a drug overdose. Soon after that, the ambulance arrived and took Anni away.

It wasn't long before news of Anni's death had spread over the entire campus. Everyone who knew her just couldn't believe she was a heroin addict. Coach Richert spoke to the football team at practice about it, mainly sugarcoating the horror of it with placid warnings about "not letting this incident with Anni keep us from preparing properly for the game on Saturday," and that "Anni wouldn't be happy with us if we lost this game because of her." He also took a minute to emphasize the dangers that drugs posed to the players. "Nobody is immune to them. NOBODY. The safest thing is not to ever use them."

Before practice, Caleb made sure he found Coach Axom. "Coach, could I talk with you a minute?"

"What do you need, Caleb?"

"Well," he said, "I just wanted you to know I accepted Christ as my savior last night in my dorm room."

A smile broke out on Axom's face. "That's fantastic, Caleb! I promise you, it's the best decision you'll ever make. If you have any questions about your salvation or anything else, for that matter, you know I'm always here for you."

Later, Caleb stood in the back of the team meeting, head down. He couldn't shake thoughts of Beth from his mind. He couldn't tell her over the phone about Anni last night, she would have wondered how he'd known.

Caleb whispered to Coach, "Can I leave for a second and check on Beth?"

Coach patted him on the back. "Take the rest of the day off. I know she's pretty traumatized by what happened."

He flew out of the locker room and into Beth's office. As soon as he saw her, he grabbed her and started squeezing her tight to him.

"Beth," he whispered, "I am so sorry. I know you and Anni were good friends." She had already started moving into Anni's office and another girl—Susan Smith, the entrance receptionist—had taken her place.

"Oh, Caleb," Beth whimpered, "it's so sad. I've known about her problem for months, but I didn't tell anyone about it. Her husband knew about it too and tried to get her to go to rehab, but Anni would have nothing to do with it. I do have peace of mind knowing Anni accepted Christ, though. As a new Christian, Caleb, one thing that should give you comfort is that we can't fall from God's grace. So even if we mess up, which we all do, God is there to pick us up. He just wants the very, very best for all of us, and I know Anni is in heaven today."

Caleb hugged her and said, "That's good news, 'cause I keep messing up a lot."

Beth smiled. It was a refreshing thing to see. "Caleb, it's so sad, but maybe in a weird way that I can't understand right now, I think it's God's plan for me."

"What?"

"Well, you're now speaking to the Vice President of Football Operations for the #1 rated football team in America."

"You have got to be kidding me," Caleb said, half confused and half elated. "You got Anni's job?"

"Yes I did! I'm just appalled by *how* I got it, but I got it. Somebody had to get it, I guess. I'm just as surprised as you."

Caleb grabbed her, kissed her, and said, "I'm so proud of you. They couldn't have found a better person."

Beth blushed. "Thank you."

"Well, Miss Vice president," Caleb said with a playful nudge, "you better get to work. I know you have a lot to do."

Beth chuckled. "You have no Idea."

Caleb left the office and went back to his dorm. Thoughts of Rod consumed his mind, and he turned the situation over and over again in his head. *What could he do? According to Anni, the last thing she told him was that I didn't have anything to do with her heroin addiction. He had no proof on me. The only thing he knew was that I was screwing his wife, and that's not illegal. You never know—after the way Anni treated him, he might be glad she's gone.*

Caleb rushed back to his dorm and flushed all of his cocaine and heroin down the toilet. He thought he would keep his weed (he hoped God wouldn't mind that so much). He had to call his dad at the hardware store and tell him that he accepted Christ. Jack, naturally, was so happy he started crying. "I have been praying and praying for you!" he said so loudly that Caleb had to hold the phone away from his head. "That's a prayer answered right there. I'm so proud of you."

Caleb smiled. "Thanks, Dad. It feels great."

***

Beth was still in her office after dinner, so he stopped by and she gladly welcomed him in.

"Have you ever seen the bathroom and bedroom in the back?" Beth asked. Caleb didn't say anything.

She showed him around, ending at a place he was familiar with. She motioned to the safe. "Did you know this was here?"

"I heard Anni kept a large amount of money in here. I know she gave me some money a few times when I was running short."

"She did?" Beth said. "I have no idea, because there are no records of anything concerning that money. I think that's the smart thing to do, don't you?"

"Yeah, you never know when the NCAA might want to look at your books or something, and giving money to athletes is against the rules."

Beth took a few steps forward and motioned for Caleb to follow. "Come here; I have to show you this." She put in the combination and swung back the door. "Have you ever seen so much money before? Unbelievable!"

Caleb said, kicking himself mentally, "Nope, that's a lot of dough there."

"I counted it today, and there's over $2.3 million dollars."

He wrapped his arms around Beth from behind, lovingly pulling her a few steps back. "Beth, don't talk about this money or show it to anyone else. Ever. It wouldn't be safe for you in here if this were to get around."

She shook her head. "Nobody seems to even *want* to know about this money. I only showed you because I trust you so much, and I promise, I won't ever tell anyone about it."

"Good," Caleb said, and as he left, he just thought, *Déjà vu.*

***

The football players were required to go to an invitation-only boosters appreciation banquet this coming Tuesday night. It was the annual Christmas event that only big boosters of the program attended. Caleb read the announcement and looked over at Lance, rolling his eyes. "Ugh, talk about something I dread doing? This just sounds awful, shaking hands and giving autographs to a bunch of rich people."

Lance laughed. "Dude, why are you so antisocial? How bad can it be, man?"

"You just don't know me, man," Caleb said dismissively. "Things like this are a nightmare to me. If you think I'm antisocial now, you should have seen me a few years ago. I was a hermit!" he said, laughing.

Lance chuckled. "You, Caleb Lewis, are a complicated man, my brother."

"You have no idea." Caleb replied, shaking his head with a smile.

***

The boosters came by and shook the players' hands one by one as they moved down the long line, and the players signed whatever they wanted signed. Caleb was the last one in line, and Luke Donaldson was next to him. Susan Smith stood next to Caleb and another secretary next to Luke.

As they came by and shook the players' hands, they were exchanging money in the handshake. Not every player

256

received money from every booster; it just depended on the booster's particular interest in a particular player.

Caleb leaned down to Susan. "What's going on?"

Susan, with a big grin, reached up and kissed Caleb right on his lips and said, "Merry Christmas."

Caleb, surprised and confused by the kiss, said, "Merry Christmas to you?"

By the time they were done, Caleb had signed for and taken pictures with all one thousand boosters that were invited. He looked over at Susan and said, "I'm done. I'm spent. I want to go home now." Caleb was the last football player left at the banquet; most had left about an hour earlier.

"Caleb, you did good!" Susan said, laughing loudly. "Would you marry me? I don't know how much money I have in this sack!" She kept laughing hysterically, jiggling the bag full of money the boosters had given to Caleb. "Boy, this is *literally* a sack full of money. Here ya go," she said as she handed him the sack.

Caleb just stared at her. He had been so busy taking pictures and signing that he hadn't even noticed Susan receiving money.

Susan couldn't stop laughing. "I've done this for six years now, and I've NEVER taken anything close to what's in this sack. I thought I was going to have to ask for another one! Enjoy, Caleb—you've earned it."

"Thanks."

Susan seemed anxious; she kept looking at him and then quickly looking away. Eventually he focused his gaze on her until she cracked. "Listen," she mumbled, "I can't believe I'm going to ask you this, but here goes. I know this is a bit aggressive, but would you by any chance like to go back to my apartment with me?" She was blushing badly. She had been secretly infatuated with him since she first saw him, and this was the most time she'd had alone with him.

Caleb's eyebrows peaked. "Susan, you're a wonderful person, and if I weren't already dating Beth, I would definitely. It would be an honor to go home with you. But I don't want to cheat on Beth. I hope you understand."

Susan drooped a little. "I wasn't sure if you two were dating; Beth's never said anything about it. I feel like a jerk for saying anything now." She chuckled. "Well, I gave it my best shot, and I respect you for staying loyal to Beth."

Caleb bent over and gave her a kiss on the cheek and said, "If for some reason it doesn't work out between Beth and me, you'll be the first girl I call, I promise."

Susan knocked him on the shoulder and said, "Get out of here, you big lug, and congratulations again."

Caleb took his sack full of money and went back to the dorms. He poured the money on the bed and started counting—$84,300 when all was said and done. Caleb ran out the door and down to the common area of the dorm. All the football player were jumping around, happy about the money they got. Caleb found Lavon gave him a friendly smack on the back. "What a night, huh? How much did you get?"

Lavon, grinning from ear to ear, said, "Caleb, it's a miracle. I tell ya, it's a miracle. I got $1,200 from them boys. Can you believe that? I didn't have $20 in my pocket, and I wouldn't have had that if Miss Anni hadn't had slipped me $100 a couple of weeks ago. I can go buy some Christmas gifts for my family back in Bossier City now, Caleb. They're going to have the best Christmas ever. Man, Caleb, talk about answered prayers! How much did you get?"

Caleb hesitated. "I—I haven't counted it yet. I'm glad for you Lavon, congratulations."

Caleb went around the room asking other players how much they got, and most of them were around $800 or less. But man, they were all so happy.

Caleb went back up to his dorm and thought about how grateful he was, and about all the wonderful things that had happened to him since he moved out to California. Sitting down at his desk, he pulled out a box of envelopes, counted out eighty of them, and put $1,000 in each one. Late that night, he went to all the rooms and slid two envelopes under the door, one for each person. He didn't sign his name or tell anyone he was doing it. The note inside just said *Merry Christmas from someone who appreciates all you do for him.*

Caleb awoke the next morning to loud screams, but not the screams he was used to hearing in his nightmares. They were screams of joy. All the players were pouring into the hallway overjoyed with the envelope they found under their doors. The nightmare had finally stopped, and Caleb giggled, stretched his arms, rolled over, and went back to sleep.

CHAPTER 40

AN APOLOGY

It was Saturday, the last game of the season before finals and Christmas break. The team was starting to show up in the locker room, and everyone was slipping into their usual routines. Caleb didn't have much of a routine before a game, nor was he superstitious in the least, but a bunch of the other players were. They wouldn't shave their beards or wash their jocks, or they always wore the same socks. There were a million different ones. Caleb just put on what was in his locker and didn't really think about it.

They came out of the tunnel at 1:50, and the crowd was as crazy as always. This game was a big deal to CAU being undefeated, but Caleb had never lost a football game. Even his junior and high school teams won every game every year; the TV announcers were really playing it all up. Stanford didn't have a great team this year—their record was 5-5, so their coaches were really talking this one up. They were telling their players, "If we win this game, we're going to a bowl game." *That's kind of sad, winning only six games and getting invited to play post-season ball.* It seemed kind of underachieving to him, but what did he know about it.

Stanford kicked off to CAU and Caleb trotted out on the field. The roar of the crowd was deafening, yelling in unison, "Caleb, Caleb, Caleb!" They huddled up on the 25-

yard line, and Caleb called for a down and out to Rory. Caleb dropped back to pass, but Rory slipped and fell. Caleb looked over at his outlet receiver, but he was blocking someone. With nowhere else to go, Caleb took off running around the right end, cut left, cut right, knocked down a cornerback, put a stop and go on the free safety, and took off on a 75-yard touchdown run on the first play. He sauntered off the field only to be mobbed on the sidelines, greeted by the cheers of his teammates and a few hard smacks on the back. The television announcers were just beside themselves with acclaim and awe for this young man who had such a terrible childhood and pulled himself out of it to become possibly the greatest quarterback of all time. And he was just a freshman.

CAU 7, Stanford 0. The game remained much the same, and Stanford had no answer for the Panthers. CAU was bigger, stronger, and faster. The game got out of hand quickly, and Caleb never saw the second half. He just sat on the bench reflecting on his life, as he had done so many times since he got to college.

How he wished he knew then what he knew now. He was hard on himself even though he understood the psychology behind it. He also didn't want to lie to Beth anymore. *But there's only so much truth a person can take.* Caleb had caused horror story after horror story in his life. Just over the last two months, Johnny Caldwell had taken care of two different girls for him!

Caleb just wanted it all over. He was drained and just couldn't take it anymore. He didn't know how many girls he had hurt in Enapay, but he just prayed to God that no more girls would come forward.

Caleb looked up at the time clock—the game was almost over, 63-0. When the final whistle blew, he tried to get off the field before anyone noticed, but the players wouldn't let him go. They lifted him and Luke up on their shoulders and carried them around the stadium to high five the fans. After all that chaos, there was a trophy presentation to be made to Coach Richert for winning the Pac 10. Caleb didn't want any of this glory, and he found it embarrassing. He slunk behind the whole team and stood at the back while Coach Richert accepted the trophy and spoke. Coach was a classy guy and thanked all the right people, then asked Luke and Caleb to come to the stage.

He just sighed and trudged up there, as requested. After Luke finished talking, Coach asked Caleb to say a few words. Caleb stood there at the microphone for a moment, uneasy, very silent, looking for words. Finally he cleared his throat and said, "First and foremost I want everyone here and watching TV to know that last week in my dorm room I accepted Jesus Christ as my Savior; to everyone in my home town of Enapay, Oklahoma, I want to apologize to you. I caused some of you a lot of pain and heartache. I did some things that I am not proud of, and I so wish I could take it all back, but I can't."

Caleb's voice was shaking and breaking up. "I hate to blame my circumstances on how I treated people back then—that seems to be the convenient excuse for my behavior. I did have some tough times early in my childhood. My parents divorced, my brother died in

Vietnam, my sister died of an overdose, and my mother was killed almost seven months ago in a home explosion. I got dealt a bad hand and didn't know how to handle it at that young age, but ultimately it is still my fault. The one constant in my life was my father. He is a great father, and I want to thank him for not giving up on me and always loving me." Caleb struggled to get his words out. "I love you, Dad. Well, I guess to end this I would like to leave one thought to the people I hurt. Christ has forgiven me, and I pray you can find it your hearts to do the same. I am so sorry, and I just want to move on with my life and pray that you can move on with yours. Now, let's go win that National Championship for the greatest university in the world, CAU!"

The coaches were sobbing, as were many of the players and fans. The crowed exploded with applause, and the TV announcers' voices were shaking as they called that speech one of the bravest, most sincere speeches they had ever heard. Each player got in line and hugged Caleb as they passed to go the locker room. The American public fell in love with Caleb Lewis that night.

Beth was watching all of this from her office window. She was overcome with emotion and couldn't stop the tears. She thought to herself, *That is MY man!* She dashed down three flights of stairs screaming, "Caleb, Caleb, Caleb!" She ran through the tunnel shouting his name and met him full speed at the 20-yard line. She jumped up in his arms and hugged him so hard, sobbing. "I love you, superstar. I love you. I love you, Caleb Lewis." Caleb just cradled her

in his arms like a baby and said, "I love you, Beth Owens,"
and they walked up the tunnel together.

CHAPTER 41

ANTONIO BRAZA

Caleb and Beth were walking back to the locker room, where the team was already showering. Caleb put his hand in the small of her back, nudging her, and said, "Come on, I have something I have to do, and you need to be there with me."

She looked at Caleb, hesitant, and said, "Okay." He walked her into the locker room. Beth tried not to look around at all the half-dressed and naked men everywhere. "CALEB!" she yelped. "I can't be in here! This is so awkward…." She closed her eyes and tried not to look, but Caleb could have sworn he saw her peeking through her fingers.

He laughed and said, "It don't seem to bother any of the guys." He took her to the middle of the locker room and shouted for all of his teammates to gather around. "What in the world are you doing?" she snapped in a sideways whisper, keeping her eyes focused on an innocent wall tile. "I've never been this embarrassed in my life!"

Once his teammates had gathered around, he suddenly grinned, grabbed Beth's hand, and got down on one knee. "Beth Owens, will you marry me?"

Beth put her hands over her mouth and gasped. She looked first at Caleb, then around the room and said, "YES, YES, YES!" Her voice came out somewhere between a warble and a shout. "It would be an honor to be Mrs. Caleb Lewis!"

He stood up, scooping her close to him as he rose, and gave her a big kiss. The locker room just exploded; all the guys were coming up and hugging her and congratulating Caleb. She accepted all the hugs graciously, but in the break between two congratulations, she looked up at Caleb and said softly, "Caleb, they're all naked, sweaty, and stinky, and they're just rubbing their stuff all over me when they hug me. I think they're doing it on purpose, too!"

Caleb was laughing so hard, he couldn't catch his breath. After about ten more minutes she looked at him and said, pleading, "Please get me out of here." Caleb guided her out to the hallway and hugged her tight.

"Go ahead and go home. I'll come by soon."

She nodded, then grinned and tiptoed over to him. "Bend down, I want to whisper something in your ear."

He bent over, and she said, giggling, "You have the biggest wiener in the locker room." Caleb just rolled his eyes and playfully pushed her and told her to get out of here. After she'd gone, Caleb showered and changed his clothes and then went to see Coach Richert.

"Congratulations, boy," Richert said, "you did good with that girl."

Caleb said, "Thanks, Coach. Could I ask you a favor?"

"Anything you want, Caleb."

"You don't know of a good jewelry store I could go to with Beth and buy her a ring, do you?"

Without a moment's pause, Coach picked up the phone and called Antonio Braza, the owner of Exquisite Jewelry. "Tony, this is Coach Richert calling; could you do me a favor?"

"Anything, anything you want!" Tony said, pumped up to get a call from Coach. "You just name it."

"Caleb Lewis needs to buy a ring tonight; do you think you and your staff could stay open a bit late and help Caleb and his girlfriend?"

"YES! I'd love to do that! Can Caleb be here around 7? I'll have everything prepared."

"Thanks, Tony. He'll be there," said Coach as he hung up. "Caleb, do you have money to buy this ring?"

"Yes, Coach; Anni kept me very well supplied."

Richert's smile soured immediately. "I don't want to hear that," he said and told him to get out of his office.

Caleb got back to his dorm, and the first thing he did was call Jack.

"I watched the game, but more importantly, I watched your speech in the end," he told Caleb. "That was a very brave speech, and it took a REAL man to spill his guts out like that on national TV." Jack chuckled. "Our phone has been ringing off the wall from people in Enapay. Every single call is how proud they are of you, and how you've taken control of your life and made the necessary changes to become a good person."

"Dad, I didn't do anything," Caleb said, and Jack could hear the smile on his face. "God changes our perspectives and makes us see what's important and what's just fluff. I'm not taking any credit for whatever changes people have seen in me—I give all that to God. Heck, I've only been a Christian a week. I'm not even sure how to be one yet."

Jack sat there on the phone in quiet for a moment. "Wow, I can't believe this is my son I'm talking to."

Caleb smiled. "I do have some big news, though, Dad."

"I don't know if my heart can stand anymore good news!" he said, laughing.

"I asked Beth tonight to be my wife—we're getting married!"

Jack was just ecstatic for Caleb, but Caleb started talking about Beth and went on and on and on about her. He had never heard *Caleb* this excited about anything.

"Have you set a wedding date yet?"

"No, but I'll let you know." The smile faded from Caleb's face for just a moment. "I wish Mom, John, and Amanda were still here, Dad. They all would have been so happy and proud. I miss them all so much. Don't you?"

Jack sighed. "I know, son. I do too, but I bet they're watching everything from heaven."

Caleb replied, "I sure hope so," and hung up the phone.

He went to his bag and got out the $30,000 he brought to CAU with him and some of the money that he got from the safe, then headed over to Beth's apartment and knocked on her door. Beth came springing to the door, and Caleb said, "Come on, let's go get you a ring."

Beth jumped up and wrapped her legs around Caleb, squealing like a little girl. "How exciting!" Caleb gave her a piggy back ride to the car.

They hopped in the Vette and she said, "I don't mean to embarrass you, Caleb, but I think I'm making a bunch of money now. Do you need me to buy this ring?"

He said with some hesitation, "I don't want to do this, but I have to tell you something." Caleb had no idea how she would react to what he was fixing to tell her.

"What?" she replied. She seemed rather undaunted and still quite bubbly.

"Anni gave me a lot of money, and I mean A LOT of money."

"Like how much money?" she asked.

Caleb shook his head. "850 thousand dollars."

Beth sat there for a few seconds and didn't say anything. Finally, she said, "Why would Anni give you that much money, Caleb?"

Caleb quickly said a silent prayer. *I'm sorry God for this lie I'm fixing to spin, but I hope you understand.* "Anni told me that the coaches said I'm bringing in millions of dollars to this university and for her to make sure I had all the money I needed. Every time I walked into her office she handed me a bundle of money, and she just kept doing it over and over again."

How in the world do you tell your new soon-to-be wife you stole the money and about Anni? I think some things are just better off left to me and God.

Beth frowned and said very sternly, "Caleb, Anni was sick and didn't know what she was doing. You shouldn't have taken all that money; you don't need it, and it isn't yours. I want it back in the safe." Caleb sighed and thought, *Yup, I was pretty sure that's how she would react; it's all blood money anyway.* He knew he couldn't be married to Beth and try to conceal 850 thousand dollars. Giving that money back ran against every human instinct he had acquired in his life. The old Caleb flashed through his mind for a second and thought, *Is this girl worth that kind of money? A lot of thought, effort, and time was sacrificed for that money, including Anni's life.*

They pulled into the jewelry store. Beth frowned. "Caleb, looks like they're closed."

He walked around and opened the car door and said, "Get out of the car please, Mrs. Lewis." When they reached the entrance all the lights in the store came on. Antonio opened the door and welcomed them to Exquisite Jewelry. All the sales people were dressed up in black and standing behind the counters.

Beth bopped him in the chest and smiled. "How did you do this?" Caleb told her to get whatever she wanted. She looked and looked—this was very important to her. She had waited 22 years to put a ring on her finger.

She saw a bunch she liked, but there was one that she just fell in love with—a Cartier flawless three-carat diamond. A single stone in a platinum setting with a wedding band and matching groom's ring. The only thing she didn't like was the price—$62,000.

"Caleb, I just love this ring, but it's too much money. I don't know how we can afford this."

Caleb didn't have enough money on him, since he promised Beth to give it all back. Thinking hard, he leaned over to Antonio and said quietly, "I'll pay you $50,000, and I can't pay you until and IF I get drafted for the NFL." He then looked down at Beth to be sure she was listening and said, "She'll also throw in a couple of good season tickets free for the next 3 years."

It's hard to change overnight, and Caleb was still used to people giving him things. Antonio, being the huge fan of Caleb's that he was, said, "You got a ring, Caleb! Just tell all your friends what a great deal they can get at Exquisite Jewelry." All the sales people at the store started clapping. They all knew who Caleb was and were excited for him.

Beth's face reddened, and not in a good way. "Outside, please," Beth whispered, suddenly angry. She stormed out of the store and then whirled to face Caleb. "Caleb Lewis, you can't make promises like that! And don't you ever, EVER again tell someone what I will do or won't do. My job is none of your business, and it's not a toy for you to make deals with. We will try do everything in our marriage the right way—God's way. If not, you're going to be really, really miserable being married to me. Do we understand each other? If not, we can call this whole thing off right now!"

Caleb looked down at her, surprised at her temper, and said," I didn't do anything wrong. I told the man I was going to pay for the ring, just after I got drafted. There's nothing wrong with making a good deal on something, but I *will* apologize to you for bringing your job into it. I'll talk to Antonio about the season tickets, but not about how I INTEND to pay for this ring."

Beth crossed her arms, still irritated, and said, "I'll just let my daddy pay for it and that will be that."

"I'll cut off my throwing arm before I let your dad buy your engagement ring," Caleb said. "I didn't do anything wrong, and there's nothing wrong with me paying for this ring when I get an NFL contract."

Beth sighed. "I'm sorry. I guess since you promised to pay for it and he agreed on your terms, there isn't any harm done. But I'll tell you one thing, Mr. Superstar quarterback—the day you sign that NFL contract, Antonio is the first thing coming out of that check!" Beth reached up and gave him a big kiss, and the two of them walked back into the store happy again. They sized her and his fingers and took everything back to the jeweler. Caleb stood around and signed autographs for all the sales people, and they had it ready for them in twenty minutes. Beth walked out of that store just staring at that ring. She didn't take her eyes off of it the whole ride home.

"Oh, speaking of your dad," Caleb said suddenly, "I have one more thing to do. I didn't propose to you the proper way."

"Well, it was certainly unique, but what are you talking about, superstar?"

"I didn't call your dad and ask for your hand first. Wasn't I supposed to do that?"

She shrugged. "Oh well. I bet my dad will understand; he's a great guy. We'll call him when we get back to my apartment, okay?"

CHAPTER 42

A NEED TO KNOW

On Sunday, Caleb went by and picked up Beth for church—he was excited to go this time. When they walked in everyone was swarming him, telling him how excited they were about his decision to accept Christ. They'd all heard him on television. For the first time ever, Caleb felt at home and at peace with himself inside a church.

Dr. Braxston spoke of trying to live the Christian life in a world full of haters. When the invitation time came, Beth nudged Caleb and said, "Get up, please; we need to go down front and talk with the pastor."

Caleb said stubbornly, "No, I'm not going down there."

She shook her head. "Get up, Caleb! The invitation will be over soon!"

"No!" he said defiantly. "I refuse to go down there. Why would I want to?"

Beth, flustered with him now, reached over and pinched him hard in the side and said, "You get up out of that pew right now, Caleb Lewis, or I will grab you by the ear and drag you down there."

"Okay, okay, OKAY! Quit pinching me."

They went to the front and spoke with Dr. Braxston about Caleb's decision to accept Christ. Beth said, "Caleb would like to be a member of the church and to be baptized tonight if that is okay with you, Dr. Braxston?" Caleb just stared at her and started to say something, but she put her finger to his mouth and said, "HUSH!"

Dr. Braxston said, "It would an honor, Caleb."

Caleb glared at her with those blue eyes and she said, "Don't you give me that look; I'm not scared of you one little bit." She turned her attention away from him. "Pastor, we'll be here at 5. Is that the right time?"

"Yes, see you then!"

As they were walking out of the church, Caleb nudged Beth. "What was that? I've heard of baptism, but what is it, exactly, and why in the world is it so important to you?"

"It's a symbol to show you're born again. It's a public declaration that you want to follow the Lord's walk. It's also to show your friends and family that you are saved. When you get baptized, you're telling the world how your life has changed. It's a symbol of rebirth. It doesn't save you, but it shows you have been washed in the blood of Christ and are reborn."

Caleb smiled. "Well, this showing up places and not telling me stuff like this has got to stop! And if you ever pinch me again, I'll pinch you back." Pointing a finger in her face, he laughed and said, "You've been getting a bit too pushy lately. You better watch yourself or I'll bop *you* in the head."

***

They went back to Beth's apartment and Caleb said, "We haven't had a chance to talk about when you want to get married."

"Friday of this week," she said casually.

"This coming Friday? Sheez, why not right now?"

"I don't want to wait until the championship game is over. I'm ready to get married now. This coming weekend is the only free weekend we have coming up that we aren't busy with something else. Also, if you don't mind, I want a small, private wedding—just your dad and my parents and maybe a friend or two. Is that okay with you?"

He shrugged. "Whatever you want to do."

"Then we can go somewhere nice for a few days and have our honeymoon!" She smiled off into the distance for a bit, picturing the places they could go. Then she suddenly giggled. "I am SO ready to make love for the first time. I've waited a long time. This is exactly the way God planned for a man and a woman to have sex." Beth bopped him in the chest, pointed her finger at him and said, "Rest up superstar, rest up."

***

They showed up at the church that night for Caleb to get his baptism instructions. Beth went out in the lobby to wait for church to start. She looked up to see that Coach Richert and Coach Axom were just coming through the door. Right after them were Jason Briggs, Lance Wood, Lavon Jackson, and Jason Allgood. She welcomed them all and thanked them for coming, and together they headed inside and had a seat. Dr. Braxston stood in the water, and Caleb came out and stood next to him. Dr. Braxton asked Caleb if he had accepted Jesus Christ as his savior, and he said, "Yes sir."

Dr. Braxston then said, "On that profession of faith, I baptize you, Caleb Lewis, in the name of the Father, Son, and Holy Spirit," and dunked Caleb in the water. Everyone stood up and started clapping.

Beth sat there with happy tears rolling down her cheeks, clapping till her hands hurt. *This is just perfect*, she thought to herself.

As the week went on, Caleb's time was consumed studying for his finals, and Beth was working 18-hour days. She was frantically trying to get preparations made, not only for the wedding and honeymoon, but for the football team going out to New Orleans in January. In between all of that, Caleb and the football team were preparing to play Miami—the best team they had played that year, by far—for the National Championship.

CHAPTER 43

BELLS ARE RINGING

The day of the wedding, the ceremony was scheduled to start at 4 P.M., and then they would fly out to Hawaii that evening at 8. They both had their bags packed and ready, and Caleb took $20,000 from the money he brought out to California with him to pay for everything. He had no idea what stuff would cost and didn't have a credit card.

Beth's parents arrived at the church at 2:15 and eagerly introduced themselves. "I'm Dr. Sam Owens, and this is my wife, Betty."

He shook their hands and said, "I'm sorry I didn't ask you before I asked Beth to marry me, but the moment just felt right."

Dr. Owens chuckled and said, "Don't worry about it. I have faith in my little girl, and if she believes you're the right man, then Betty and I are 100% behind it."

Beth nudged her mom, then cast a sidelong glance at Caleb. "I bet we have the prettiest babies ever, Mom, don't you think?" Betty looked over at Caleb and sighed. "Beth sure is right—you are one handsome young man. I bet you two will have some lovely babies."

What's up with all this baby talk all of a sudden? "Your daughter is one beautiful lady inside and out, and I consider myself lucky to be her husband."

About that time, Jack, Mary, and Billy were walking up to the entrance. When they came in, Beth dashed over and swooped Jack into a hug. "You look a lot better than the last time I saw you."

"I feel a lot better too!" he laughed.

Caleb hugged Mary, then shook Billy's hand and said, "Billy, you've grown up on me now. Are you eight?" Billy was a huge football fan, but he couldn't remember Caleb very well because he didn't hang around their house much. Billy was awestruck and asked if he would sign his football. "I'll sign anything you want, Billy," he said, ruffling the boy's hair. Caleb picked up Billy and put him on his shoulders and they all went out front to get caught up with each other.

After all the introductions and small talk, Betty gave Beth a package and said, "Open this, honey."

It was the most beautiful wedding dress she had ever seen. "Mom! I wasn't going to bother everyone with this stuff."

Betty replied matter-of-factly, "My daughter is getting married in a wedding dress. I've waited 22 years for you to get married, and you're wearing that dress!"

Beth hugged her and said, "Come on, let's see if it fits."

Betty followed quickly. "I brought my sewing kit in case I need to make some adjustments."

While Beth slipped into the dress, Betty grabbed a needle and made a few small changes. "Honey, did you buy some nice lingerie to wear tonight?"

"Mother! HUSH!"

Betty, a bit embarrassed asked, "Beth, have you ever even seen a penis? Do you know how they operate? I feel bad, but I never really talked with you about sex." She paused, mouth open, trying to figure out how to describe it. "It's all about friction, you know? Do I need to go over a few things before tonight?"

"MOTHER. I am *not* having this conversation with you!"

Soon after, Susan Smith came running through the door and handed Beth a bride's bouquet of flowers—a beautiful arrangement of small white roses and little footballs and baby's breath. Beth hugged Susan and thanked her.

By 3:30, Caleb's four buddies and Coaches Richert and Axom had arrived. They were all sitting in the front pew, and Beth had John Westinghouse and a couple of the secretaries from work there on her side. Jack was going to be Caleb's best man, and Betty would be the bridesmaid. At about 3:40, the front doors opened up and the entire CAU football team poured in, and behind them, all the other people from the church. Caleb looked over at Jack and said, "Well, so much for a small private wedding, huh?"

At 4, the back doors finally opened and the organ started playing "Here Comes the Bride." Caleb looked out to see the most beautiful woman God had ever created walking down that aisle. He was trying hard not to cry, but he couldn't help it. Dr. Owens got up and took Beth's hand, and Dr. Braxston asked, "Who gives this woman away to matrimony?"

"Her father," Sam replied.

Beth and Caleb turned to face each other, and simple vows were given. Dr. Braxston then said, "By the power vested in me by the state of California, I now pronounce you Husband and Wife." Caleb just stood there looking around; he had never been to a wedding. Beth just laughed and said, "Come here, superstar, and give me a kiss." Everyone stood up and clapped and hollered. Then all of a sudden, the entire CAU marching band came marching through the front door, parading up and down the aisles playing music. In the end, they played the Panther fight song, and all the cheerleaders got on the stage and cheered.

Beth and Caleb were just beside themselves. As the band marched out, Beth told the crowd, "I'm so embarrassed, but I didn't know all you people were coming—we hadn't planned a reception."

She heard her mother say, "Oh Beth, you know better."

Dr. Braxston intervened and said, "Beth, all your girlfriends have been working non-stop all night to make sure you had a nice reception. You are all invited to the fellowship hall right next to the church."

All the girls had fixed the fellowship hall up like a football field. The football team tore into the food, and Susan said, "You guys come over and look at the cake we made for you." Beth and Caleb followed her hand-in-hand until they found the cake—in the shape of the CAU stadium. They cut it together, and she handed him the first piece and then crammed it into Caleb's face. He stepped back, confused, and said, "What the hell was that for? What did I do?" He looked over at the preacher. "Oops, sorry."

Everyone started laughing, and Coach Richert said, "That's a tradition of good luck, Caleb."

"Really…," he said, one corner of his mouth pulled into a smile. He grabbed Beth and pushed her head face-down into the cake. "I need all the luck I can get!" Beth came up totally covered in cake, gasping for breath but laughing. After the girls had cleaned her up, Beth lined them all up, then turned around and threw her wedding bouquet; Susan caught it.

They had a wedding day far, far beyond what they planned. It was just perfect.

After about an hour, Caleb found Jack. "Dad, hate to say it, but we've got to get out of here and catch our plane. I'm so happy you, Mary, and Billy came out here. Tell Billy I'll mail him lots of autographed stuff when I get back, okay?"

Jack hugged him tight. "Get out of here and go have some fun." The last thing Jack said to Caleb, with a smirk on his face, was, "Son, do I need to explain sex to you?"

Caleb looked back and laughed and said, "I could probably give *you* a pointer or two." Jack just turned around, laughing to himself.

Caleb and Beth waved goodbye to all their unexpected guests, hopped in the Vette, and took off to LAX for their honeymoon.

CHAPTER 44

ALOHA

The lady at LAX told Caleb it'd be $5,000 for the tickets. Caleb sighed. "Do you just gravitate to the most expensive things?"

"Hey superstar," she said, pointing her finger in his face, "I booked these tickets on short notice and they cost more when you do that. Do you want me to pay for them?" Caleb laughed and pulled out the money and paid.

When they boarded the plane, they went to their first-class seats and snuggled, talking about all they were going to do in Hawaii. Beth had been to Hawaii with her parents a couple of times, and she just loved it. She knew all the things to do and wanted to show him everything. She'd booked a suite at the Four Seasons hotel right on the beach. To be honest, she felt a little guilty.

"This hotel is really expensive," she said quietly, "and so were those plane tickets. It also costs lots of money to eat and do things in Hawaii. I just wanted you to know I brought my credit card, and I'll pay for all of this."

Caleb chuckled. "I'm pretty positive we're staying at the most expensive place in Hawaii. I think I'm beginning to notice a pattern here."

They got to their hotel around 11 and made their way up to their room—it was five rooms and bigger than Beth's apartment by a long shot. They traded kisses and small talk, and the hotel had brought a big gift basket and a bottle of expensive champagne in an ice bucket.

Beth had never had a drink of alcohol but thought, *What the heck, you only get married once, and this might relax me a bit.* The taste seemed extremely strong to her.

They passed the next few uncomfortable minutes in silence. After Beth had downed two glasses of champagne, she finally said, with some hesitation, "I guess I should go change. I'll be out in a minute." She sat in the bathroom for a long time, so uneasy she felt a little sick. She put on her lingerie and fixed her makeup, then took one final glance in the mirror. *Well, this is as good as I get. I hope he thinks I'm pretty.*

Beth stepped out to the living room nervously. She stood in front of Caleb timidly and said, "I hope I look cute for you."

Caleb's jaw dropped. "You look stunning, Beth." Beth then reached up to her chemise straps, closed her eyes, took a big breath, and let it drop to the ground. Caleb just gazed at her for a minute, amazed by her body. Then he smiled. "You are the sexiest woman I have ever seen." She stood there shyly, breathing very quickly, trying to catch her breath.

Caleb got up from the couch, lifted her up, and cradled her in his arms. He carried her into the bedroom and laid her down. The two made love the entire night. It was the most tender, loving sex that Caleb had ever had.

At 5 the next morning, Beth rolled over and purred, "Put on your swimsuit, I want to show you the most beautiful thing you'll ever see." She sighed. "I'm so glad I waited to have sex until I got married. Tonight just couldn't have been more perfect. But come on, let me show you something."

Beth was a gym rat who ran five miles a day three days a week and did aerobics the other days, and you could tell. She was only 5'2" tall, and she weighed about 105. She'd bought one of those itsy bitsy bikinis, and she looked incredible in it. There were just three little bitty pieces of fabric on the whole thing, and her tight little butt was totally exposed except for one little string going up her crack. Caleb wondered why she just didn't go naked—there wasn't much difference. Beth would never dare wear such a skimpy outfit at home, but she didn't know anyone in Hawaii, so what the heck.

She had also bought Caleb a tiny, tight Speedo. Caleb looked at it skeptically and said, "Really? It looks uncomfortable to me, babe."

"*Please* try it on! I think you'll look sexy in it."

He reluctantly said, "Okay," and he put it on. It took Beth's breath away. *What a body my man has.*

He shifted uncomfortably. "Beth, I'm too big for this tight little thing. Everyone can see the outline of my stuff. Look how far out my bulge is! I feel silly."

She grabbed his hands and replied, begging, "Oh *please* wear it. I think you look fabulous."

He just grumbled and said, "I think I look like a sissy, but whatever." Between her body and his body, it was a sight for all to see.

They walked out on the beach just as the sun was starting to peek up over the horizon. The sound of the waves rolling onto the beach and the wind coming in off the surf calmed them as they sat cradled in each other's arms, watching the most magnificent sunrise. "How can anyone not believe there is a God after looking at that sunrise?" Beth mumbled, maybe just to herself. They soon fell asleep on the beach in each other's arms.

After they woke up, they went back to their room and made love. They got up at noon and put back on their bathing suits. Caleb refused to wear that sissy suit again, and went downstairs to eat. It was Saturday and their plane was leaving on Tuesday, so there was a bunch to do according to Beth. "We don't have a minute to waste!" she'd said.

Everywhere they went, men and women were just staring at the two of them. Beth saw women nudging their husbands as she walked by, and she just giggled every time. Beth was strutting her stuff for everyone to see.

"You do know if someone takes a picture of us it's going to wind up in every magazine in the country, don't you?" Caleb whispered. Beth thought about that for a moment and in a panic sprinted back to the hotel and put on a more modest swimsuit.

Over the next few days they took a helicopter ride around the islands, had sex, ate, paraglided, had sex, ate, surfed, had sex, ate, hiked, had sex, ate, took a boat ride, had sex, ate, rented sea doos, had sex, and ate. They did just about everything there was time to do on that island. They even made love on the beach one night. Beth was just ravenous about sex, insatiable. Caleb had never seen anything like her—she was killing him! "You're going to use my wiener plum up, and we aren't going to ever be able to do it again."

Beth bopped him in the chest and said, "That's silly, that can't happen." She paused. "Can it?"

On Monday night, Caleb just couldn't go anymore; they had barely slept. He was lying in bed talking and laughing. "Do you mind if we don't do it tonight?"

Beth looked disappointed. "I told you before we left you had better toughen up, superstar. I've beaten you. I am stronger than the big tough quarterback. Do you give up?"

Caleb, feeling defeated, replied, "Yes, yes, you won; you're tougher than I am. Now please, please, *please* let me go to sleep. No more sex!" Caleb then laughed and said, "I bet you aren't like this ten years from now."

She said, beaming, "I will always be like this. I can't believe how friggin' great sex is. What a spectacular gift from God!"

He just smirked and said, "We'll see about that sex part in ten years."

He rolled over and went to sleep. "I'll be ready when you are, superstar, just wake me up okay?" Caleb just grumbled.

They awoke the next morning and made love one more time before heading back to the mainland. After they had packed up, he went downstairs to settle up the bill. He counted his money—he had spent almost $15,000 on this trip. He looked over at Beth and asked, irritated, "Is there anywhere else we can spend some money? I still have $5,000 left." She bopped him in the chest, growled at him, and huffed off.

Once on the plane, she asked him if he thought they should move into a bigger apartment. He said, "I have no opinion on that. Whatever you want to do and whatever we can afford on your salary. How much money do you make, anyway?"

She shrugged. "I'm not sure; I haven't received a check since Anni died. I was making $12,000 a year as a secretary, and John told me I would be getting a nice increase in my pay when I took over Anni's job."

"Well, don't do anything till you know how much money you're making, okay?"

She nodded.

As the plane landed at LAX, Beth wrapped her hands around his arm. "Caleb Lewis, I love you so much, and I am so looking forward to spending my life with you. This has been by far the best vacation I have ever had." She started pecking him quickly all over his face like a mother does to a child.

Caleb replied with a serious look, "Beth Lewis, my wiener has hurt so much since I married you!" and started laughing.

"CALEB. Oh you make me so mad sometimes. Well, that wiener had better toughen up, superstar," she said as she bopped him the chest. She was just radiant. She grabbed his hand and said a short prayer for them thanking God for their marriage and especially sex.

CHAPTER 45

SOMETHING STINKS

Beth was still frisky but slowing down just a bit. She was working so hard and still trying to learn about Anni's job; it was something new every day. Beth had put the 850,000 dollars from Caleb back in the safe as soon as she got back to work, and she felt comfort with that, but there were parts of her job she detested, the primary one being that safe in her office and sliding money under the table to the football players; she knew it is wrong and needed to be stopped. She had read every page of the NCAA rules and regulations books so many times now she had it memorized. CAU was in non-compliance on a bunch of it. Beth knew that at some point there was going to be a reckoning, and she wanted no part of it. She wanted to head it off before it came. For a 22-year-old girl who had only had this job for a month, she was pretty gutsy. She would not compromise her principles for anyone.

She went to John Westinghouse, the athletic director, to talk about everything she had learned. John sat there quietly and listened to her. John already knew everything that she was saying, and on top of all of it, he had second thoughts about how the football program was being run by Coach Richert. He knew all the rules and also knew that trying to stop this beast of a program was going to be tough. The majority of fans don't care how you win, just win. Things had been this way so long, and so many other football programs did the same thing, that he wasn't sure if he could stop it.

"I agree with all your concerns, but right now isn't the time to put an end to it. Let me talk with Coach Richert after the National Championship game and see what we can do to get this under control."

"John, there is a right way and a wrong to do things, and we are wrong," Beth said, putting a hand down on the table firmly. "I would like us to run a clean program that nobody would be ashamed to be a part of, and right now I am very uncomfortable with how we do things. It's just a matter of time before all of this comes crashing down. Our sins will always find us out." She took a deep breath. "We need to start running a squeaky clean program or I am resigning from my job."

John leaned back in his chair and said, "Don't overreact here. It's been done this way for years."

She leaned forward and looked at John very sternly and said, "Just because it can be done, doesn't mean that it *should* be done." Beth stood up and turned to go. "I want that safe out of my office, John. I refuse to pay any more football players, and I'm not selling players' tickets anymore. If you want to move that safe into your office I could care less, but I want it gone. CAU agreed to abide by the NCAA rules, and by God we are going to do it if I have anything to say about it." She wrote the combination down and tossed it to him. "There's 3.6 million dollars in that safe. You worry about it." As she was closing the door, she added, "You can fire me, or I'll resign today, but I can't do this dishonest stuff anymore." And she left.

She went to her office bedroom, laid down, and just sobbed. That had been building up in her since she took this job, and it took a lot of courage for her to walk into John's office and speak to him that way. She had prayed and prayed about this, and she was sure this was what God wanted her to do. Beth wasn't concerned about her job even though she was making $120,000 a year now. She wasn't selling her soul for any amount of money. One hour later, the maintenance crew appeared in her office moving that safe to who knows where. She didn't care, she was just glad it was gone.

The National Football Championship was coming up fast on January 1st at the Superdome in New Orleans. The football team had about two weeks left to prepare for it. Coach Richert was trying to keep everything normal for the players—same schedules, same practice routines, same weight and film viewing schedules. The Miami Hurricanes were going to be a big challenge. They were also undefeated and had played a much tougher schedule than CAU. They were as big, strong, and fast as the Panthers, but the Panthers had one thing they didn't have—Caleb Lewis. He would be the difference-maker in this game. Miami had lots of problems trying to neutralize Caleb; it was very dangerous to blitz him, because if you missed, the last thing you wanted him to do was run. It was also very dangerous to sit back in coverage and let Caleb pass. His arm was deadly accurate at any distance, and the four receivers CAU had were the best in the nation. Miami wanted to make Luke run the ball the whole game, but wanting something and actually making it happen is a different story.

After studying all the matchups on paper, the coaches felt they had a slight upper hand over Miami. But the problem with football is always the intangibles. You can't measure things like toughness and the heart to win the game at any cost. To completely sell out to yourself, and your teammates, no matter what.

Caleb had studied and studied and studied. The team had put in the game plan and was working on the execution. Coach wanted everyone to understand what they were trying to do. It wasn't any different than any other game plan—it always comes down to execution.

The team was flying out to New Orleans the day after Christmas. That gave them six days to get used to their environment, plus there's a ton of stuff that New Orleans had in store for them. New Orleans is a great town, but for a bunch of 18- to 24-year-olds, there were temptations galore. Beth made sure there were lots of escorts to watch over the boys. The escorts were to be out on the street every night until 1 A.M. looking out for football players.

Caleb was both happy and sad about not being able to sleep with Beth for six days. It gave his stuff some time to heal (and it needed it). Beth was not happy about it at all, though—she just couldn't imagine going six days without sex. Caleb smiled at her and said, "Sheez baby, you were a virgin for 22 years and now you can't go six days?"

She looked up at Caleb with a very concerned expression and said, "Caleb, I may be addicted to sex."

He just laughed and said, "Trust me babe, compared to other addictions, that's not so bad." They were truly in love and enjoyed each other's company. They laughed all the time, and both were anxious every day to get home to see each other. Caleb had never been this happy. He also couldn't wait to go to church every Sunday. He had read the Bible so many times now he had lost count. He couldn't get enough of God's word, and even Beth was having a hard time keeping up with his knowledge.

It was Christmas Eve, and for the first time, they weren't at home with their families. With the team leaving the next day, there was no way they could go back home and spend it with their loved ones. Caleb had bought a gigantic Christmas tree and put it in the living room. Beth was just aghast—it was the ugliest tree she had ever seen. It was too big, half-dead, and terribly crooked. But he was so proud of it; he had bought decorations and just piled them on the tree. It was the most hideous thing she had ever seen, but she didn't say anything.

The night of Christmas Eve, they put on their best clothes and went to church to worship and watch the Christmas program. A full choir and orchestra, real donkeys, goats, and a manger and hay just assailed Caleb's senses. He sat wide-eyed like a little child listening to the beautiful music and the acting. He was telling Beth all about the birth of Christ and the wise men and the star. Beth sat there listening to Caleb and just let him talk. Of course, she had studied this Bible story since she was a child and knew it by heart, but Caleb was so excited, Beth acted like it was her first time hearing it. When the play finished, Caleb started clapping loudly, a big old grin on his face. He had never seen anything like this before.

He talked and talked on the way back to their apartment about the birth of Christ and about what that meant to the world. "Beth, isn't it amazing that the birth of Christ was over 2,000 years ago, and he's still changing the world today! Isn't that the most remarkable thing you ever heard?"

Beth smiled, her heart warming. "Yes, superstar. It's truly amazing."

"Beth, there has never been someone as sick as I was. I was the worst of the worst. I hurt so many people and did so many terrible things in my life. I didn't believe anyone could forgive me. But God loved me so much! What a mind-boggling, incredible, astonishing gift that is this Christmas!"

Beth sighed. *What a remarkable man, and what a remarkable savior we have.*

CHAPTER 46

TROPHY?

The team is in New Orleans, and Caleb is tired of it the second he gets off the plane. Caleb is irritated at the CAU media relations people; it seemed all he did this week were television interviews. One after the other, it is getting tiresome to him. They all wanted to talk about his life in Enapay and the struggles he went through. Caleb understood that is interesting to folks, but to him it is his real life and a hard time, and frankly he is tired of talking about it.

He told the CAU media relations people that is it. "Do not schedule me any more interviews about my life in Enapay. If they would like to talk about football, that is fine. If they would like to talk about my salvation, that is even better. If they want to talk about world peace or any other subject in the world, I will do it. But I refuse to talk about Enapay anymore." The media people just looked at Caleb and could tell he is getting mad. When Caleb starts getting angry, people take notice. Luke Donaldson is also run over with requests for T.V. Luke had won the Heisman Trophy three weeks earlier. He is sick of it also.

Caleb couldn't get out much because he was just inundated with people wanting autographs and pictures. When Friday finally arrived and he was off-limits to everyone, he breathed a sigh of relief. He had hardly seen Beth, either—

she was so busy making sure everyone went where they were supposed to go that there just wasn't any time for them.

The day of the game had come. Kickoff was scheduled for 6 P.M. There was more of pre-game entertainment than usual, starting hours before kickoff, so it threw both teams off their typical schedules a bit.

Coach got the team together in the locker room for the team prayer. Caleb had always thought this was a bit silly—he figured the other team was praying the same prayer. God couldn't care less which team won a football game.

***

"This is Joseph Jack tuning in from KXRT Los Angeles, the home of the CAU Panthers. It doesn't get any better than this, fans—your #1 Panthers undefeated and playing the Miami Hurricanes for the National Championship Title! Behind the play of Meadville, PA native and Heisman Trophy winner Luke Donaldson and the freshman phenom from Enapay, Caleb Lewis, this teams hopes to cap off the season undefeated as the undisputed National Champions."

Coach Richert pumped a fist in the air and shouted at the top of his lungs "LETS GO GET THAT CHAMPIONSHIP TROPHY MEN!" and out the tunnel they poured.

"CAU has won the flip of the coin and deferred to the second half," Jack continued. "There goes the kick and Miami returns it to the 45. Miami is cutting through the CAU defense like a hot knife through butter. Miami scores on their first possession of the game! That was just too easy! I see the defensive coaches already making adjustments on the sideline. Miami 7, CAU 0.

"And Miami lines up for the kick. Thad Thompson catches it—he's at the 10, cuts right, 15, spins off a tackler, 20, 25, 30, he may go! Ahhhh brought down at the 48 yard line. Lewis huddles up the team."

Caleb crouched down. "This may be the only chance we ever have to play for the National Championship. Give it everything you have on every play. Don't you be the guy to screw this up." He called the play and broke the huddle.

"Lewis drops back, throws a flair pass to Thad for 13 yards. 1st DOWN PANTHERS, Caleb hands off to Luke on a power play, ohhh our offensive line just crushed their defense and Luke goes for 25. Lewis back under center, A QUARTERBACK DRAW, LEWIS RIGHT UP THE MIDDLE…SCORE! Tie game!" Caleb trotted off the field to the tune of the coaches still yelling and making adjustments for the defense.

***

"We are deep in the second quarter, and Miami is punting to CAU. Thad Thompson catches the ball at the 10. LOOK AT THAT HOLE! Nobody is going to catch him! HOT DIGGITY DOG! TOUCHDOWN PANTHERS! CAU 14, Miami 7.

"The defense and special teams are starting to make a difference in the game. CAU kicks off, and Miami returns it to the CAU 45. Well, it looks like the defense has stepped up, and Miami has had to kick a field goal. CAU 14, Miami 10. And that is your halftime score, folks!"

In the locker room, the coaches had their players in separate rooms working on adjustments for the next half. They were pretty pleased for the most part but kept telling the players to tighten the noose. "We still have a half to play, and this game isn't decided by a long shot yet!" they said. Caleb had a good first half—he threw for over 280 yards and had 68 yards rushing.

Joseph Jack seemed eager to get back in on the action when the players flooded the field again. "Coming out for the second half, Miami kicks off to CAU. Thad catches it in the end zone and tries to come out—no! He's blasted at the two yard line. CAU has 98 yards to go to score. Lewis tries another quarterback draw but gets nothing. 2nd and 10 Lewis hands off to Luke. OH NO, Luke fumbles! Miami picks it up and scores, DAG NABBIT! CAU 14, Miami 17."

Miami kicks off, and Thad lets it roll out of the end zone. The official places the ball on the 20.
Caleb is irate; this game is too close for comfort now. "Everything you've got, guys. It's time to sell out."

***

"What a game so far, folks. In the third quarter, Caleb Lewis passed on every down that series and ran in from the 10 on a quarterback bootleg. We stand at CAU 21, Miami 17 now starting the fourth quarter, and CAU has the football on their own 39. Caleb drops back to throw a screen, but Miami is all over it. Caleb takes off around the left end, HE IS GOING TO SCORE! 50, 45, 40, 35, 30, 20, 10, TOUCHDOWN! 61 yards untouched for Caleb Lewis! HOT DIGGITY DOG! Your score is CAU 28, Miami 17."

Caleb came off the field and shouted to his team, "We have some cushion, and now all we have to do is hold on!" As the game finished up, CAU managed one more touchdown. The final score clocked in at CAU 35, Miami 17.

Confetti came pouring down from the stadium rafters, and the players had just drowned Coach Richert with Gatorade. Caleb sat on the bench watching everything, then bowed his head and offered a quick prayer thanking God for the blessings he had given him. As he was sitting there, he heard Beth screaming and jumping around as she bolted across the field. It made him happy to hear her voice, and he stood, opening his arms. Beth jumped up and wrapped him in a hug and told him how proud she was. Caleb was the MVP of the game. He had rushed for 140 yards and thrown for 423. CAU were the National Champions for the fourth time in their history. Caleb was happy, and life was good. But there was no denying that he was ready to go back home with his wife and relax a bit. "Let's get out of here, okay?" he shouted to her over the crowd.

Beth gave him a sour look and said, "Caleb, you need to stay here with your teammates and accept the awards and say some nice things. YOU are the team, and this is very important to all your friends. You need to celebrate with them."

Caleb just sighed and said, "You go stand by the locker room; I'll find you after I change clothes, okay?"

Caleb trotted out on the field and hugged all his buddies, and they stood cheering as Coach Richert and John Westinghouse were presented the National Championship trophy. Caleb walked up and received his MVP trophy after them, and when the master of ceremonies asked Caleb to say something, all he said was, "I give all glory to God, it's that simple," and walked away.

Caleb sprinted off to the locker room with what seemed like every national TV reporter trying to catch him, but he didn't want to talk—he was tired of it. Caleb got showered and changed his clothes. He went around the room and hugged each and every player in the locker room and shook every coach's and trainer's hand, thanking them for their hard work. Their plane was leaving at midnight, and he was ready. He went outside the locker room to find Beth, but those dang reporters were just swarming him.

Caleb dragged Beth back to the locker room (she didn't bother to cover her eyes this time), and Caleb asked Coach if the team could clear out a path for him and Luke to get back to the bus. Coach walked out to the locker room and summoned the offensive and defensive linemen.

"I have one more assignment for you guys tonight. Surround Caleb and Luke and don't let the reporters bother them and get them to the bus." They grinned and formed an impenetrable circle around the two, shepherding them to the bus amid the surge of people with microphones.

CHAPTER 47

MOVING ON UP

It was early February now, and Beth and Caleb were able to relax a bit. Caleb had been on quite the whirlwind tour of the country since CAU won the National Championship—he'd decorated the covers of Sports Illustrated, The Sporting News, and even made an appearance on the Johnny Carson Show. He had become a hot commodity, not only in football but for fashion and modeling as well. It was next to impossible for him to walk out in public anymore without being inundated with autograph requests.

It wasn't much of a surprise, then, that the two of them wanted to move to a house and out of that apartment. Fans and reporters were knocking on their doors all hours of the day and night. It felt unsafe, and Caleb worried about Beth when he wasn't home. Caleb had called Dr. Owens, his father-in-law, and asked him for some help. Houses were very expensive in L.A., so Caleb asked Dr. Owens if he would buy the house and make the payments on it, and he would send him the money every month. "Sure, Caleb. But if you have the money, I don't understand why I need to make the payments."

"Well, my mom left me some money when she passed away, but I'm not sure if I can qualify for a loan like this. That's why I'd like you to buy it and I'll send you the payment every month."

"Okay, I'll do whatever you two need me to do."

"Thanks so much," Caleb said. "And your daughter has exquisite taste."

Sam chuckled loudly. "Don't I know it! But I have plenty of money, Caleb. Go buy the house my baby girl wants."

Caleb told Beth to go pick out a *reasonable* house in a gated community with lots of security if possible. When she finally chose one and brought Caleb to take a look, his immediate response was, "Good Lord, honey! Is this the biggest one you could find?"

"But it's just perfect! It is 3,200 square feet and has four big bedrooms and a huge kitchen, a den, two fireplaces, and a big, beautiful back yard with a swimming pool."

"How much?"

"It also has a three-car garage and the house is brand new, never lived in, and it's in a very secure gated community. If you aren't invited, you don't get through the gates. The realtor told me that a bunch of high-profile people live here."

Caleb just raised an eyebrow and said again, "How much?"

"It has the most modern appliances, and the landscaping is just to kill for!"

"HOW MUCH?"

Beth closed her eyes and quickly said, "1.6 million dollars." She peeked through one eye—Caleb was just staring at her like she had lost her ever-loving mind. "Caleb, we *have* to buy this house! It's *perfect.*"

Caleb just shook his head and said, "You offer a million and let's see what happens." Beth squealed loudly and ran back to the realtor's office. The counter offer came back at $1,250,000, and Caleb told Beth to sign the papers. Caleb still didn't feel comfortable bringing Sam into this. He went to see the John Westinghouse to explain the problem he was having.

"Mr. Westinghouse, Beth and I just don't feel safe living in an apartment. People are coming and knocking on the door day and night wanting interviews or autographs. It's becoming a real problem. We found a house we want to buy, and I don't really want any help from anyone, but if you could call one of your booster buddies and see if they would loan us the money on Beth's salary and at a low interest rate, it would really help us out."

"How much is the house, Caleb?"

Caleb, embarrassed by the price said, "We signed a contract for $1,250,000 already."

John snorted. "Nice house. Let me make some phone calls, and you guys just get ready to move, okay?"

Caleb smiled. "Thanks Mr. Westinghouse, I appreciate it." John was going to get Caleb Lewis whatever he wanted, and John knew how to do it.

John called Caleb a couple of days later and told him to go to L.A. Savings and Loan and talk to a Mr. Burdoll. Caleb and Beth walked in, and Mr. Burdoll welcomed them with a happy, "Congratulations, you two! Caleb, we've got your down payment of $300,000—that's half the money your mother left you, including the interest it has earned so far. Beth, you easily qualified for this loan. All I did is give you two a nice break in the interest rate. I just need you to sign a few papers and you'll be the new owners of your dream house! You guys would have qualified without my help."

As they were leaving, Mr. Burdoll gave them the house keys and said they could stay there immediately. Beth seemed like she was going to explode. "How fun! We get to camp out in our new house tonight."

Caleb told her, "I'll grab some guys, and then we'll start moving stuff tomorrow, okay?"

Beth put her hands on her hips. "No."

"No what?"

Beth replied matter-of-factly, "We are *not* taking that old, ratty furniture in my apartment and putting it in this brand new home. We're going shopping, superstar."

Caleb looked at her, shook his head and said, "That's hard to believe."

Beth laughed and said, "My dad said he would furnish the house as a wedding gift, so it's not costing us anything!"

Caleb just sighed. Dodged a bullet there.

Over the next week, furniture truck after furniture truck arrived. Couches, drapes, five TVs, beds, linens, cookware—everything in that house was brand new. Beth and her interior decorator spent over $150,000 getting everything she wanted and more. It was fabulous, though. Beth snuggled up to Caleb in their brand new king size bed and said, "Let's break it in, superstar."

CHAPTER 47

KORI & LORI

Friday night, Caleb wanted to go out to eat and to the movies. He asked Beth to call downtown to that movie theater that had the V.I.P room and see if it was available. She said, "Great, I'll give them a call."

They left around 7 and had a really nice supper. Caleb signed a few autographs and took some pictures with some folks, but it wasn't overwhelming; it had become a part of his life now. After the movie, Caleb took Beth's hand and they started on the long walk back to the car—they'd had to park a long way from the theater because there wasn't much parking.

"Let's take a shortcut," Caleb said, tugging on Beth's hand. They turned down a dark alley, giggling at the thought of this little mini-adventure, when two men in dark clothes materialized from the shadows.

"Hey, big fella, I bet you have a lot of money. Why don't you hand some over?"

When Caleb didn't immediately drop his wallet and run, the two took a step closer and flipped open two knives. The steel stood out white in the darkness.

Caleb immediately reverted back to his street smarts. He knew by looking at them that they were drug addicts. They had seen him pull up earlier in that Corvette and knew he was rich. Beth looked up at Caleb, afraid, and saw something she had never seen. Caleb's demeanor had completely changed. He was an entirely different man, with a look in his eyes that was almost…evil. There wasn't any Jesus coming out in this man right now.

"Beth, stand behind me," Caleb growled suddenly. He instantly lunged at one of the guys. The man stepped back, swung his knife in a flash, and cut Caleb deep across the forearm. It started bleeding badly, leaving red trails down to his fingertips.

"After we take all your money, we're going take your girlfriend," one man said, nudging the other, and they started laughing hysterically. Caleb's forehead veins were throbbing, and adrenaline was rushing into him full force. Caleb took another step towards the drug addict, and when he did, the other man ran around Caleb, dodged his attempt at a grab, took hold of Beth, and put his knife to her temple. Caleb knew drug addicts were very unpredictable, and this was a mess. If it were just him these two guys would already be dead, but Beth caused a whole other set of problems. He had to protect her, no matter what.

"CALEB!" she screamed, stumbling back into her attacker as he led her deeper into the darkness. She was bleeding from the pressure of the knife to her temple. Caleb's brain was hitting on all cylinders—he was aware of anything and everything around him.

Suddenly, he stepped back and raised his hands. "Let her go and I'll give you my money." Caleb was trying to keep an eye both men, but it was tough to do. One had Beth, and the other one was staying well behind him. They weren't stupid.

The man said, laughing, "I'll take your money *and* your honey!" He ran his tongue over Beth's neck and put his free hand to her crotch, rubbing it up and down.

Caleb's head was about to explode. Through a snarl, he growled, "It's time for you to die now." His blue eyes glittered, their gaze sharp enough to slice through the man in front of him.

Beth was gasping for air, crying and terrified. "Caleb, just let him have the money, baby, give him the money."

"You want my money?" He couldn't have cared less about the money, but this guy had a knife to the only girl he had ever loved, and by God hell was going to rain down on him.

Caleb had laser-like focus watching the man's eyes. He reached into his pocket and pulled out a wad of money and threw it in the guy's face. The second he blinked his eyes, he lunged forward and grabbed the hand holding the knife. He tried to pull it away from Beth, but the man fought back and dragged the blade down her face, leaving a deep cut from her temple to her Jaw.

 Caleb went bat crazy mental on this man.

He was screaming from the bottom of his gut, the guttural sound echoing down the alleyway as he grabbed the man's knife hand. He lifted the guy up and slammed him into a brick wall with everything he had.

Beth was laying on the ground, bleeding and crying, scared to death and trembling so much she couldn't stand. Caleb grabbed the man's hand and began forcing the blade up to the man's face. Caleb was growling over and over again, "Are you ready to die now!" With a final shove, he forced the blade through the man's eye and into his brain. Suddenly, he buckled forward and lost his breath as a sharp pain jolted into his back. The other guy stood behind him, with a look of confusion. He whirled and grabbed the man, lifted him up over his head, and smashed him to the ground.

Beth was trying to watch Caleb, but blood was pouring down all over her face. It made it difficult to see, but Caleb was scaring her more than the assailants. She had never seen such anger, rage, and fury in all her life; she couldn't believe this was Caleb.

As the man was laying on the ground trying to get his senses back, Caleb scrambled to a corner where a cinder block sat stopping the wheel of a rolling trash bin. Caleb dug his fingers into the block and picked it up over his head. He heard Beth scream, "No Caleb, don't! Please!" And with all the strength he could muster, he turned and slammed the sharp corner of the block into the man's face. His attacker's head exploded, speckling the wall behind him. Beth just laid her head down and passed out.

Caleb turned around and dropped to his knees next to Beth. "It's going to be okay, baby; I'll get you some help." He had seen a hospital about two blocks from the movie theatre. He picked her up, cradling her in his arms, and started running. She was bleeding badly, and he had no idea how severely hurt she was. As he entered the emergency room, he screamed at the woman, "My wife has been stabbed! Please help her NOW!"

The lady receptionist hit the "Need Help Now" button and the ER people were out in a flash. Caleb was getting very weak but was able to put Beth on the gurney. She opened her eyes again, crying Caleb's name as they wheeled her off. After they had taken her, Caleb fell down on his knees, then face forward to the floor. The woman at the desk looked and saw the knife still sticking out of his back and hit the button again. Caleb was bleeding to death.

They wheeled him into the same room with Beth, just a curtain separating them. She was screaming Caleb's name, but he wasn't saying anything. "I need lots of blood here! Get some oxygen going on him immediately!" Beth was trying to look and see what was going on, but the nurses were holding her down telling her to be still.

The surgeon snapped open part of the curtain and peeked in on the doctor helping Beth. "If she's okay, I need another hand NOW." The nurses had hooked Caleb up to three bags of blood, and it was just gushing out his back. "That knife cut the thoracic aorta. Get me a scalpel and more blood." The surgeon cut about a twelve-inch incision along his back and violently spread the tissue apart. There wasn't a second to waste.

"Doctor, we're losing him!" the nurse hollered urgently.

Beth, with all the strength she had, pushed the nurses away and ran over to him, ripping out her IVs and dragging down her machines as she crossed the room. Blood was pouring down her face, but she ignored it and grabbed his hand. "Baby, you can get through this. Come on superstar, you can do this." Then, abruptly, the heart monitor quit beeping. Just a long, continuous tone. Beth looked up at the monitor, drew in a breath, and then raised her fist to God. In anguish, she started screaming, "No, no, NO! You can't do this!" In screams so loud that her voice cracked, she cried, "I won't allow this, God! You make him live, damn it!"

Total silence.

Caleb Lewis was dead.

Beth let out a groan deep from the bowels of her soul and laid her head down on her husband's chest. Even as the nurses tried to pull her away to treat her injuries, she fought back and kept talking to him.

Caleb looked down. *What in the world is happening?* He hollered, "Beth? Beth, it's okay, baby, I'm fine." Caleb had never felt such peace before. He looked up, heading for the most wonderful light he had ever seen. He stopped and looked around and thought, *I...must be in Heaven.*

Caleb had to shield his eyes to look right into the bright light, where he noticed a group of people approaching. Maybe they were angels. When they got to him, Caleb just broke down. It was his mom, his brother John, and his sister Amanda. Caleb couldn't speak, but they all grabbed him and hugged him. He finally said so softly, his voice cracking, "I've missed you all so much, you just don't know."

Caleb could barely talk he was crying so much, and he wouldn't let go of any of them. He had never, *never* felt so much comfort and safety. He looked at his mom, guilt heavy in his heart, and said, "Mom, I'm so, *so* sorry for the way I treated you those last few years."

Lillie looked at him tenderly and cupped his face in her hands. "I loved you regardless, son. Quit beating yourself up over it—it's time to let it go. I have never been better."

"Mom," he asked. "Have you seen Jesus?" Lillie stepped back, and from behind her, he saw him. Jesus was standing there. Caleb fell on his knees just bawling like a baby, and he couldn't look up. The most beautiful light surrounded him, blinding in its brightness.

"Caleb, you need to go back," he heard the voice say, more gentle than the booming thunder he'd expected. "You still have a lot to do."

Caleb replied, "No Lord, I want to be here with you and my family."

Lillie lifted him up and cradled him in her arms. "Your family is back home, son, and Beth is with child. You're going to have twins, Caleb. I'd like you to name them Kori and Lori."

Caleb was back on the gurney. It had been four minutes and thirty seconds since he flat-lined. The surgeon wasn't giving up and looked up at the heavens in desperation and said, "God, I need some help here." He was still feverishly trying to fix that aorta.

Beth was just in shock looking into those beautiful dilated blue eyes of his. She pleaded over and again, "Caleb, come back baby, please come back." She would never give up on this man that she loved. He was strong enough to come through this. Beth thought she heard a beep and looked up absently, mind dull from what had been the worst hour of her life. Then another beep, and another, and she saw Caleb's eyes return to normal. The heart monitor started beeping up a storm.

The surgeon just sat down and let out a sigh of relief. "Coach Richert owes me big time on this one. Nurses, pull those tubes out of his throat and let him breathe."

When the tubes came out, Caleb took the breath of all breaths and looked at Beth and said, "Kori and Lori" and passed back out. She had no idea what that meant but didn't care—she fell to her knees sobbing, thanking God for sparing his life. The surgeon told the nurse, "Give him some morphine; I didn't have time to give him a general anesthesia, and he's fixing to hurt like the dickens."

All the coaches came pouring into the ER. They had heard Caleb was dead. TV trucks were already pulling up outside the hospital, trying to catch the scoop. "We just don't know much right now, but we're working on the story." It was breaking news across the nation.

The doctor helped Beth back to her feet, then sat her back down on the bed. "Nurse, she's going to be fine; hand me some sutures."

The surgeon working on Caleb overheard him and said, "Doctor, I'm pulling rank on you. Call Dr. Oslowoedski. He's the best plastic surgeon in L.A., and I'm not going to let you scar that beautiful face of hers."

After the doctor had sewn Caleb up, the attendants wheeled him over to ICU. Beth had to wait for the plastic surgeon to stitch her up before she could follow. The surgeon went out to talk to Coach Richert, who had arrived as soon as he could. "Just so you know, I'm not ever paying for season tickets again." Richert nodded, though it felt odd to smile. "Caleb is very lucky to be alive. He was dead when he got to me. The knife had cut his thoracic aorta; we lost his heart beat for almost five minutes. It's a pure miracle he's still here with us. Caleb also had a terrible cut across his forearm, but I stitched that up and it'll be fine. Beth has a deep knife cut from her temple down to her jawbone. I have the best plastic surgeon in L.A. on his way to stitch her up."

Coach Richert just sat down in the middle of the floor trying to catch his breath. He looked up, distraught, and said, "Doc, are they going to be okay?"

The doctor said, "I think so, but he went a long time without oxygen to his brain, so we'll have to see. He will definitely need some rehab—I tore a ton of muscle and tissue in his back trying to get to that aorta. He's going to be in ICU for at least a week, maybe longer. Beth will also be fine. She just needs time to heal, both physically and emotionally. She's still in shock from the assault."

***

The next morning, the doctor came by Beth's room to check on her. As he was looking over her sutures, he said calmly, "I have some great news for you, Beth."

Both her eyes were blood red and black and blue as the night, but her whole face lit up. "Is Caleb doing better?"

The doctor grinned and said, "After seeing your blood work and urine results, it looks like you're going to have a baby!" Beth couldn't help it—she started sobbing again. She had prayed more in the last ten hours than she had ever prayed in her life, and folks, that is a *bunch* of praying.

 The doctor dismissed her two days later, and she went immediately up to ICU. Caleb was still on a ton of pain medication. They didn't want him to move at all for fear of disturbing that aorta. It needed time to heal. Beth didn't leave the hospital for two weeks. Her mom and dad came immediately upon hearing of the assault. They stayed at their daughter's new home and took care of it.

She sat next to Caleb and held his hand and just prayed and prayed, thanking God for sparing their lives. Many times she would look at Caleb, aggravated, and say, "Who are Kori and Lori? If they're some of your old girlfriends, I'll bop you in the chest for saying their names at a time like that!" She kept telling him, "We're having a baby!"

318

Caleb went home two weeks later. He did hurt, but he was so tired of taking pain medication. All Beth wanted to know was who the heck Kori and Lori were; Caleb always just laughed and grinned. "I have no idea what you're even talking about." Caleb and Beth both healed just fine, with no permanent damage to either of them.

Six months later, two children were born to Caleb and Beth Lewis—a healthy baby boy and girl. Those babies had the most beautiful bronze skin, big dimples, silky black hair, and the most transparent blue eyes you ever saw. Caleb stood grinning from ear to ear as the nurse placed the babies on Beth's breasts.

He said proudly, "Beth Lewis, I would like you to meet Kori and Lori Lewis."

She looked up at Caleb. "First thing, how did you know that I was pregnant even before *I* knew I was pregnant? Then, how in the world did you know it was twins, and *THEN* a boy and a girl?"

Caleb walked over and sat on the side of the bed, reaching for Beth's hand. "Would you like to know how I knew all that?"

Beth looked up anxiously and replied, "Yes! Finally. I can't wait to hear this. How?"

Caleb looked at Beth, tearing up. He wrapped his arms around the three of them and said, "Because my mom told me, that's how."

THE END